Resounding praise for Agatha and Anthony Award winner

MARCIA TALLEY
and
HANNAH IVES

"Hannah Ives is an appealing, believable heroine who would rather face a killer than her own post-cancer emotions, and Marcia Talley perfectly catches her ambivalence."

Margaret Maron

"[Characters] so real they must exist somewhere beyond the page."

Anne Perry

"Talley's thoughtful handling of Hannah's bout with breast cancer and the emotional and physical recovery . . . add depth . . . [Her] characters shine."

Ft. Lauderdale Sun-Sentinel

"A writer and a character we
again—and soon.'

Washington Times

"[Her] characters are well d
the dialogue sparkle

Baltimore Sun

"Hannah Ives is a welcome a
the mystery landscap

Laura Lippman

Hannah Ives Mysteries from Marcia Talley

This Enemy Town
In Death's Shadow
Occasion of Revenge
Unbreathed Memories
Sing It to Her Bones

MARCIA TALLEY

This Enemy Town

A HANNAH IVES MYSTERY

AVON BOOKS
An Imprint of HarperCollins*Publishers*

This is a work of fiction. Names, characters, places, and incidents are products of the author's imagination or are used fictitiously and are not to be construed as real. Any resemblance to actual events, locales, organizations, or persons, living or dead, is entirely coincidental.

AVON BOOKS
An Imprint of HarperCollins*Publishers*
10 East 53rd Street
New York, New York 10022-5299

ISBN-13: 978-0-06-058739-0
ISBN-10: 0-06-058739-3
www.avonmystery.com

First Avon Books paperback printing: September 2005

Printed in the U.S.A.

10 9 8 7 6 5 4 3 2 1

"To the men and women who are faithfully serving in enforced silence to secure for America the freedom that is denied to them"

—Servicemembers Legal Defense Network,
Conduct Unbecoming

My birth-place hate I, and my love's upon
This enemy town. I'll enter: if he slay me,
He does fair justice; if he give me way,
I'll do his country service.

WILLIAM SHAKESPEARE, *CORIOLANUS*, ACT IV, SC. IV

ACKNOWLEDGMENTS

To the real-life Pair-o-Docs—Barry Talley and David White—who together have produced musicals that have thrilled, delighted, and astonished Annapolis audiences for two decades. Thanks for agreeing to go on sabbatical for the duration of this book so those two other guys could direct *Sweeney Todd*.

To Helen Arguello for help building sets, and Ensign Paul Wood, USN, producer of the 2004 Glee Club musical and backstage guide extraordinaire. From the dressing rooms below to the dizzying heights of Mahan Hall's amazing clock tower . . . ooooh, thanks, especially for manning the camera while I was cowering on the balcony. And to Randy Martell, who has all the keys.

To Vice Admiral Ronald A. Route, Naval Inspector General, for advice on Navy policy and procedure; Capt. Keith Bowman, USN, who responded to my request for information by inviting me on a tour of the Pentagon; Lt. Jonathan Glass, MC, USNR, for valuable help with the medical bits; and Special Agent Marina Murphy, Federal Bureau of Investigation, Annapolis Regional Authority, who answered a bazillion questions about FBI investigations. If I got it wrong, it's my mistake, and not theirs.

I have been overwhelmed by the generous outpouring of support from my Naval Academy friends—midshipmen, faculty and staff, both past and present. I based all the cool characters on you, of course. The rotten ones I made up.

To friend and fellow mystery author, Donna Andrews, who was nearly arrested while checking out a location for me in Fairfax, VA. Be careful where you point your camera, and of course I would have bailed you out! Does Homeland Security take VISA?

To Luci Zahrey, the "Poison Lady" who would be very, very dangerous should she ever turn to crime.

To my writers groups—Sujata Massey, John Mann, Janice McLane, and Karen Diegmueller, in Baltimore, and Janet Benrey, Trish Marshall, Mary Ellen Hughes, Ray Flynt, Sherriel Mattingly, and Lyn Taylor, in Annapolis—for tough love.

To my amazing editor, Sarah Durand; her can-do assistant, Jeremy Cesarec; to my publicist, Danielle Bartlett, and everyone at Harper Collins who makes it such an incredibly supportive place for a mystery writer to be.

To my web diva and lunch buddy, Barbara Parker. Come see what Barbara can do at *www.marciatalley.com.*

To Marisa Young and James Cheevers, whose generous bids at charity auctions sponsored by Malice Domestic, Inc. and the Friends of the Annapolis Symphony Orchestra, respectively, bought them the right to be characters in this book.

And to Kate Charles and Deborah Crombie—Plot Fest Forever! And, when are we going to do another one?

This Enemy Town

CHAPTER 1

Pay it back or pay it forward?

That one's easy. If I had to pay back every saint who left a fresh-baked loaf of bread or a hot casserole on my doorstep during the worst of my chemotherapy days, I'd be standing in the serving line at the Clay Street Helping Hand shelter, dishing up baked beans and mashed potatoes until the next coming of comet Kahoutec.

So I pay it forward, like in the movie. Out of the blue and for no reason, I do favors for strangers. And when they ask how to pay me back, I say they have to pay it forward. To three more people. Each.

When I first met Dorothy Hart at the Naval Academy Wives Club luncheon in January, I never dreamed that paying it forward would involve the use of power tools. Don't get me wrong. I'm as much a handy-mom as the next woman on Prince George Street. You have to be when you live on Prince George, a three-block section of gorgeous, but chronically needy, eighteenth-century homes. My husband Paul signed us up for cable, in fact, so I could watch *Talk2DIY* on Home and Garden TV and *House Doctor* on BBC America. And, I was first on the block to raise my hand when Home Depot started offering Do-It-Herself home-improvement workshops.

When our upstairs toilet overflowed, ruining the living room ceiling, I turned DIY into a family affair, dragging my sister Ruth along to their session on plastering. She went grudgingly, lured out of Mother Earth, her New Age shop on Main Street, not by me, but by Home Depot's catered veggie platters and dark, gooey brownies. Ruth needed the workshop, heaven knows, even though she probably planned on meditating away the plaster that rained on her head every time she opened her store's storage room door.

In March, I'd be learning to lay brick. My neighbor, Brad Perry, the Corporate Lawyer, elaborately sidesteps the loose bricks on our front porch and warns me, congenially, that they're a lawsuit waiting to happen.

So, I'm not opposed to power tools, *per se*. It's just that there are hundreds of other ways I'd rather spend my time.

Paul gave me a nifty Barbara K Toolkit for my birthday. I use it occasionally, but store it in the basement, so if I'm up on the third floor with a nail between my lips, holding a picture against the wall, trying to decide where to hang it, I'm not going to be wild about laying everything down and trotting downstairs for a hammer. The heel of my shoe works just as well, thank you very much.

In the kitchen, I have a steak knife with a broken tip that doubles as a screwdriver (both Phillips and regular), and I can't imagine how anyone manages without a good pair of chopsticks. When my grandson chucked my Timex down the toilet? Chopsticks. A hint for Heloise. I should send it in.

When I told Dorothy yes, I didn't know about the power tools, of course. I had been grazing around the hors d'oeuvres table in the Midway Room of the Naval Academy Officers and Faculty Club—part of architect Ernest Flagg's "New Academy" of 1899—sipping a glass of indifferent but deliciously cold Chablis, when Susan Fuquea, the petite, effervescent blonde married to the deputy commandant, introduced us. "Hannah, I'd like you to meet Dorothy Hart, Admiral Hart's wife. They've just moved to Annapolis."

Dorothy was a rail-thin brunette badly in need of a hair stylist. The bouffant "do" that bloomed from her head had gone out with Lady Bird Johnson. At least I hoped it had, but these days one can never be sure. If it's really retro, it's probably back.

I stuck out my free hand and tried to think who Admiral Hart was. The only admiral assigned to the Academy was its superintendent, and the superintendent's name certainly wasn't Hart. "Nice to meet you, Dorothy," I said, and because in military circles wives are often defined—rightly or wrongly—in terms of their husbands, I quickly added, "My husband's on the faculty here. Paul teaches math."

Dorothy squeezed my hand, then dropped it to pluck a plump, chilled shrimp from a passing tray. "Ted's stationed at the Pentagon," she said, following my lead. "He's Deputy Assistant Secretary of the Navy for Weapons Acquisition and Management. Or maybe it's Under Secretary for Weapons Management and Acquisition." She chuckled. "I don't even think the Navy knows for sure."

"The Pentagon?" I couldn't imagine why anybody in his right mind would choose to live in Annapolis and work at the Pentagon. The Pentagon is a grueling commute to northern Virginia and back, one hour or more in the best of traffic. Each way.

Susan Fuquea's smile dazzled like an ad for Crest White Strips. "And Dorothy's son, Kevin, is a second classman."

Dorothy's cheeks grew pink as she nervously tucked the empty toothpick she'd been holding into a fold of her napkin. "Kevin loves being here, so when Ted was offered his choice of Hawaii or the Pentagon, we didn't think twice."

"It must be nice to have your family together for a change," I commented. "Where do you live?"

"We rented a condo near Reston for a while, but recently we bought a place in Davidsonville."

I sipped my wine and nodded in approval. Davidsonville was near the intersection of 50 and 424, midway between Annapolis and Washington, D.C. Admiral and Mrs. Hart, I soon learned, had split the difference, and bought a ten acre lot in the heart of an area that had once been a prosperous horse farm.

Dorothy was describing how Homestead Gardens was transforming her flower beds into a bower of delight when Susan Fuquea waved a beautifully manicured hand to someone across the room. "Don't mind me, ladies," she said, turning in the newcomer's direction. "Carry on. You two have a lot in common."

A lot in common. I knew what that meant. I studied Dorothy's pale, sunken features and felt my face grow hot. Her hairdo. That mushroom-shaped disaster I'd been so critical of a few minutes before was, I realized now, a wig.

I nibbled the dark chocolate off a strawberry while considering how best to bring up the C-word.

Dorothy saved me the trouble. Clearly Susan had filled her in on my medical history, and the introduction to Dorothy was no accident. She tugged on her bangs, sliding her wig to and fro over her scalp. "Chemo," she said simply. "Three months to go. You?"

"Done!" I declared, instantly warming to a sister in arms. "Ages ago, thank goodness. I've been in remission for almost five years."

"I hope you don't mind," Dorothy said, leaning toward me and speaking in an exaggerated whisper. "But I'd like to appoint you my new role model. You look terrific. It's good to know that someday I might get my hair back."

"Guaranteed," I reassured her. "My hair grew back with a vengeance. It used to be straight, now look at it!" I spread my fingers and combed through the tight auburn curls that cascaded over my forehead. I decided not to mention my eyebrows, battalions of tiny hairs that had gone permanently AWOL. Each morning I fill in the blanks, brushing on eyebrows from a box labeled "Shaping Taupe." "Where are you going for treatment?" I inquired.

"Hopkins," she said.

"Ah. Another good reason for choosing the Pentagon over Hawaii."

Although the medical care in Annapolis is first rate—Paul theorizes that doctors like to set up practice near their sailboats—we're just thirty miles from Baltimore and Washington, D.C., and if you need them, the best hospitals that Philadelphia and New York City have to offer are only a few hours north by train.

"After the mastectomy, my follow-up treatment was definitely a prime consideration," Dorothy continued. "And then there's Kevin, of course."

I didn't know Midshipman Hart, but I wondered how gung-ho the young man would be about a mother hanging over his shoulder. My own daughter, Emily, had attended Bryn Mawr College in Pennsylvania—two hours flat from our doorstep to hers. She'd been a capable student, but a difficult and headstrong young woman. Back then, two hours had been about right: it kept us from killing one another. But now . . . ?

"Do you have children, Hannah?" Dorothy asked as if reading my mind.

"A daughter," I replied.

Dorothy had acquired a glass of wine from a passing server and I watched as she sipped at it, cautiously at first—as if testing the bouquet—then more thirstily.

"Emily lives in Virginia, near Staunton. Her husband works at a chi-chi health spa up in the mountains." I took a rejuvenating swig of my own wine and thought how much I envied Dorothy having her son so close by. Staunton—and my two adorable grandchildren, Chloe and Jake, were more than three hours away.

Dorothy asked a few polite questions about my son-in-law, Dante, and the health spa he worked in, but she looked so washed out and worn that I actually considered calling up Dante and ordering an emergency full-body massage for the woman. Compliments of moi.

Then I did the next best thing. I set my wineglass down on a cloth-covered serving tray, smiled reassuringly at Dorothy, took a deep breath and paid it forward. "Is there anything I can do to help? Anything at all?"

Dorothy paused, nibbled on a miniature totem pole of cheese, olive, and salami and considered. "Actually, there is."

I snagged a shrimp for myself and waited for her to continue.

"Kevin's landed a role in the Glee Club musical," she told me, "and in some insane moment, I agreed to help out. But, I'm just exhausted, Hannah. Some days I can barely put one foot in front of the other." Her eyes went wide and shone with desperation. "But I hate to disappoint Kevin."

I nodded. The Glee Club is the Naval Academy's premier musical organization. Every February they take time from their busy academic schedule to produce a Broadway musical that's so good it routinely outdraws all the amateur theaters in the Baltimore/Washington area. Combined. Paul and I never miss a show. The year before they'd staged a spellbinding version of *Fiddler on the Roof*. Everyone was still raving about it.

And the competition is stiff. Kevin would have had to beat out dozens of other singers for a role—any role—in the show.

"What are they doing?" I asked.

"Sweeney Todd."

I was working on a second shrimp, and I swallowed it then, practically whole, in my haste to respond. "Oh my God!" I croaked. "I love *Sweeney Todd*! When the DVD with Angela Lansbury finally came out, I ran straight out to Tower and snatched one up. I must have played it a hundred times already."

"It *is* wonderful," Dorothy agreed. "Kevin's excited about being given the opportunity."

"What role's he playing?"

"Jonas Fogg," she said, "the guy who runs the insane asylum. It's not a huge part, but Kevin's a fine tenor, so they use him in all the company numbers. And he's understudying the role of Beadle Bamford, so there's always the possibility . . ." Her voice trailed off and she blushed, as if embarrassed about where that thought was taking her.

"I'm surprised I haven't seen the posters yet," I commented. "*Sweeney Todd* is a mega hit. It should really pack them in."

"Who's Sweeney Todd?" someone warbled from the direction of the crab dip. I turned to face one of my least favorite people, Margaret Atkins, wife of the chairman of the math department, aiming an overloaded slice of melba toast directly at her mouth. Even though Paul had been completely cleared of sexual harassment charges brought against him several years before by a former student, Margaret still regarded him, and me, with deep suspicion.

"Dorothy Hart, meet Margaret Atkins, who, clearly, has spent the last two decades living under a rock." I said it with a smile so Margaret would know I was teasing, but she took my remark the wrong way, as usual.

"I still *work*, Hannah," she snorted, pointedly reminding me that since I'd been riffed from my job in Washington, D.C., I didn't. "*I* had to take a day *off* to come to this luncheon."

Out of the corner of my eye I caught Dorothy in mid-gape, so I knew I wasn't the only person in the room who found the woman's behavior boorish. Margaret was round and stumpy, stuffed like a sausage into a tailored two-piece suit of the same improbable red as her hair. She was also the pain-in-the-ass manager of the Academy branch of the Naval Federal Credit Union, so I had to deal with her on occasion, like it or not.

It was an effort, but I decided not to walk down any mean streets with the woman. "It's about a barber named Sweeney Todd who was unjustly exiled to Australia," I explained with exaggerated sweetness. "He escapes back to London where he goes into business over Mrs. Lovett's pie shop—"

"The worst pies in London," Dorothy chimed in.

"Exactly. And the two of them plot revenge against the lecherous judge who framed Sweeney and raped his young wife."

Margaret took a step back, one hand pressed flat against her bosom. "Oh, yuck!"

"Sweeney uses his razors to knock off his customers," Dorothy added, leaning toward Margaret and emphasizing every word, "by slitting their throats."

The hand bearing the melba toast began to waver. A glob of crab dip slid sideways onto the floor.

"But Mrs. Lovett's pretty darn resourceful." Dorothy threw me an exaggerated wink, clearly enjoying herself at Margaret's expense. "Pretty soon all of London's lining up for a taste of her delectable meat pies."

" 'Shepherd's pie peppered with actual shepherd . . .' " I sang softly.

Dorothy smiled mischievously, then toasted Margaret with her empty wineglass. "Think about *that* the next time you stick your fork into a meatball, Margaret."

I laughed out loud. I couldn't help it. I'd swallowed a good bit of wine on a nearly empty stomach, after all, which probably upped my silliness quotient by fifteen or twenty percent.

Margaret gasped, then looked down, staring with embarrassment at the creamy, cheesey glob on the rug next to the toe of her patent leather pump. She waved down a passing server. "Somebody's dropped some crab dip," she informed the young woman. "It needs wiping up."

I caught Dorothy's eye. *Somebody?* she mouthed.

Margaret turned on me as if *I'd* delivered the line about the meatball. "Well, I can't imagine anybody wanting to see a show about . . . about *that!*" And she flounced through the double doors that led to the club lobby, heading in the general direction of the ladies' room.

Dorothy selected a chicken strip from a chafing dish and waved it in the air while chanting Mrs. Lovett's line from the musical. " 'It's priest. Have a little priest . . .' "

" 'Since Marine doesn't appeal to you, how about rear admiral?' " I quoted back, giggling, then stifled myself with a hiccup when I remembered that my new friend was actually married to a rear admiral.

" 'Too salty,' " Dorothy chirped, not appearing to mind in the least. " 'I prefer general.' "

I couldn't resist. " 'With or without his privates?' "

And we fell about laughing, as if we'd been best friends since junior high. Lord knows, we were certainly acting like eighth graders. I was glad Dorothy felt good. Endorphins are good medicine.

When we'd recovered sufficiently to rediscover the bar and order a couple of sensible club sodas with lime, I studied Dorothy's pale blue eyes blinking away tears of laughter behind her rimless eyeglasses and thought it might be fun to help out with *Sweeney Todd*. I visualized driving midshipmen up to A.T. Jones in Baltimore and watching while George Goebel and his pros fitted the cast with elaborate nineteenth-century costumes designed especially for the show. I thought about makeup: painting Mrs. Lovett's cherry-red cheeks, making Sweeney's eyes look dead and sunken, and about how much fun it would be to create the zombielike faces of Sweeney's victims. I grew excited about prowling the antique shops of West Annapolis in search of Victorian-era props to furnish Sweeney's barbershop or Mrs. Lovett's pie shop.

"Sure," I agreed with new enthusiasm. "How can I help?"

Dorothy grabbed my hands in both of hers and squeezed her appreciation. "Oh, Hannah, would you? You've saved my life." Then she said the words that made my heart drop to my shoes, as if she'd explained it all to me before. As if I had known from the very first moment we met. As if I had always known.

Dorothy was building the sets.

My mental gears ground violently as they shifted from romantic visions of frock coats and tea trays and wing-back chairs with antimacassars to images of a bleak industrial cityscape where soot-stained brick walls stretched out of sight into the fly gallery. I visualized a huge, elaborate set featuring barred windows and fuming chimneys, a complicated revolving structure of stairways and platforms, with Mrs. Lovett's pie shop (downstairs) and Sweeney Todd's tonsorial parlor (upstairs), all connected by bridges, trapdoors, and hidden chutes, set pieces that moved in and out of the wings with the smooth silent menace of icebergs.

I thought about Mrs. Lovett's belching oven and Sweeney Todd's deadly barber chair.

I thought about saws and hammers and screwdrivers and drills.

"Wonderful!" I lied brightly. "When do we start?"

CHAPTER 2

Dorothy and I arranged to meet at Mahan Hall the following Tuesday, where I would have my first opportunity to visit the auditorium, check out the sets, and see exactly what I'd gotten myself into.

Just before three o'clock, I bundled myself into a coat and scarf, pulled on a pair of boots—it had snowed overnight and the brick sidewalks were treacherous with slush—thrust my hands into my pockets and trudged down Maryland Avenue toward Gate 3, one of three heavily guarded entrances to the Naval Academy, and the one closest to my house.

After threading my way around the security barriers—none-too-subtly disguised as humongous planters—I produced my civilian ID for the earnest young Marine at the gate, who scrutinized it closely, his brown eyes flitting up and down between my face and the one pictured on the ID in his hand. His caution didn't surprise me. I had shoulder-length hair in that prehistoric picture, and pink, chipmunk cheeks, but I must have passed muster because he returned my ID with a cheerful, "Have a nice evening, ma'am," and glanced only briefly at my backpack before smiling and waving me through.

The Yard—what any other college would call its campus—is 330 acres of dormitories, offices, classroom buildings, state-of-the art sports facilities, officer housing, parade grounds, memorial parks, and playing fields that roll gently down to the seawall that during high water holds back the Severn River. To my right, opposite the guardhouse, was the Administration Building, where the superintendent had his offices; behind that rose the majestic dome of the Naval Academy Chapel.

Avoiding the icy patches, I hustled down the walk, passing Preble Hall, the building that housed the Naval Academy Museum and one of the finest collections of ship models to be found anywhere, until I stood within the welcoming arms of Mahan Hall, a national Historic Landmark, and, like the Officers and Faculty Club and the other buildings in the immediate vicinity, a turn-of-the-nineteenth-century Beaux Arts treasure.

Named for Rear Admiral Alfred Thayer Mahan, Naval Academy Class of 1859, author of the definitive book on sea power, Mahan (the building, not the man) sits at the center of the Yard, across a grassy square from Bancroft Hall, the colossal, eight-wing dormitory, constructed in a double H, that houses and feeds all 4,200 midshipmen.

Mahan itself has only two wings—Maury and Sampson, home to the Engineering and Humanities departments respectively—and rising from the center, a monumental four-faced clock tower. As I approached, the bell in the tower tolled six. Six bells in shipspeak; 1500 military time, 3:00 P.M. for landlubbers. From behind me came the answering bells of the chapel carillon, playing the Westminster chimes—the long version. I stood quietly, breathing slowly, my breath condensing like smoke before my face, enjoying the moment, waiting until the last bong had faded into the crisp late afternoon air before moving on.

I climbed the steps of Mahan and pushed through the bronze-studded oak doors that led into the lobby, which, in spite of their enormous size, opened silently and effortlessly on massive, perfectly balanced hinges.

No matter how many times I visit, it always takes my

breath away to step into that magnificent foyer, with its wide expanses of black and white marble and its pair of grand interior staircases. The architect had built clerestory windows at each landing so that whatever the weather, the interior spaces would be flooded with light.

I paused in the lobby, trying to decide whether to go left or right, figured it didn't matter—the wings were identical—and walked around to my left, up a couple of steps, and through a glass door that led to a long hallway with windows on one side and carved wooden doors leading to the auditorium where I had agreed to meet Dorothy. I opened the door nearest the stage end, slowly, so as not to disturb any rehearsal that might have been in progress, and slipped in.

As I eased along an aisle between two rows of seats, moving toward the center of the auditorium, I glanced at the stage and was relieved to see that set construction was well under way. A wooden superstructure was already in place—the bleak windows of Fogg's Asylum stared at me blankly from the left, and to the right, a skeleton of two-by-fours outlined what was soon to be Mrs. Lovett's pie shop with Sweeney's tonsorial parlor just above.

The air was heavy with sound: the hum of voices punctuated by occasional shouts, the pounding of hammers, the screech and whine of a power saw emanating from somewhere nearby.

Midshipmen were scattered about the hall—singly and in groups—dressed in a variety of uniforms, depending upon where they'd just come from—class or athletic practice. Off in one corner, a trio dressed in WUBAs—working uniform blue alpha: black trousers and black, long-sleeve shirts—appeared to be practicing lines, holding their scripts behind their backs and glancing at them from time to time as if to jog their memories.

Other midshipmen in bright blue and gold track suits were sprawled in seats about the auditorium, their feet propped up on the backs of the seats in front of them, books open on their knees, studying.

I didn't see Dorothy, so I sat down to wait.

A midshipman in gray sweats wandered onstage, carrying a hammer. He gazed upward, pointed the hammer at the lights, gestured with it to someone behind me—in the light booth, I presumed—then wandered off, stage right. What was that all about? Nothing changed about the lights—they remained a bright pinkish hue—so I figured no one in the light booth had been paying attention.

Suddenly, as if a bell had rung somewhere—this was a school, so perhaps it had—the room began to fill with midshipmen. I checked my watch: three-fifteen. The tech crew disappeared through a door at the rear of the stage, and a tall midshipman holding a sheaf of papers and looking very much in charge did an impressive, one-armed thrust and sprang onto the stage, "Listen up!" he shouted. After thirty more seconds of to-ing and fro-ing, the hammering stopped, someone pulled the plug on the power saw, the room quieted and he began passing out rehearsal schedules for the remainder of the week.

"Hannah!" Dorothy breezed in from a door on the north side of the auditorium, smelling winter-fresh, a combination of cold air and wet wool. She plopped down in the chair next to me. "Sorry I'm late," she whispered. "I got tied up at the grocery. You wouldn't *believe* the crowds. Must be because of the snow."

"Oh, yes I would," I whispered back. It was a mystery to me why in these parts ordinarily sane people, at the slightest hint of snow from some know-it-all on the Weather Channel, would rush out to stock up on milk, bread, bottled water, and toilet paper. Even in Annapolis, which rarely saw more than one or two inches of the white stuff, a prediction of snow turned everyone bonkers.

"Did you notice our setup out there?" She gestured with

a gloved hand toward the door through which she had just entered.

"So that's where the sawing was coming from! I wondered. I came in from the hallway on the south side, so I missed it."

Dorothy pulled off her gloves, stuffed them in her pocket, then shrugged out of her fur-lined jacket. "There's no scenery shop in the building," she told me. "But we've got a huge workshop over in Alumni Hall. We'll go over there tomorrow."

I helped Dorothy arrange her jacket over the back of the chair in front of her, where it could dry out, then nodded toward the stage. Two actors in long raincoats had wandered on. "What's up?"

Dorothy squinted at the stage for a few minutes, getting her bearings. "They're getting set to rehearse the opening number. Those two guys are grave diggers."

I leaned back comfortably in the cushioned seat, waiting for rehearsal to begin.

"This is a wonderful theater," Dorothy mused. Her head rested against the back of her seat and she stared up dreamily into the impressive, sky-blue dome with its enormous, Phantom-of-the-Opera-style chandelier.

"You should have seen it a couple of years back," I told her. "Tiny stage, no fly gallery, piss-poor sound, and a lighting system from World War Two that was always blowing fuses." I explained how a $750,000 donation from a former thespian had allowed the Academy to restore Mahan Auditorium to its former grandeur, with enough money left over to hire a paint expert to recreate the historic polychrome painting that decorated the elaborate and unusual proscenium arch.

"And you won't believe what they found during the renovation!" I waved my arm in an arc that took in the entire U-shaped balcony. "When the workmen pulled down the acoustical tile up there, and scraped off the adhesive, they uncovered six enormous display cases set into the walls. Inside were souvenir flags from the War of 1812 that had been lost for half a century." I drew quotation marks in the air around "lost."

Dorothy shaded her eyes and squinted up into the darkness, trying to see what I was talking about. "Some idiot simply tiled over the glass?"

"Yup. I'll take you up there later for a closer look. I mean, who knew? You'd think the Navy couldn't lose track of something that important. They were British pennants from the Battle of Lake Erie, for heaven's sake, captured by Oliver Hazard Perry in 1813 or thereabouts. That was one of the most strategic naval battles in U.S. history. It helped secure the Northwest Territories for the United States."

Dorothy was staring at me as if I'd grown another head.

I made a fist and poked her playfully on the arm. "That's Paul talking, not me. He goes on and on about it. When he's not diddling around trying to solve Reimann's Hypothesis or some other bit of mathematical esoterica, he's quite the history buff."

On stage, the midshipman in charge was reaming out some hapless plebe who was making himself as small as possible in the front row. "I warned you that we'd be working through the weekend, Parker! What do you mean you have to go to your cousin's wedding?"

"I'll take care of it. *Sir,*" the plebe added glumly.

I bet Dorothy a double latte that if the kid had a cell phone, he was already on it, cancelling out on his cousin rather than seeing his Navy career shot down in flames.

Suddenly a hand went up, tracing a languid O in the air. The hand belonged to a bearded, tweedy gentleman, professorially attired in a gray wool jacket over a blue cashmere V-neck sweater that stretched gently over his modest paunch. "Move on, Mr. Lattimer, move on."

"That's Professor Black, the director," Dorothy whispered. "He's absolutely amazing."

I was familiar with Professor Medwin Black, having

read his résumé printed in the "Cast" section of every Glee Club program for each of the previous ten years. During summer vacation, Professor Black directed summer stock in upstate New York. Several of his protégés were currently on Broadway. The Academy was incredibly lucky to have him.

Dorothy leaned toward me once again. "And the guy at the piano's the music director, Professor John Tracey. The mids call them both 'Doc.' "

In the rosy light from the stage, Dorothy's face looked young and unlined. I made a mental note to find out what kind of lightbulbs they were using so I could install them around my vanity at home.

"Everyone has nicknames around here," Dorothy continued. "I imagine the mids will give you one, too, if you stick around long enough."

"Oh, I plan to stick around," I said. Even though the sets were well under way, it looked like a good deal more work had to be done before opening night in two and a half weeks' time. I had never been one to give up easily. And if I'd made a promise? I'd stick to it.

"Do *you* have a nickname?" I asked.

Even in the subdued light I could see Dorothy blush. "They call me 'Mom.' "

"That figures," I chuckled. "You should be flattered."

"Oh, I am." Dorothy leaned toward me and pointed. "See that mid there?"

I recognized the fellow I'd seen earlier, the one in sweats who'd been gesturing at the lights with a hammer.

"He's on the tech crew. His name is Jonathan Lyon, but they call him 'Cher.' "

"Cher? As in Sonny and?"

Dorothy chuckled. "No, Cher, as in clueless."

It took a moment for it to register that she was talking about Cher, the teenage heroine in the movie *Clueless*. I smiled. The film was a family favorite. "I see. But why Cher?"

"He looks busy, doesn't he? But every time you need actual work done, he's clueless. Either that or nowhere to be found."

I was both amused and appalled. "Midshipmen take no prisoners, do they?"

"And see those two over there?" Dorothy pointed to two female midshipmen, wrestling what looked like a meat grinder the size of a washing machine up the left-hand flight of stairs, one of a pair that flanked the proscenium arch. "They're Frick and Frack."

We watched while Frick (or was it Frack?) tipped the contraption forward while Frack (or Frick?) seemed to be trying to set it down on the top step and got thwacked in the head by the handle for her trouble.

"Isn't that just perfect?" Dorothy cooed.

I was confused. "Getting thwacked in the head by a giant meat grinder?"

"Nuh-uh. It's actually a bone crusher. I found it at an antique store in Savage Mill. I couldn't believe my luck, I mean, who has bone crushers simply lying around the house?"

I had to agree the contraption was perfect. It had an air of menace, enhanced by that giant crank handle, a wheel eighteen inches or more in diameter. And the machine was large enough to be seen from every corner of the auditorium.

Frick and Frack duck-walked Mrs. Lovett's meat grinder across the stage and set it in place behind the curtain at stage left. As I recalled from watching the DVD, it wouldn't be required until the second act.

"Anderson! Toreno!" This from Professor Black, clearly eager to get started. "Places! Places everyone!" He clapped his hands. "Let's go, let's go, let's *go*!"

Immediately, there was a scurrying sound, like raccoons in the attic.

I watched Professor Tracey's long thin fingers fly over the electronic keyboard, playing arpeggios, presumably to get everyone's attention. His wedding ring flashed as he flipped a switch on his console, and suddenly the room was filled with tortured, dissonant organ music, the lugubrious chords that Stephen Sondheim wrote to mark the opening of his remarkable opera.

Nothing else happened.

Professor Tracey leapt to his feet, upsetting the piano stool. The stage lights gleamed on the polished surfaces of both his glasses and his bald spot. "The director begins the music," he shouted at the stage, "in the hopes that action will, in fact, commence." He stooped to right his stool, eased his backside onto it, and, with eyes fastened on the cast members already on stage, began playing again. Slowly at first, then faster and faster, building, building, driving forward with a manic intensity that was unsettling, just as Sondheim meant it to be.

Suddenly the air was split by the piercing shriek of a factory whistle that, even though I was expecting it, made me gasp. I thought about checking my eardrums for bleeding.

The music abruptly stopped.

"Not now!" screamed Professor Black, twisting in his seat to reproach the midshipman who was in charge of the sound board at the back of the auditorium. "And turn it down, for pity's sake!"

"From the top!" Once again, John Tracey's hands attacked the keyboard.

" 'Attend the tale of Sweeney Todd . . .' " sang a young man in a ragged overcoat. He was helping another man drag a body bag onto the stage.

" 'He served a dark and an angry god . . .' " sang the second player.

"Yes! Yes!" Professor Black was pleased.

Actor by actor, the stage filled as the chorus arrived to lay out the background story of the Demon Barber of Fleet Street. I watched as a disheveled woman poured ashes from an urn over the "body." Dorothy punched my arm. "There's Kevin!"

"Where?" I asked. She couldn't have meant the woman with the urn.

Dorothy pointed a finger with a badly chewed nail. "The one in the ridiculous wig." She turned to smile at me in the semidarkness. "I should talk about ridiculous wigs, shouldn't I? Like mother, like son?"

"Don't be too hard on yourself," I said as Kevin, dressed in a long frock coat and an unruly white wig, opened his mouth.

" 'His needs were few, his room was bare . . .' " sang Kevin in a clear, high tenor.

" 'A lavabo and a fancy chair . . .' " sang another.

We watched appreciatively while Anthony and Sweeney, fresh off the boat from Australia, made their entrances. And then the beggar woman arrived sporting a remarkable petticoat under a bundle of colorful rags. "Alms, alms for a miserable woman . . ."

Another elbow in my ribs. "That's Kevin's friend, Emma."

I squinted at the beggar woman. She looked vaguely familiar. I wondered if Kevin's friend was "our" Emma, Emma Kirby, one of several midshipmen we'd been sponsoring since they were plebes, providing them with a "home away from home," particularly during their difficult first, often lonely, plebe year. That pile of rags could have been Emma Kirby, I supposed, but it was hard to tell exactly what was under all that makeup.

" 'Wouldn't you like to push me parsley?' " Emma sang, turning to Todd pathetically. After a few more naughty but hilarious measures, Todd shooed the beggar woman away, and she scuttled to the edge of the stage, sat down on the steps and peered out into the audience, such as it was, while shading her eyes with a hand wearing a tattered, fingerless glove. She waved at me. I waved back. Definitely our Emma.

Except for sporadic e-mails, I hadn't talked to Emma since the previous May, when she left on her summer "gray hull" cruise. I wondered why she hadn't been by to see us. We needed to catch up, and I promised myself I'd give her a call.

On stage there was a subtle lighting change. Professor Black yelled, "Where is it? Where is it? Go back and get it!" while the midshipman playing Mrs. Lovett cooled her heels, rhythmically slapping her rolling pin against her open hand. Within seconds the tech crew scurried in with a long narrow table, set it down firmly in front of Mrs. Lovett's pie shop, and scurried away again.

Now that she had her pie-making table, Mrs. Lovett launched into the intricate patter song about the worst pies in London and I was really getting into it, until I became distracted by a midshipman, costumed like an inmate of Fogg's Asylum, who slouched down the aisle and planted herself in the seat next to Dorothy. "Hi, Mom," she said.

This puzzled me, until I realized she was addressing Dorothy by her nickname.

"Hi, Greta," whispered Dorothy. "You looked good up there."

Greta sighed a long-suffering sigh. Clearly she didn't agree. From my vantage point, Greta was a sullen piece of work, sitting with clenched jaw and narrowed eyes, mouthing Mrs. Lovett's lines, loudly filling in missing words. Fortunately there were few, or the actress on the stage—who seemed more than capable of handling the challenging role—might have leaped off the stage and strangled her.

Then Mrs. Lovett fluffed a line.

"What a mistake they made casting *her*!" Greta groused. "I tried out for the part and would have been so much better in the role. Just because she thinks she can sing . . ." She heaved another sigh. "Professor Black is nuts."

Professor Black didn't seem nuts to me. He seemed extraordinarily competent, coaching quality performances out of what were, after all, young engineering students, using firmness, tempered with humor. Greta needed to take a pill.

I returned my attention to the stage, where a new scene was beginning. The actor playing Beadle Bamford entered from stage right calling, "Mrs. Lovett! Mrs. Lovett!" crossed to the plain box that would become a harmonium—one of the projects that would soon end up on my To Do list—sat down and started singing, " 'Sweet Polly Plunket lay in the grass, turned her eyes—' "

"Stop! Stop!" Professor Black flailed his arms.

All eyes turned to Beadle Bamford, whose hands remained gracefully poised over the fake keyboard.

"Midshipman Monroe, what have you done to your head?"

The midshipman caressed his glossy, hairless scalp. "I shaved it, sir."

"Why, pray tell, did you do that?"

"Last night was Service Assignment Night, sir," he said, as if that explained everything.

"Tell me what that has to do with you showing up for rehearsal today wearing a bowling ball on your shoulders."

"I'm going Marines, sir."

"I see." Medwin Black rested both hands on the back of the theater seat in front of him, bowed his head, and seemed to be consulting the toes of his brown oxford shoes. A deathlike silence fell over the auditorium until he looked up again and said, "So, you and the other jarheads went out to celebrate, I presume."

"Yes, sir. With the senior Marine, sir."

"And then you came back to the Hall and shaved your head."

The midshipman playing the Beadle shrugged. "It seemed like a good idea at the time, sir."

Professor Black sighed. "Never mind, we'll work around it." He waved an arm. "Continue!"

Beadle Bamford's parlor song was interrupted once

again by the arrival of box dinners. Rehearsal ground to a halt while the midshipmen launched a full-frontal assault on the food tables. Dorothy and I decided to avoid the stampede and wait until after the midshipmen had eaten before picking up our boxes.

In the meantime, Dorothy invited me up on the stage, where she spread out the sketches the set designer had made on top of Mrs. Lovett's pie-making table and discussed with me what still needed to be done. "A lot will be taken care of by the backdrop we're renting," Dorothy said, to my great relief. "How would you like to be in charge of the barbershop?"

I turned and tipped my head back to get a better look at the structure. From where I stood, perhaps a dozen steps led up to the platform that would eventually be transformed into Sweeney Todd's place of business. There was a back wall—wallpaper would cover that—but other than that, the room was open on three sides, nothing to keep me from tripping and tumbling ass over teacup onto the stage eight or nine feet below.

I shook my head. "I don't do heights," I explained. "I went to Paris once. At the top of the Eiffel Tower there are iron girders that still carry the impression of my fingernails."

In the end, I volunteered to construct the oven, while Dorothy would work upstairs, concentrating on making Sweeney's diabolical barber chair—also rented—function properly.

Suddenly I grew light-headed, whether from hunger or from the stage lights raining relentlessly down on us, it was hard to tell. Sweat prickled my scalp and gathered under the sweatshirt I wore, running down my back and between my breasts.

Dorothy noticed, and tugged at her wig. "Are you hot, too, Hannah, or is it just me?"

I managed a laugh. "My late mother always said, 'I

don't have hot flashes. I have short, private vacations in the tropics!' " I gathered up my bag. "Let's get out from under these lights."

We moved to the edge of the stage, where the lighting was less ferocious, and sat down, side by side, dangling our legs over the lip. "Remember when you said you wanted me for a role model?"

Dorothy wiped her forehead with the tail end of her shirt. "Yeah."

"Well, I hope you don't mind, but I've brought you something." I set the bag I'd been carrying on her lap. "Open it."

Dorothy grabbed the handles of my duffel and pulled them apart. She peered into the bag, and I watched a smile spread slowly across her face. "Hats!"

"Friends gave them to me," I confided, "more than I could ever use. I don't need them anymore, thank goodness. I thought you might find wearing a hat more comfortable than a wig, at least while you're working. I know I did."

Dorothy pulled out a blue canvas hat with *Sea Song* embroidered on it in white script. "*Sea Song* is my sister-in-law's sailboat," I told her. "We should go sailing sometime."

The next hat out of the bag was one decorated with red, white, and blue sequins. Dorothy settled it over her wig. "This seems appropriate," she announced, turning her head from side to side as if examining herself in an imaginary mirror. "How do I look?"

"Patriotic. When you get home, you can experiment with wearing it without the wig."

Dorothy's smile faded. She removed the bespangled hat and placed it, along with the blue canvas one, in the bag with the others. "I'll have to think about it," she said. "I'm not sure that Ted . . ." She clutched the duffel bag to her chest. "Let's say I'll take them home. And, thanks, Hannah. Thanks a lot. I really appreciate it."

Kevin appeared—without being asked, he had fetched box dinners for his mother and me—then just as quickly, he disappeared. Dorothy and I ate passable ham and cheese sandwiches in companionable silence, cardboard boxes balanced smartly on our knees.

After rehearsal ended, Dorothy dragged me into the hallway, where the lumber, Sheetrock, and power tools were being temporarily stored. I gasped. There was enough material in the hallway to build a home for Habitat for Humanity. Maybe two or three of them.

"Let's go," I said with a smile. "I hope we're not going to need all this material! Way too depressing! I'll deal with it tomorrow."

"Need a ride?"

It was after eight o'clock, but I wanted to walk. "No, that's okay, Dorothy. Prince George is one way, so you'd have to drive the long way around. It's shorter for me to go on foot. Really," I added when she looked doubtful. "But I'll walk you to your car. Where is it?"

"Out front."

On our way to the parking lot, we noticed Kevin and Emma standing next to one of the empty coatracks at the end of the hallway. Dorothy opened her mouth to call out to her son, but I threw out an arm to restrain her. "It looks like a private conversation," I warned.

Whatever the two young people had been discussing, the conversation was clearly over. "I'm really sorry, Kevin," Emma was saying, her voice small and tight. "But I'm not going to do it. I'm just *not*!" She hoisted her book bag over one shoulder and hurried down the staircase that led to the exit on the lower level. Kevin stood in stunned silence for a moment, then ran after her, his words echoing hollowly off the marble walls. "Emma! Wait up!"

"Oh, dear, I hope there's nothing wrong," Kevin's mother said, her brows drawn together in a frown. "I think he has a bit of a crush on that girl."

"Uh-huh."

"Well, you know what they say?"

"What's that?"

"The course of true love never runs smooth."

"So they say."

The fact was, in the course of the past two years I had grown to know Emma Kirby fairly well. Kevin might be standing on the platform, but that train was not coming into the station for him.

CHAPTER 3

Seeing me at the musical rehearsal had appar-ently pegged Emma's guilt-o-meter, too, because when I got home that evening, Paul told me she had called.

"She leave a message?"

Paul looked up from the crossword puzzle he was working. "She apologized profusely for ignoring us and asked that you call her back. She left a number. I think it's her cell."

I returned Emma's call at once, because I wanted to see her. I was keen to find out why she had returned to the Academy. The last time we talked, she had been planning to call it quits.

Emma and I arranged to meet before rehearsal the following day in the Hart Room of Mahan Hall, which had been, until Nimitz opened in 1972, the main reading room of the Naval Academy library. In the years since then, the Hart Room had been used for everything from wedding receptions to spare office space, but had recently been converted into an elegant student lounge. When the cappuccino bar went in, I rejoiced, and occasionally met Paul there for coffee.

Flags representing each of the fifty states flanked the marble staircases that led from the center of Mahan lobby up to the Hart Room. Because the cappuccino bar was on the south side of the building, I chose the staircase to the left. As I climbed to the second floor past Ohio, Iowa, and Indiana, I wondered what Emma wanted to talk to me about, and if it had anything to do with why she'd returned to the Academy, or what I'd overheard of her conversation with Kevin the night before.

On the phone, she'd sounded worried, but when I pressed her for details, she put me off, saying it wasn't a good time. Privacy, I knew, was a rare commodity in Bancroft Hall, where everyone had one, sometimes two, roommates, doors were rarely locked, and first classmen—"firsties"—could walk in on you, unannounced, at any time.

I was early. Emma hadn't arrived, so I bought a Tropicana grapefruit drink from the cashier at the counter and settled into an upholstered chair to wait.

The room was magnificent—like Cinderella's ballroom—with enormous windows that stretched all the way to the ceiling some thirty feet over my head, highly polished wooden floors, and a Romeo and Juliet–style balcony that overlooked the terrace below. As long, I swear, as a football field, the room had doorways at each end that linked it to classrooms in Maury and Sampson to the north and south, respectively.

Midshipmen were sprawled, some of them sound asleep, on sofas and chairs that had been arranged in conversational groupings about the room. Several mids were seated at tables, talking in low voices over open textbooks, and if the mid clicking his way from website to website on his laptop at the next table was any indication, computer services had thoughtfully provided wireless computer access to users of the room.

I checked the clock that hung over the doorway leading to Maury. It was two-forty. Emma was late. It wasn't like her. I had just tossed my empty Tropicana bottle into the recycling bin labeled "glass" when she breezed in, full of apologies and out of breath, her books and uniform cap tucked under one arm.

"Want anything to drink?" I asked. "My treat."

Emma shook her head. "No thanks. I brought my own." She produced a can of Sprite from under her cap.

"Cookies? Chips?"

She grinned and patted her thigh. "Uh-uh. Gotta watch out for that Severn River hip disease." The midshipmen diet was calorie-rich, to support their active regime. It proved particularly hard on the women.

"Like you need to worry," I teased, envying Emma's solid but trim figure. "Any particular place you want to sit?"

Emma glanced around, then gestured with her soda can to a pair of chairs set at precise right angles to one another on the fringed edge of a Bokhara carpet. "How 'bout over there," she suggested. "More out of the way, and nobody'll bother us."

"I was glad to see you last night," I told her as we settled comfortably into the plump leather cushions. "When we didn't hear from you in September . . ." I shrugged. "Well, after our heart-to-heart last spring, I assumed you'd decided not to come back to the Academy."

Emma popped the top of her Sprite and took a long swig. Without her stage makeup, without makeup of any kind, in fact, Emma was a beautiful young woman. She was blessed with clear, almost translucent skin and rosy cheeks, a look that millions of women aspired to but no regimen but diet, exercise, and . . . well, youth could even begin to duplicate. Her dark hair was cut in a neat bob, curling gently under at each ear, well off her collar, as required by Navy regulations; a swoop of bangs was caught to one side and secured at her temple with a plain silver barrette.

"I thought about it all summer," she said, "while I was on cruise." She gazed at me with serious green eyes flecked with amber, inherited, no doubt, from her father, an Irish Catholic from Boston. But their almond shape, and her blue-black hair, came directly from her mother, a native of Taiwan.

"Tell me about your summer," I urged, steering the conversation gently in another, less land-mine-strewn direction.

That seemed the right tack. Emma's frown vanished and she launched cheerfully into an account of her summer training. "For most of June, I was on the *USS Bonhomme Richard,* an amphibious assault ship," she said.

Despite Paul working for the Navy for years, I'd never thought much about ships. I must have looked puzzled, because she hurried to elaborate. "It looks like an aircraft carrier," she explained, "with a flat deck for the planes, but it's much smaller. I was one of a thousand crew members, but if we needed to, like helping with the war in Iraq or something, we could have taken on as many as sixteen hundred troops."

I'm not particularly good with figures, but even I could do the math for that. "That's twenty-six hundred people, give or take. That's huge!"

"Bigger than my hometown," she joked. "But an aircraft carrier is almost twice as big. Take the *Nimitz,* for example. It carries six thousand people, is approximately eleven hundred feet long by two hundred fifty feet wide and is taller than an eighteen-story building. The *Bonhomme Richard* is just 844 by one hundred six. Quite a difference."

My synapses were firing on all cylinders as I struggled to put those statistics into context. I thought about Connie's sailboat, the only boat I'd ever sailed on. It was a mere thirty-seven feet long and probably as wide as the average Volkswagen Beetle measured bumper to bumper.

"Holy cow," I said at last.

Emma reached for her notebook and extracted a postcard from between the pages. "Here's a picture of her," she said, handing the postcard to me across the table.

The *USS Bonhomme Richard, LHD6,* had a nickname, I learned: the Revolutionary Gator. And Emma was right; it did resemble an aircraft carrier, with airplanes lashed, like children's toys, to the deck. Unlike an aircraft carrier, though, amphibious vessels could drive home, straight into the gaping black hole in the vessel's stern. "A ship like that," I said, handing the postcard back, "you must have been rocking and rolling. I'd have been barfing nonstop."

"It wasn't so bad," she said. "They keep you pretty busy, so you don't have time to think about getting sick. The Navy assigns us to petty officers—they call them running mates—and we follow our running mates around, learning the enlisted side of things." She leaned forward, resting her elbows comfortably on her knees. "Most of our training comes from books, so it's great to see what *really* goes on. I can tell you one thing." She gestured with her soda can. "You haven't lived until you've spent a couple of weeks following a petty officer around. Those people really work *hard*."

"I guess they want you to walk in enlisted shoes, see what it's like before they make you an officer and put you in charge."

She nodded. "Next summer, part two. We'll shadow officers." She tipped up her soda can and finished it off.

"Where did you sail?" I asked.

"From Hawaii to San Diego. And in a way," she continued, rolling the empty can back and forth between her palms, "being on that ship really cinched it for me. You know I've never wanted to do anything but fly helicopters. The *Bonhomme Richard* carries forty-six Sea Knight helicopters, some ASWs and six Harrier attack planes. It made my heart sing just to stand on deck and look at them. And when they practiced night takeoff and landings . . ." Her eyes took on a faraway look and I could tell she was standing again on that pitching deck with wind from the prop wash tearing at her hair. "When push came to shove, there really was no choice. I *had* to come back."

For a midshipman, the summer between youngster and second class year was fish-or-cut-bait time. It was the last chance a midshipman had to tell the Navy, "No thanks, not for me," without incurring a five-year military obligation, or more. Once a midshipman started his second class, or junior, year, he owed the Navy (and the taxpayers) big-time. Emma was now committed to the Navy. The ships and the choppers had apparently changed her mind.

"Have you talked to your parents?"

Emma sat up as if she'd been shot. "God, no! You met them on parents' weekend, Hannah. American Gothic all the way. Can you imagine? Dad would go ballistic if he found out I'm gay." She pointed to one of a series of oil paintings that lined the walls on both sides of the room, portraits of famous admirals. "See that painting up there?"

I nodded. It was a full-length portrait of Admiral William J. Crowe, USN, former Chairman of the Joint Chiefs of Staff and ambassador to Britain during the Clinton administration. Crowe was standing behind a chair, smiling benevolently, like a favorite uncle, with his hat tucked under his arm.

"Well, picture Crowe with a poker up his butt and frowning, and that'd be my dad."

I had to smile. I'd met Emma's father one Parents' Weekend. I didn't know about the poker, but there *was* an uncanny resemblance between the two men. "How about your mom, then?" I asked.

"That's a laugh. She'd insist that I *change.* She'd sic her prayer group on me, and if that didn't work, she'd find somebody to kidnap me and drag me off to some Bad Girl Camp for deprogramming. The Baptists have their ways."

"You're not serious about the deprogramming."

She tapped her mouth with an index finger. "Read my lips. *I'm deadly serious.* Dad owns the only farm supply store in Galena, Iowa. Can you imagine all those good ol' boys dropping by, tonguing their chaw from one cheek to the other just to tell Daddy how supportive they are of his only daughter's alternative lifestyle?" Emma slumped into the cushion and crossed one black-clad leg over the other before continuing. "I got appointed to the Academy by Senator Tom Harkin, for heaven's sake. Harkin was a jet pilot in the Navy during Vietnam. I'm doomed!"

I opened my mouth to say something reassuring, but Emma cut me off. "It gets worse. I was grand marshal of Galena's memorial day parade, sitting on top of the mayor's stretch Caddy, riding down Church Street to Courthouse Square behind my high school band playing 'I'm Proud to Be an American.' Oh, this'll go over just great in Galena." She raised her arm and used an index finger to write an imaginary headline in the air. "Galena Girl Goes Gay."

She sighed deeply, stretching her legs out straight on the carpet in front of her. "Well, you know what they say. If they don't ask, I'm certainly not going to tell."

Emma blinked rapidly, fighting back tears.

"This is going to make life difficult for you here, isn't it, Emma?" I said gently.

"Well, it's not like I've actually *done* anything, you know," she said, swiping at her eyes with the back of her hand. "As I told you last spring, I've had these feelings since junior high, but I didn't do anything about it. I thought that being attracted to my girlfriends was normal. That one day I'd grow out of it. I've read the storybooks! I thought that eventually some guy'd walk into my life and bells would start ringing and my heart would go pitter-pat. And when that didn't happen, what did I know? I thought I just hadn't met the right guy."

"But . . ." I struggled for the words. "If the Academy finds out . . ."

Emma waved a hand dismissively. "I know, I know. But, they won't. If I don't *act* on my feelings . . ." A sly smile crept over her face. "I figure if I leave my black leather jumpsuit in the bottom drawer and lock up my nipple ring—"

"Nipple ring?" I interrupted in a hoarse whisper, but I could see from her ready grin that she was just kidding about the nipple ring. I wasn't so sure about the jumpsuit.

"Is there anybody special?" I dared to ask.

Emma was staring at another one of the admirals, two or three portraits down from Admiral Crowe. "This summer, while on leave?" She stared at the wall dreamily, and I knew Emma was miles away, on some deserted South Pacific beach, perhaps. She shuddered, dragging herself almost physically back to the present. "Well, let's just say that something crystallized for me on Waikiki, and after that I knew there was no going back."

"I'm glad you told me," I said.

"You're right, though, Hannah. It's not going to get any easier. Take Kevin, for example." She closed her eyes and tilted her head heavenward. "Take Kevin, *please*!"

"Kevin Hart, you mean? The guy who plays Jonas Fogg?"

She nodded. "*That* Kevin. Kevin's not the only guy who's asked me out. I've actually gone on a couple of dates since I came to Annapolis, but nothing. You know?" She glanced away. "And if I don't start dating soon, I'm afraid somebody'll guess."

"Nobody will guess, Emma, if you don't tell them—" I shut my mouth as an officer dressed in Navy khakis walked by the back of my chair on his way into Maury. When he'd disappeared through the door, I continued. "They'll just think you're a Hall Rat, a dedicated mid, working hard and sacrificing your social life to stay at the top of your class."

We sat in silence. "Kevin does seem to be attracted to you," I said after a few minutes had ticked by.

"Well, if I ever did decide to have a go with a guy, it certainly wouldn't be with Kevin. He's driving me bonkers!"

"What's the problem? He's certainly attractive."

"Oh, right. In a me-Tarzan-you-Jane kind of way. I should take out a restraining order."

I laughed out loud. "His dad's an admiral, I hear."

"And Kevin never lets us forget it. What a prick!" I imagined she was thinking about Kevin when she pressed her empty soda can between her palms and squashed it flat. "And now his mom's hanging around, too." She laughed uneasily. "One big happy family."

"I was with Kevin's mom last night," I told Emma, as if she didn't know. "I'm helping with the sets for *Sweeney Todd*. I don't mean to be nosy, Emma, but when we were leaving the building, we saw you talking to Kevin. You didn't seem very happy."

"Oh, *that!* Kevin asked me out—again!—but I told him no. We're in the same company. Mids aren't allowed to date other mids in their company."

"But that's the perfect excuse! You can remind Kevin that you *can't* go out with him. It's against the rules."

"You'd think, but he was pressuring me to take a love chit. Can you believe it? I told him to pound sand."

"A what chit?" I couldn't believe that I'd heard Emma correctly.

"A love chit. That's not its official name, of course, but if you fall in love with somebody in your company, and you want to date, you can request permission to be moved to another company." She moaned. "As if I'd take a love chit for Kevin, or for anybody else, for that matter! I *like* my company; my best friends are in my company."

Emma began playing with a button on the front of her shirt, twisting it absentmindedly until I began to fear for the thread. "So, I figure I'll just go on as I have been. Mind my own business. Graduate. Take my commission. The worst that will happen is that someday the Navy will find out I'm a lesbian and they'll kick my ass out anyway, but at least I'll go out proud, holding a B.S. degree in engineering and knowing how to fly a goddamn airplane."

I couldn't imagine living a double life like that. What if the strong physical attraction that Paul and I had for each other were suddenly against the law, the lovemaking we enjoyed not even legal in the privacy of our own bedroom? What if Paul could lose his job simply for loving me? It was unthinkable.

"Emma?" I touched her hand where it lay gripping the arm of her chair. "Are you sure?"

She nodded. "They're not supposed to ask, of course, but if they do, none of this honesty bullshit for me. I'll lie through my teeth if I have to. Make 'em prove it." She threw both hands in the air. "Isn't it *stupid*?"

I had to agree. The military's "Don't Ask, Don't Tell, Don't Pursue" policy had to be the most wrong-headed compromise in the annals of legislation, and that was saying something.

Emma looked at me with wide, honest eyes. "If I can hold on, tough it out, maybe they'll change that ridiculous law."

I knew where that was coming from. *Where there's life, there's hope.* How many of my desperately ill friends had felt that way? If I can just hold on—one day, one week, one month at a time—perhaps they'll find a cure before my time runs out.

"I understand, Emma," I said. "And if there's anything I can do . . ."

Emma reached out and squeezed my hand. "Oh, Hannah, I feel so comfortable talking to you. Sometimes I think you're the only person I can trust."

She was right to trust me; I hadn't even told Paul. I knew *I* could keep Emma's secret. But, I wondered, could *she?*

CHAPTER 4

Over the course of the next week I saw Emma every day, quite literally, in passing. I'd wave cheerily while on my way to or from the set shop in nearby Alumni Hall or we'd exchange pleasantries when I happened to run into her—surrounded by several dozen of her cast mates—in the dressing room.

On Saturday afternoon I paused in the hallway of Mahan, paint bucket in hand, to watch as Emma, dressed like a Victorian bag lady, perfected her timing, a complicated choreography made considerably more difficult by the demands of her bulky costume: a tattered shawl pinned over a tightly laced bodice, a red bonnet sporting a nosegay of wilted pansies, and skirt upon skirt upon layers of petticoats over the most extraordinary pair of hot pink pantaloons Victorian London had ever seen.

The midshipman playing Judge Turpin was stalking the hallways, too, flinging his judicial robes about like a latter day Dracula, dropping to his knees again and again to recite *mea culpa, mea culpa, mea maxima culpa* for a pivotal but disturbing scene that had been cut—for obvious reasons, it seemed to me—from the original Broadway production. As I watched, fascinated, Turpin clutched a Bible and sang about his obsession for Johanna, his teenage ward, then produced a whip from his sleeve and began flailing himself: *God! Deliver me! Filth! Leave me!*

All activity in the hallway ground to a halt. Actors, tech crew, and midshipmen simply passing through on their way to athletic practice were sucked into Turpin's orbit. Eyes closed, accompanied by music nobody else heard, Turpin sang a cappella with unrestrained passion and an intensity that was almost scary. *Soft. White. Cool. Virgin. Palms.* His final E-flat faded into several seconds of palpable silence, followed by the echoing patter of spontaneous and enthusiastic applause.

Whatever one might think about the propriety of a self-flagellation scene in a college production, one thing was certain—the audience would be mesmerized.

Turpin shook himself out of his trance, adjusted his silver wig—which had slipped crookedly over his left eye—bowed deeply to his impromptu audience, and gave a high five to the midshipman playing Beadle Bamford, who'd been standing nearby with the script open, following along.

"Whoa!" The comment came from a midshipman who was lounging against the wall directly behind me.

"Whoa, indeed," I agreed, glancing at the young man over my shoulder.

Without his mad scientist disguise, I hardly recognized the kid, but it was definitely Kevin, I decided: tall—at least six-foot-two—with blue eyes, fair freckled skin, and a fuzz of reddish hair cut "high and tight," like the U.S. Marine his mother told me he aspired to be. "That'll give some old admiral a coronary," Kevin chuckled.

"I daresay you're right." I eased into a vacant spot next to him and leaned back against the cold stone wall. "And how about that block of tickets reserved for Manresa?" I wondered aloud, referring to the upscale assisted living center, a former Jesuit retreat, built high on the banks of the Severn River, just opposite the Academy.

Kevin jerked his head to the left. "Emma's bit is going to give the blue hairs apoplexy, too, I'll bet."

I followed his gaze. Emma was working on her number,

the center of attention once again, now that Judge Turpin had swanned off, cape tails flapping. " 'Hey! Hoy! Sailor boy! Want it snugly harbored?' " She sashayed across the marble floor, flipped up her skirts and aimed a couple of pelvic thrusts—half taunting, half teasing—at the Beadle. " 'Open me gate, but dock it straight, I see it lists to starboard!' " she sang. Then, just as quickly, she switched off the beggar woman and became Emma again, bending at the waist to adjust the laces on her high-buttoned shoes, revealing yards of frothy petticoats.

Quite frankly, I was surprised. Emma had to know that Kevin was watching. And he was, too, a goofy grin splitting his face. What was Emma thinking? Didn't she know he'd take it as a sign of encouragement? I'd have to speak to that girl. But before I could corner her for a motherly word, Emma had snatched the bonnet off her counterfeit ringlets and scampered down the stairs in the general direction of the dressing rooms.

" 'Scuse me, ma'am." Kevin pushed away from the wall and bounded down the stairs after her. "Emma, wait up!"

"Don't mind me," I grumped to his departing back. I fought back the urge to run after the pair. But Emma was a big girl, I told myself. Time she learned to deal with the consequences of her complicated love life without any assistance from me. Besides, I needed to get busy on Mrs. Lovett's oven.

My project, the oven, was actually well underway and, like every prop in *Sweeney Todd,* was intended to be oversized, exaggerated in scale, not only so that it'd be more menacing, but for a more practical reason: so it could be seen from every corner of the theater.

The size and shape of your average refrigerator, the oven was built out of quarter-inch plywood. A thin sheet of metal covered the door, which opened with a downward tug on a large iron handle. On top, we'd installed a squat chimney stack. I say "we" because I'd had the assistance of a pro, Midshipman First Class Bennett Small, who had turned up backstage in the tech room one day, tossed two quarters into a can on top of the minifridge, helped himself to a Coke, and cheerfully introduced himself as my assistant.

"Help yourself," he invited, indicating the fridge. He stretched out full-length on the ratty sofa and propped his feet up on the arm. "Anything that doesn't have a label on it is fair game."

I opened the fridge and peered in. Cokes, Diet Cokes, Sprites, a few Gatorades, some with labels and some without, were stacked neatly inside like cordwood. I selected an unlabeled Coca-Cola and, following Midshipman Small's example, fished a couple of quarters out of my purse and tossed them into the coffee can.

Midshipman Small took a long swig from his soda. "Don't touch the Dr Pepper, though, or Adam will go ballistic."

"Adam?" I popped the top on my soda.

"Adam Monroe. The mid playing Beadle Bamford."

"No chance of that," I told my assistant. "Can't stand the stuff. Way too sweet."

Bennett Small, I soon learned, was called Gadget. The nickname was apt. He could turn nuts and bolts, odd scraps of metal and miscellaneous gizmos from Radio Shack, into inventions as diverse as a receiver that could pick up signals from *Voyager One* or, in a recent more down-to-earth effort, a high-tech, radio-controlled miniature robot known in collegiate circles as a BattleBot. That fall, he'd entered the competitive BattleBot arena with a lightweight 'Bot he'd named Skeezicks. Skeezicks successfully evaded killer saws, pulverizers, and the dreaded vortex before reaching out its skinny metal arms and short-circuiting its opponent for the well-deserved win.

During the first week of our partnership, Gadget and I reached what I considered a fair and equitable division of labor on oven construction: Gadget ran wires, installed electrical switches and lightbulb sockets. I bought the red lightbulb at Safeway, screwed it in, and—tah-dah—flipped on the switch.

We'd been waiting around all week for the smoke machine to be delivered, and by the time it appeared on the loading dock, we'd become a well-oiled team. I held the tool bag, passing tools to him like an operating room nurse while Gadget unpacked the equipment, secured the smoke machine to the floor just behind the oven, and got the whole thing going.

"You are wasted on the Naval Academy," I told Gadget as we stood in Row C, arms folded across our chests, admiring our handiwork. The oven crouched on four stubby legs, stage left, belching smoke and glowing crimson, like a malevolent Easy-Bake oven. "You should be working for NASA."

Gadget blinked pale blue eyes at me from behind his rimless eyeglasses. "I'm going nuke," he said.

"Submarines?" The news didn't surprise me. Only midshipmen at the very top of their graduating class were selected for the nuclear Navy. Gadget was so smart he'd probably be the first midshipman in history to graduate with *more* than a 4.0.

"Yoo-hoo!" It was Dorothy, standing "upstairs" in Sweeney's tonsorial parlor, shading her eyes against the glare of the stage lights. "I could use a little technical expertise up here!"

Actually, Dorothy had seemed hyperenergized that week, banging away with little help or complaint on the scaffolding above my head—the second floor of Mrs. Lovett's pie shop. "Get me while you can," she had chirped down to me on one occasion. "I go back to the oncologist on Tuesday, so by Wednesday, I'll be back to barfing."

I could relate to that. I'd once been so ill from my chemotherapy that I'd watched all of *Killer Klowns from Outer Space* because I was too exhausted to reach across the bed for the remote. So, I took Dorothy at her word.

Earlier in the week, we raided the antique shops in West Annapolis, furnishing Sweeney's chamber with a coat tree, a low bookshelf, a sofa-sized painting in a rococo frame entitled *The Barque Geelong Off Hong Kong,* and a large wooden chest with brass studs and leather straps, just the thing to hold the body of Perelli, rival barber to Sweeney Todd and Sweeney's first victim.

For a mere $120 plus tax we'd scored an actual red and white barber pole at Absolutely Fabulous Consignments, then celebrated our coup over luscious, grilled Reuben sandwiches—three napkins required—at Regina's German deli just next door. We figured we'd earned it.

All the props were in place now at Sweeney's except the most important—his chair. Rented from a theater company in Virginia, the Victorian-style barber chair had made its appearance on the loading dock about the same time as our smoke machine, and Dorothy, Sweeney, and the two midshipmen in charge of trapdoor and body chute construction were wasting no time getting it installed. Made of solid wood with a seat and back of woven cane, the chair was a veteran, having dispatched hundreds of Sweeney's victims in theaters all the way from Maine to Florida.

"Guinea pigs!" Dorothy shouted. "I need guinea pigs!" Behind her, Sweeney and one of the tech crew were carefully aligning a short pipe that extended from the bottom of the chair with a metal plate on the floor. "Come *on!*" she urged when nobody made any effort to step forward. "I need volunteers to go down the chute, otherwise we won't know where to position the chair."

Professor Black materialized at my elbow. "Don't need any cracked heads on my watch," he muttered.

"Hellooooooo?" Dorothy warbled.

Still nobody stepped up to the plate.

I gently elbowed Professor Black. "What's the problem?"

"Beats the heck out of me."

And me, too. Midshipmen maintain themselves in peak physical condition. They are required to run a mile in under six minutes, jump from a forty-foot tower into a tiny pool of water, and leap tall buildings in a single bound, or they don't graduate. You'd think a trip down a chute the length of your average playground slide would be, well, child's play.

Professor Black apparently agreed. He began pinwheeling his arms. "Murphy! Crenshaw! Tyler! Get out here, the lot of you! It's show time!" Surprisingly spry for a man of his girth, the professor hopped onto the stage, and as each actor straggled in from the wings, began herding them like some tweedy sheepdog into a line that snaked, single file, up the stairway leading to Sweeney's tonsorial parlor.

Gadget and I watched as the first victim settled himself into Sweeney's chair, a mix of anticipation and apprehension alternating across his face. The actor playing Sweeney, standing just behind, pantomimed the throat slitting bit and yanked on the back of the chair, causing the seat to shoot forward, depositing his victim feet first through the trapdoor. "Next!" sang Sweeney in a lyrical baritone.

Two more victims were successfully launched through the trapdoor and down the chute. After each, Dorothy and the technician would confer, slightly reposition the chair and adjust the mounting plate accordingly.

By the time everything was screwed down tight, the trials had attracted a handful of daredevils, midshipmen who probably spent their leave time driving their SUVs from theme park to theme park, riding roller coasters with names like Anaconda, Shockwave, and Screamin' Demon. Queued up rather haphazardly on stage, they jostled for position, waiting for the opportunity to sit down in the chair, have their throats slit, and play dead as the floor gave out beneath them. For these guys, everything, even mealtimes, could turn into a competition, and pretty soon

Saturday morning rehearsal had become an Olympic event.

"Eight point seven!" somebody shouted as another victim shot out the end of the chute.

"Nine point three!" said another.

And we all fell about the auditorium laughing.

"Hey, Hannah. How about you?"

I gaped at Dorothy. "Me?" I tapped my chest with my thumb. "You talking to *me?*"

Dorothy waved me onstage. "You said you wanted to give it a try."

"I don't remember saying that." I smiled uncertainly, watching as Sweeney skillfully dispatched another victim. He was practicing with his razors now, big scary metal objects with seven-inch blades that had been modeled on a traditional straight razor and fabricated out of a single piece of steel by a local company that usually manufactured hard-to-find parts for boats. There was no edge, of course, and therefore absolutely no danger of Sweeney cutting anyone's throat for real, but from the audience, the razors looked menacing. Between victims, Sweeney twirled the razors, and the metal flashed between his fingers, filling the darkened theater with twinkling shafts of light.

I swallowed hard, considered the chair and the razors, thinking how embarrassed my family would be if my obituary read, "Killed in a bizarre accident involving a barber chair."

"Hannah?"

Some cheeky mid behind me began making discreet clucking noises.

"Oh, all right!" Holding onto the rickety wooden railing for dear life, I climbed the steps to Sweeney's shop, where the pseudobarber welcomed me into his chair with a polite bow. The Pair-o-Docs, Professors Black and Tracey, clapped encouragingly from the wings. Dorothy bounced up and down on her toes. I imagined everyone else was holding their breaths.

Keeping one cautious eye on Sweeney, I backed into the chair, squirmed a bit and took a deep breath myself.

Slice'a da throat, light-a da light, shriek-a da whistle. My head shot back, the ground opened up beneath me, and I was completely at the mercy of gravity. *Yee-haw!* One second later I lay in an untidy heap on a wrestling mat inside Mrs. Lovett's pie shop, laughing my head off.

Gadget extended a hand, helping me to my feet. "Bravo zulu," he said. Navy speak for well done.

"Thanks." I brushed sawdust off my sweat pants. "That's almost as exciting as the Volcano Pool at the Polynesian Village Resort."

"Disney World?" he asked.

I nodded. "We took the grandkids down last summer. You climb to the top of this fiberglass mountain, then shoot down a long slide built inside it—whoosh!—into the pool."

Gadget and I headed for the tech room at stage right, down a short flight of steps and into a weirdly shaped cubbyhole of a room furnished with an odd assortment of castoff furniture, its walls densely painted with the names of cast members who had appeared in Academy productions going well back to the 1930s. A computer, a television, a VCR, piles of cheap paperback novels and videotapes—I saw *Mulan, Rambo, Shakespeare in Love*, and *Animal House*—a gooseneck lamp and loose wires and extension cords leading God knows where. All the comforts of home.

"We spent a fortune on Magic Kingdom tickets," I said as Gadget held open the door and waited for me to go through ahead of him. "But forget about Mickey! I think the kids would have been happy to spend the whole four days at the pool, sluicing down that lava tube."

I helped myself to an oatmeal cookie from a package

sitting open on the table. "I did it a couple of times," I added, taking a bite. "Damn thing was over thirty feet long, twisting and turning." I gestured upward with the cookie in the general direction of the stage. "Much more dangerous than *that,* anyway."

Gadget rapped three times on the battered tabletop. "Knock on wood."

"You think that's necessary?"

Gadget shrugged. "You never know. We put it together pretty fast."

I finished off the cookie and licked the crumbs off my fingers. "I'm not worried. This is an engineering school, isn't it? You're engineers. You're supposed to be able to build things." I grinned back at him, then, thinking about the rickety handrail, rapped three times on the tabletop, too.

As my mother always said, "Better safe than sorry."

CHAPTER 5

Victorian London: it surrounded me. Gentle-men in top hats. Ladies in bustles and bonnets and bows. Butchers and bakers and candlestick makers. Beggars, grave diggers, Gypsies, the odd escapee from Bedlam, and a stick-twirling bobby or two. I'd been teleported—T-shirt, paint-smeared blue jeans, Nikes, and all—directly into a set for Charles Dickens's *Christmas Carol.* When I closed my eyes, I could even *smell* the nineteenth century—but when I opened them again, it was only a half-eaten steak sub with onions that an actor had abandoned on a nearby chair.

The theater was filled with sound, too, a glorious cacophony as the orchestra members wandered into the pit, unpacked their instruments, and began tuning up. They were accompanied by saws, drills, and hammers, musical themselves in their whines, drones, and rat-a-tat-tats as, working frantically together, we neared the firm deadline imposed by opening night.

I'd finished painting the steps leading up to Sweeney's parlor, cleaned my brushes in turpentine, and took a well-deserved time-out to watch with some amusement as Gadget helped the sound engineers fit the leads with body mikes. He'd lined the mikes up along the edge of the stage, marked each one with an actor's name using masking tape, and was checking their batteries—the square, nine-volt kind—for juice. Gadget being Gadget, he'd chosen the high-tech way, by pressing his tongue against both terminals.

My cell phone vibrated against my ribs. It was Dorothy, leaving a message that she wanted to consult with me about something. Not seeing anything productive in watching Gadget systematically destroy his taste buds, I returned her call. She didn't pick up, so I went looking for her.

Dorothy wasn't taking a break in the tech room as her message had indicated, so I hustled off in the opposite direction, through a narrow, almost invisible doorway and down an even narrower flight of stairs. I paused on the half landing that opened into the other hidey-hole where actors and amorous, in-the-know couples seeking privacy often hung out: the Jabberwocky room. Painted flat black, the walls of the Jabberwocky room were decorated with large-scale, surprisingly faithful copies of Tenniel's illustrations from *Alice in Wonderland.* Alice had been swimming up the stairway wall with the Dormouse ever since the 1940s, and on the far wall, behind a rickety bookshelf, she had spent decades sipping endless cups of tea with the Mad Hatter et al. Alas, there was no sign of the Jabberwocky, who at some time beyond recent memory had been painted over with an enormous map of Tolkien's Middle Earth by someone with little skill and even less taste. Because of her recent chemotherapy treatment, I had suspected that Dorothy might be resting on the large white sofa that dominated the room, but she wasn't there.

I toddled down the remaining steps that took me to the lower dressing room level and stuck my head through the door. "Hello? Anybody home?"

I was talking to myself. Everyone appeared to be somewhere else, except for a chorus line of Styrofoam heads that stared at me eyelessly from a shelf. The heads were wig stands, but at that moment they simply sat there on their necks, eerily; wigless and bald, reminding me, sadly, of Dorothy. The last time I'd seen her, she was still wearing that moth-eaten wig. Maybe she hated the hats I brought her? Plan B was to lure Dorothy and that wig of hers down to Karen James's beauty salon on Maryland Avenue. If anyone could coax it into a more updated hairstyle, Karen James could.

Wondering if Karen's place had an emergency entrance, I turned my back on the wig stands and wandered into the dressing room proper. Mirrors covered the walls on both sides, and makeup, book bags, and assorted articles of clothing were strewn about everywhere. Mounted on the wall next to a pair of gigantic pipes at the far end of the room was a strange, dark gray box, which on closer examination appeared to be a radio. I flipped the switch on and nearly jumped out of my Nikes.

"Tobias! Don't talk to me, talk to the audience!"

I spun around, but Professor Black wasn't anywhere in the vicinity. When I could breathe again, I realized that the box had to be an intercom piping sound in directly from the stage some twenty feet overhead. "Plot, plot, plot!" the director shouted above the strident scrape of student violins not yet ready for prime time and the relentless pounding of the electric piano. "If they can't understand the words, they won't know what's going on! Talk to the people in the back row!"

Grinning to myself, and feeling a bit sorry for the actor playing Tobias, I continued into the hallway, past the rooms that housed the Academy's telephone switchboard—always locked up like Fort Knox, for some reason known only to AT&T and the head of building and grounds—and out the back door onto the lawn. I was heading toward the set shop in Alumni Hall. Unless Dorothy had gone home sick, I couldn't imagine where else she could be.

The enormous cargo door in the back of Alumni Hall yawned open, thank goodness, so I didn't have to walk all the way around the building and let myself in the front. I passed through its jaws into the belly of Alumni Hall, where the staff seemed to be getting ready for a basketball game.

Completed in 1991 with hefty contributions from the United States Congress and individual contributions from well-heeled alumni and friends, the massive arena could seat the entire brigade of midshipmen, plus staff and faculty, too, for a total of 5,700 souls. Got half a million bucks? You, too, could have part of the building named after you, like the USO, which bankrolled the colossal stage that descended from the rafters five or six times a year, transforming the east end of the building into the Bob Hope Performing Arts Center.

Room 1061, the set shop, was open, its door rolled up, accordion style, like an old-fashioned rolltop desk. The concrete floor was spattered with paint in a rainbow of colors, and the frigid air was filled with the delicious, piney smell of freshly sawed wood.

I found Dorothy there, on her hands and knees, looking fairly chipper, considering, and painting pink and white stripes below the chair rail of a flat that would soon be installed as one wall of Mrs. Lovett's parlor. The wall above the chair rail was decorated with wallpaper, a whimsy of hearts and roses.

"Hey," I said.

On the far side of the cavernous room two midshipmen, a man and a woman dressed in sweats, looked up from their work and waved. They were putting the finishing touches on a backdrop, a stylized black and white representation of the rooftops of London.

Dorothy sat back on her heels and wagged a paintbrush at me, dripping pink paint onto one of her neatly executed white stripes. "There you are! Oh, damn." She dabbed at the drips with a rag that she kept tucked into the waistband of her jeans. "There's gloves over there," she said, wiggling the fingers on her free hand in the direction of the workbench. "In case you don't want to ruin your manicure."

Not having a manicure that I could ruin, I passed on the gloves. I was pleased to see that Dorothy was wearing both a big smile and one of the ball caps I had given her. Wisps of blond hair peeked out, more or less at random, from under the brim. Big gold hoop earrings bounced gently against her neck.

"Great hat," I said.

She reached up and patted it with a gloved hand. "I thought the crab went well with my ensemble."

The crab, embroidered on blue denim in tomato-colored thread, exactly matched the red T-shirt Dorothy wore under her cardigan. "*Excellent* choice," I commented.

Dorothy went back to her stripes while I looked around for a place to stash my my handbag. "What did you want to talk to me about, Dorothy?" I asked, unzipping my jacket a few inches but leaving it on for warmth.

Dorothy looked up from her painting, took a deep breath as if to say something, then shook her head. "Nothing, really. I was just starting to panic about the signs."

I knew precisely which signs she meant. "Not to worry." I tried to sound more self-assured than I felt. "I think I can finish them by tomorrow." Using a screwdriver, I pried the top off a can of black paint, snatched a dry brush from the workbench, and began painting the bold letters that spelled FRESH HOT PIES on a rectangular board with several screw eyes installed across the top.

While the letters were drying, I went looking for the jars of tempera I planned to use for the sign's only decoration: a pie. Not much of an artist, I'd downloaded a clip art picture of a pie to my computer, enlarged it, printed it out. Using a pencil, I copied the design, inch by painful inch, to Mrs. Lovett's sign. Then I got my colors together and filled in my outlines with them. That done, I opened a jar of gray and added a twist of steam coming out the hole in the top of the pie. I stepped back to admire my handiwork. "Voilà! What do you think?"

Holding one paintbrush in her teeth and the other in her

hand, Dorothy strolled over to check it out. "Thass goot," she mumbled around the paintbrush. She removed the paintbrush and grinned. "Thanks. That looks absolutely super."

I wasn't so sure about the super, but it would certainly do, especially from the vantage point of three rows back. "Guess I better attack the banner now."

The banner I was referring to was the one used by Pirelli to hawk his elixir. I'd frame the edges of the banner with gold curlicues, I thought, and in ornate script, neatly centered, I'd paint in crimson edged with gold:

Signor Adolfo Pirelli
haircutter-barber-toothpuller
to his royal majesty
the king of Naples

And under that, in big, bold black:

Banish baldness
with
Pirelli's miracle elixir!

Since Pirelli was supposedly Eye-talian, I'd decided on a fancy script, appropriately called Informal Roman. I was shameless: I used a package of stencils I found at Michael's crafts store.

I'd painted as far as "the king of Naples," trying to decide if "king" should begin with a capital or a small K when a bell rang and the two midshipmen who had been working on the backdrop plopped their brushes into jars of paint thinner and hurried away. Dorothy and I were alone, and the silence lengthened between us.

Finally, Dorothy spoke up.

"Hannah?"

"Hmmm?" I'd given the king a small *k* and was working on a capital *N* that would have made a medieval monk proud, so I didn't even bother to look up.

"Hannah?" she said again.

I turned to see that Dorothy had finished with the parlor flat, stripped off her rubber gloves, and was sitting on the concrete floor with her back resting against the wall.

"Can I ask you something?"

"Sure."

"Did your husband . . . ?" she began, her voice echoing hollowly in the cavernous room. She folded her hands as if she were praying, then pressed them tightly against her lips.

I waited, knowing something important was coming and not wanting to rush her.

"I feel ugly as sin," she announced. She grabbed the crab cap by the bill and lifted it off her head. "Look!"

The wisps of hair I had noticed earlier were about the extent of it. Except for a line of peachlike fuzz along her forehead, Dorothy was bald. Before I could say anything, she clapped the cap back on, quickly covering her baldness. "Gross, huh?"

"We've all been there," I said reassuringly. "You hair will grow back. Trust me!"

But Dorothy refused to be reassured. She sat on the concrete, stone-faced, her feet tucked up under her. "After your surgery," she said after nearly a minute had ticked by, "did your husband lose interest in you?"

I knew where Dorothy was going with that question and decided to make it easier for her.

"Sexually, you mean?"

"Uh-huh."

I balanced my paintbrush on the rim of the open paint jar and crossed the room to sit next to her. Even though we were the only two people in the set shop, I didn't feel comfortable shouting across the room about my sex life. "Actually, Paul couldn't have been more loving and supportive," I told her after I'd gotten settled. "It was me who pushed him away."

Dorothy turned to me in surprise. "Why on earth would you do that?"

I shrugged. "I took it into my head that since I was damaged goods, Paul was only being nice to me out of pity."

A tear rolled down Dorothy's cheek, and she quickly brushed it away. "Pity? I'll take pity, but Ted shows absolutely no interest in me whatsoever."

I reached across and took her hand. "Sometimes post-surgery, men are at a loss about what to do. Ted might be afraid he's going to hurt you, for instance."

It had always amazed me how many support groups there were for cancer survivors, but I could probably count on the fingers of one hand the support groups that were available for their families—their husbands and children.

Dorothy shook her head sadly. "Ted doesn't even try. He spends hours and hours at the office. And when he gets home, he says he's too tired."

"But he's an admiral at the Pentagon! Didn't you tell me he deals with supplies and matériel? There's a war on in Iraq, Dorothy. Surely it's not so hard to believe that he has to spend a lot of time at the office."

Dorothy snorted. "Well, if he *is* at his office, he sure as hell doesn't answer his damn telephone."

"Maybe he's somewhere else?" I offered helpfully. "Like at a meeting?"

She shook her head emphatically. "That's what cell phones are for, right? No, this has been going on for some time now. Long before my surgery. Frankly, Hannah, I think Ted is having an affair." She looked at me with her sad clown face: circles of color reddened her cheeks, mascara bled into her smudgy blue eyeliner.

She rose up on one hip and dug into the pocket of her

jeans with two fingers. When she found what she was looking for, she held it out to me. "I found this in his toiletry kit, the one he takes with him on business."

The pill on her palm was encased in a foil bubble, like the last cold tablet I had taken. The pill was triangular and blue. I recognized it from the ads I'd seen on TV: Viagra.

I stared at Dorothy stupidly for a few moments, trying to think of something reassuring to say and coming up with nothing, zilch, nada. "Uh—" I began.

"Exactly," Dorothy interrupted. "Ted's not taking Viagra to enhance *my* sexual experience, that's for sure." She leaned her head back against the wall and closed her eyes. "Oh, Hannah, sometimes I think I'd be better off dead. If it weren't for Kevin—"

"Don't say that!" I shouted. I leaned toward her and added in a quieter voice, "You are an interesting, talented, and very attractive person. Hair or no hair!" I began pedaling as fast as I could. "Think of that Irish singer, what's-her-name . . . Sinead O'Connor! And Demi Moore in *G.I. Jane!* And Sigourney Weaver in *Alien*^{3}."

Dorothy sniffed and dabbed at her nose with a tissue she'd extracted from her sleeve.

"Emma Thompson was fabulous in *Wit*!" I added, "and that wasn't just makeup, Dorothy. Those women shaved for those roles and took their bald heads home with them."

Dorothy tucked the tissue back up her sleeve, leaned back against the wall and, to my very great surprise, began to laugh. "Hannah, you crack me up! Where do I go to get that kind of optimism? Laughs-R-Us?"

I didn't know about the optimism, but I had a good idea where I could go for information about Admiral Hart. Paul had taught at the Academy for a million years. He had students who had gone on to be senators and congressmen, CEOs of Fortune 500 companies, captains in the U.S. Navy and, yes, even admirals. One former student was an ambassador; one or two others had been Deputy Assistant Under Secretaries of the Navy for This,

That, and the Other. Paul had to know somebody at the Pentagon who could shed some light on the extracurricular activities of a certain Theodore E. Hart, Rear Admiral, USN, and I planned to ask my husband about it the moment I got home.

CHAPTER 6

As it turned out, it was a good thing I'd made Dorothy no promises, because begging with my husband to find me an informer inside the Pentagon was going to have to wait.

I left Dorothy with a hug and good intentions, but what is it they say about good intentions? That the road to hell is paved with them.

My personal hell started when I left Alumni Hall and headed home along the path that skirted the sea wall. As I approached the footbridge that spanned Weems Creek, connecting that part of the campus to Hospital Point, I noticed Emma talking to a female officer. All Naval Academy staff wear plastic name badges, usually black with white lettering and a miniature Naval Academy seal in the corner. I could see that this officer was wearing a name tag, but I wasn't close enough to read it. I knew she was a lieutenant, though, by the two broad stripes circling the hem of her uniform sleeve.

Emma was animated, waving both hands around in the air as if she were directing traffic. Finally, she turned on her highly polished Corfam shoes and stalked away in the direction of the library.

What was that all about? Hardly a career-enhancing move, I thought, for a mid to argue with a superior officer. It was against the rules.

I opened my mouth to call out to Emma, but thought better of it. Instead, I watched until she disappeared around the corner of Nimitz Library, heading in the direction of the temporary trailers that had filled the parking lot since Hurricane Isabel caused the Severn to crest at eight and a half feet, wiping out more than half of the Academy's classrooms.

When I turned back to see what the lieutenant was up to, she was nearly out of sight, halfway across the footbridge.

"Who's that?" I asked Dorothy, who had just caught up with me on her way to retrieve her car. "Do you know?"

Dorothy stared into the setting sun, shading her eyes with her hand. "Can't say for sure, not from the back, but she walks like that woman who's been hanging around rehearsal lately. I saw her talking to my son, but I didn't think anything of it. Next time you see Kevin, why don't you ask him?"

The next time I saw Kevin, it was the following afternoon in the basement of Mahan, and he was actually wrapped up in a conversation with the lieutenant, his broad shoulders blocking the narrow hallway just outside the dressing room door. The officer shrugged. Kevin snapped to attention, delivered a proper salute, did a textbook about-face and left. The lieutenant stared at his back for a few moments, then turned, walking down the hallway in my direction.

The first thing I noticed was her lips. Fat cupid's-bow lips slathered with lipstick in a nonregulation shade of frosted pink I hadn't seen since college.

The next thing I noticed . . . boobs. A prodigious pair, straining the dark fabric of her uniform, challenging the brass buttons that held her jacket together. And teetering precariously on her right breast pocket, pointing in my general direction was her name tag: LT GOODALL.

I started. Blood pounded in my ears. I stood frozen in the hallway, staring so hard at the woman's name tag, willing the letters to slide around like Scrabble tiles and spell something, anything else, that she couldn't help but notice. She glanced down, then up, one pale, puzzled eyebrow raised.

I should have said something, apologized maybe, but I was trying too hard to breathe.

Goodall.

Jennifer Goodall?

I'd never met the woman face-to-face, but I was all too familiar with the black and white photos in the Baltimore *Sun* that had spoiled my breakfast every morning for two and a half months. Five years had gone by, but the blond hair seemed right. And the breasts. Jennifer Goodall, the midshipman whose baseless accusations of sexual harassment had nearly cost my husband his reputation and his career. What was *she* doing back at the Academy?

"Excuse me, ma'am," Jennifer Goodall said crisply.

I was standing stupidly in the doorway, blocking the exit.

"Sorry." I stepped aside and she chugged past me, leaving traces of Irish Spring soap in her wake.

I backed into the dressing room, found a chair and sat down in it, struggling to assemble a single coherent thought. Jennifer Goodall was back.

One thing for sure. I had to tell Paul. I fumbled at my waist for my cell phone, but when I flipped it open to a screen devoid of bars, I remembered you couldn't get a signal down in the bowels of Mahan, so I hustled outside. I stood by the memorial fountain and had paged down to Paul's number before it occurred to me that I was practically at his office anyway, so I hurried over to see him.

I found him grading papers at a long flat table in Chauvenet Hall, a pen in his right hand and a mug of coffee, probably stone cold, in his left.

He smiled up from his work when I came in, "Hannah! To what do I owe . . ." The smile vanished and a puzzled expression took its place. "Hannah, are you all right?"

"You'll never guess who I just ran into," I said, plopping down heavily in the armchair next to his worktable.

"Who?" He put his pen down and turned toward me, giving me his full attention.

"Jennifer Goodall." I waited for this news to sink in.

Paul didn't even blink.

"She was down in the dressing room, talking to one of the mids."

Paul's features hardened. They could have been chiseled into the face of Mount Rushmore. He dragged his chair over to face mine. "I know," he said. "I've been meaning to tell you."

Rage boiled up inside me. "What? You knew?"

Paul nodded glumly. "I ran into her in the sandwich line at Dahlgren one day."

"And you didn't think to tell me?" I exploded, each word a piece of shrapnel aimed straight at his heart.

"I thought it would upset you."

"Upset me?" I sputtered, fighting for breath. "*Upset me?* Why do you think it would upset me?"

Paul leaned forward and captured both my hands. He stood up, dragging me along with him, enclosing me in his arms, crushing me to his chest. "And I see I was right."

I wormed a hand between us and pushed him away so I could look into his face. "Of course I'm upset, you idiot! I can't believe you didn't tell me! And if you're keeping that little secret from me, I can only wonder what else you may have to hide!"

"Don't start that again, Hannah. I thought we laid that to rest a long, long time ago."

"I thought we had, too," I said quietly, remembering the cruise we took to the Virgin Islands that had gone a long way toward mending our damaged relationship. I fell back into my chair, then leaned all the way forward and rested my forehead on my knees. "I think I'm going to be sick."

Paul wisely kept his distance while I struggled to calm the lurching going on in my stomach.

"But what is she *doing* here?" I sputtered, looking up at him through wet lashes. "Tell me she's just visiting."

Paul shook his head. "I wish. But no, she's stationed here. She's Twenty-ninth Company officer."

"How lucky for them." I sat in my chair and pouted, barely aware of the Mozart symphony drifting from his radio, the volume set to low. "Why did the Navy send her back? I simply can't *believe* it, not after all the trouble she caused, not just for you . . ." I ticked them off on my fingers. ". . . but the legal officer, not to mention the supe and the 'dant and the Secretary of the whole damn Navy!"

As if Paul needed reminding. It had been a nightmare. The press had jumped all over it, of course: NAVAL ACADEMY MID ACCUSES PROFESSOR OF SEXUAL HARASSMENT. The *Sun* and the *Post* had had a field day, using the news as an excuse to dredge up every scandal that had taken place at the Naval Academy for the past twenty years, from car theft rings to athletes cheating on exams to a female midshipman being handcuffed to a urinal, with sidebars about similar troubles at the Air Force Academy and West Point thrown in for good measure.

Paul managed a slight smile. "I don't know, Hannah. Goodall's detailer certainly didn't consult *me*." He pulled up his office chair, the rollers squeaking. "The military staff changes every two or three years. You know that, so maybe they didn't know her history."

Paul, a tenured professor, jokingly refers to the Academy's military staff as "the temporary help," but I didn't buy it. "That incident *had* to be included in her jacket, in her fitness report?"

Paul swiveled his chair so he could look me in the eyes. "After Goodall dropped the charges against me, the Naval Academy graduated her and sent her off to the fleet. End of story."

"You mean she went sailing off with a clean slate?"

Paul nodded. "Conduct issues that are resolved before graduation don't become part of an officer's official record."

I thought about Jennifer Goodall's blue eyes, pouty pink lips, and great big breasts blocking my passage in that narrow hallway. "What a good idea *that* is." I crossed my arms across my own, comparatively inadequate chest and scowled at my husband. "Frankly, I was hoping she'd gone to sea and taken a long walk off a short, slippery deck."

" 'Hard-hearted Hannah—' " Paul started the song, but I cut him off with a glare, thoroughly unamused.

"But surely *somebody* at the Academy remembers," I insisted. "Or," I said as a new thought occurred to me, "maybe she's sleeping with her detailer."

"Unlikely. But perhaps she knows where certain bodies are buried. That makes it easier when you need to call in some favors."

We sat in awkward silence while I tried to make sense of the Navy's stupid-ass decision.

Paul tried again. "I deal with the students, Hannah, not the company officers. Unless one of Goodall's mids gets into academic trouble, I'm not likely to cross paths with the wretched woman."

"With women like Jennifer Goodall," I fumed, "even three-hundred-some acres is too small. I don't want you within a hundred mile radius of that—that—" I cast about for the perfect word. "—that *bitch*," I finished triumphantly.

"Don't worry, love. I have no interest in her whatsoever." Paul waved a hand toward his papers. "Look, I'm almost done. Let me take you out for a drink?"

I sat in my chair, arms still folded, mouth still pouting.

Paul laughed out loud.

"What's so funny?" I snapped.

"You look like a malevolent Buddha."

"I feel like a malevolent Buddha," I grouched. "I'm thinking up Buddhist curses."

"Buddhists don't curse," Paul corrected me. "They're all about peace and harmony."

"You're right," I conceded. "But I'm still thinking up curses. And it'll take more than a drink to get you off the hook. If you think I'm going to cook for you tonight, you are out of your freaking mind. Buy me dinner."

Paul attempted to kiss the tip of my nose, but I turned my head and he connected with my earlobe instead. "Hannah!"

"Don't worry," I said. "I'll get over it. Just give me time to stew."

I waited for Paul to put on his coat, and as we walked in silence out Gate 3 and down Maryland Avenue toward the State House, he reached for and captured my hand. He squeezed it—one, two, three—our private code for "I love you"—and I felt my load lighten, my doubts begin to evaporate. By the time we reached Galway Bay, I was pretty sure about Paul. But Jennifer Goodall? Who knew what that scheming bitch might do?

CHAPTER 7

I'd forgotten until we got there that Tuesday is Pub Quiz Night at Galway Bay, the Irish pub and restaurant on Maryland Avenue that was our regular hangout. After hugs all around, Peggy, the hostess, showed us to a table for two near the front, and we'd just gotten settled with the menus when my sister Ruth breezed in, out of breath and unwinding a long bright purple scarf from around her neck. She'd knitted it herself, I knew, row after row, longer and longer, until the yarn she bought on sale had run out.

Paul and I picked up our coats and cheerfully moved to a nearby table for four. "I thought I'd find you here," Ruth said, breathing hard. "Hutch will be along shortly."

Hutch was short for Maurice Gaylord Hutchinson, attorney at law and my sister's live-in boyfriend. The previous fall they'd bought a house together on Southgate, a gracious Victorian with a lawn that sloped gently down to the quiet waters of Spa Creek. *Must be nice.*

"You're just in time, too," Paul announced with a narrow-eyed look at me. "Hannah and I were running out of things to say to one another."

Precisely the opposite was true. I had just attacked Paul for not having the sense that God gave a houseplant, chiding him repeatedly for not warning me about Jennifer Goodall, et nagging cetera, until he'd lost what was left of his savoir faire and suggested I put a lid on it.

"That's true," I agreed, with a withering glance at Paul over the top of my menu. "Your brother-in-law is a nincompoop. I have nothing further to say on the matter."

I had decided to order an ice cold margarita. Maybe that would help quench the fires of rage still burning up my stomach lining. Or maybe I'd pour the drink directly over Paul's head. Only time would tell.

The server took our orders, with Ruth asking for a Bass ale for the still absent Hutch. Ruth was bringing us up to date on the buying trip she was about to make to Hong Kong, when Fintan Galway, who managed the restaurant for his brother, appeared at our table. He was clutching a sheaf of papers, the first of two trivia quiz sheets, each bearing fifteen questions. "Eight P.M.," Fintan announced, laying a quiz sheet on the table in front of us. "Your team's playing tonight, right?"

Paul slipped his wallet out of his pocket and laid a ten dollar bill on the table. "The Puddle Ducks are ready!" he announced.

The previous week the Puddle Ducks came in second, losing out to the Sea Dogs by one question when the Sea Dogs knew that topless saleswomen were legal in Liverpool, England, but only in tropical fish stores. All the money went to charity: soup kitchens, needy local families, the SPCA. That week it was the Box of Rain Foundation that honored Lee Griffin, a local sailor, who had been brutally murdered during a senseless car jacking just a short block away from where we were sitting.

Paul, our resident brainiac, moved his beer to one side and spread the sheet out on the table in front of him. He started filling in the blanks, while Ruth and I chatted about some renovations she was planning for Mother Earth. Her shop was a perpetual work in progress.

Paul looked up. "What color is Mr. Spock's blood?"

Ruth and I had been discussing carpet tiles versus wall-to-wall, so alien blood was a huge leap. We looked at each other. Ruth shrugged. "Ask me about native island cultures," she suggested blandly. "I got an A-plus in cultural anthropology."

It'd been ages since I'd seen an episode of *Star Trek*, but I couldn't imagine alien blood being anything but green. Blue maybe; red in some galaxies. "Green?" I guessed.

"Is that your final answer?" Paul asked.

"Final answer."

Our three heads huddled over the quiz sheet, and we had moved on to puzzling over what a turkey was in bowling alley slang when Hutch arrived, reeking of cigarette smoke and full of apologies. "Sorry, got caught outside my office by a client. Wanted to tell me all about this idea he has for investing in the company that's going to start developing Parole."

Parole was Annapolis's first shopping center, long ago deserted by the department stores and specialty shops where my daughter and I used to shop for her school clothes. Sears had been the last holdout, moving to an anchor spot in nearby Annapolis Mall in the mid-nineties. Once Sears was gone, poor Parole had become a blot on the cityscape as deal after deal with its out-of-state owner had fallen through. In recent days, the bulldozers had been busy, pulverizing Sears, flattening Woodward and Lothrop, demolishing Hickory Farms and the Hallmark store, loading their remains in dump trucks and hauling them away. Old Parole was only a memory.

Hutch's lips brushed Ruth's cheek and he sat down. Ruth slid an ale in his direction. Hutch took a long sip, sighed, and smacked his lips. "So, where are we?" he asked, referring to the quiz.

" 'Who was the first U.S. presidential candidate to attempt the macarena in public?' " Paul read out loud.

Hutch knocked back another slug of ale before answering with some confidence, "Al Gore."

Paul wrote "Al Gore" in the blank. "Okay," he forged on. "How about this? What game begins with a corking?"

"Your fiftieth birthday party." Ruth laughed.

I shrugged. "Don't have a clue."

Darts. The word buzzed around the restaurant like gossip about the latest scandal on Capitol Hill. *Darts. Darts. Darts.* Everyone, it seemed, had arrived at the question simultaneously.

"Darts," I said with confidence.

Paul scribbled *darts* in the blank. "What soft drink, introduced in 1982, was the number three U.S. seller within two years?"

Ruth raised her hand for this one. "Diet Coke," she said. "I remember it came on the market when Eric and I were on our honeymoon in Atlanta. But that's another story."

Eric was Ruth's ex. And the story wasn't pretty. They'd been married for nine years when Eric began easing the pain of advancing middle age by taking up with a succession of bimbos-du-jour. Until recently, he'd maintained a half interest in Mother Earth, but last summer, with Hutch's help, Ruth had bought the jerk out.

Ruth's knight in shining armor took her hand, tucked it under his arm, and leaned forward over the quiz sheet, reading aloud flawlessly, although the page was upside down. "What 'founding mother' was the first real woman to appear as a Pez dispenser head?"

We guessed Martha Washington on that one, but we were wrong. It was Betsy Ross.

After all the forms were collected and the scores tallied, we narrowly lost the game to the Axis of Evil team, playing from the cozy comfort of the bay window in the adjoining bar.

Looking a trifle crestfallen, Paul excused himself to go to the restroom, while Hutch wandered off in the direction of the bar, carrying his empty mug. I seized the moment to tell Ruth about Jennifer Goodall.

"Shit."

"My sentiments exactly. And why the hell is she hanging around Mahan Hall? She doesn't have anything to do with the musical."

Ruth looked surprised. "You sure?"

"Positive. I've been working on it for over two weeks. If she were doing sets or costumes or makeup, I'd have noticed by now."

Ruth frowned. "That girl you said she was talking to, Emma? Perhaps she's in Goodall's company."

I shook my head. "No, she's not." I turned my glass by the stem until a fresh layer of salt was facing me. I raised the glass to my lips.

"I think I know," said Paul.

I nearly dropped my glass. Until he spoke, I didn't realize he'd been standing right behind me.

"I just ran into Jim Harle in the men's room." He smiled down at me. "You remember Jim. Computer services?"

I nodded.

"Well, Jim told me that Goodall's the academy's SAVI officer."

"Savvy?" Ruth and I said it at the same time.

"S-A-V-I." Paul spelled it out. "It stands for sexual assault victim intervention. One of her duties would be to provide the victims of sexual assault with an advocate."

"Sexual assault . . ." I could barely go on. "You have *got* to be kidding!"

"Ironic, huh?"

Ruth stuck in her oar. "The I-word I'm thinking of is 'insane.' "

"Knowing her," I grumbled, "I bet she probably requested the assignment."

Paul settled back into his chair, but whatever he'd been intending to say was interrupted by the arrival of our order—fish and chips for Ruth and me, Irish stew for Paul, and, I couldn't help laughing, shepherd's pie (without any actual shepherd) for Hutch, whenever he returned from the bar, that is.

As I munched my way through the succulent fish, I thought about the concerns Emma had shared with me about Kevin. I'd seen her talking in an animated way to

Jennifer Goodall; then I'd seen Jennifer talking to Kevin. If Goodall was the SAVI officer, was it possible that Emma had been reporting Kevin as a harasser? Kevin was showering Emma with attention, it was true, mooning over her, but that didn't necessarily count as harassment. But then, who knew what went on between them when they got back to Bancroft Hall?

All the same, I thought I might mention it to Dorothy. If Kevin had his sights set on flying FA18s for the Marines, a charge of sexual harassment would quash any dream he had of becoming a flying cowboy pretty damn quick. In this PC environment, he'd leave the Academy with a rocket tied to his tail.

Dorothy had lost faith in her husband. If Kevin were kicked out of the Academy, it would be more than a disappointment. She would probably survive the cancer, she might even survive a divorce, but that kind of news about Kevin could very well kill her.

CHAPTER 8

At Tuesday's rehearsal Dorothy pooh-poohed my concerns about Kevin, but thanked me for them anyway.

We sat together in the center of the theater with Professor Medwin Black in the row just in front. On stage, the woman playing Joanna finished singing a sweet version of "Green Finch and Linnet Bird" that nearly broke my heart.

"My God," Dorothy whispered. "That girl should be on Broadway."

A few seats over, the unpleasant Greta James was muttering under her breath. If she was trying to impress the good professor, it wasn't working. He uncrossed his legs, stood up, leaned across several rows, tapped her lightly on the shoulder and growled, "Enough!"

"Sorry." Greta hunkered down; the hat she wore for her role in the chorus caught on the back of the chair and tipped over her eyes.

"The minute the cast is announced," Professor Black complained to me, *sotto voce*, "the women all turn on each other. All the girls *hate* the female lead." He waved a finger at the back of Greta's head. "Sometimes I think we should be doing *Cats*."

I laughed out loud.

It was nearly time for Greta's entrance, so she gathered her costume about her and scurried away.

"That little missy," Professor Black went on after Greta was out of earshot, "sent me a six-page letter outlining the flaws in our casting process and detailing how much better she'd be in the role of Joanna. She's a good actress, but she couldn't carry the role vocally. It's always a balancing act."

Dorothy shifted uncomfortably in her seat, then seemed to gather confidence. "How come Kevin didn't get a lead?"

"Ah. Good question." Professor Black leaned back in his chair, his hands folded prayerfully across his chest. "With Kevin, it was a tough call. He could easily have handled the role of Beadle—that's why we've got him understudying it—but Adam Monroe did a terrific job, too, and he's a firstie, so that had to carry some weight." The professor smiled at Dorothy in the semidark of the auditorium. "Kevin will get his shot at the big-time next year."

"Oh, yes? What show are you doing?" I asked.

Professor Black half belly-laughed, half snorted. "That's what everyone wants to know, and we haven't even gotten through this year's musical yet!"

"Ballpark it for me," said Dorothy.

"Well, if I were guessing, I'd say Gilbert and Sullivan. *HMS Pinafore*, to be exact. It's one of the music director's favorites and he's been after me for years to do it."

I turned to ask what Dorothy thought about the music director's choice of *HMS Pinafore* and caught her staring at the stage, her face alight with pride, as Kevin as asylum keeper, Jonas Fogg, began his big scene with Anthony, the romantic lead. Anthony was aiming a pistol at her son, but he wavered, lost his nerve, dropped the gun. Joanna caught it and shot Kevin point-blank dead, but a few minutes later Kevin had sufficiently revived to join us.

Dorothy pulled down the seat of the chair next to her, but Kevin decided to sit at the end of the row just in front of us.

"That was terrific, Kev," Dorothy said.

Her son whipped off his wig and arranged it carefully over one knee. "Thanks. You didn't think I played it too weird?"

"It was just right," I cut in. "Loved the way you handled the scissors. Reminds me of the mad scientist in *Back to the Future*. What's his name?"

"Christopher Lloyd?"

"Yes, that's the guy."

"Thanks, ma'am."

Suddenly Kevin stiffened. In the semidark he turned to scowl at his mother. "What's Dad doing here?"

Dorothy's head spun around so fast that I thought she'd get whiplash. Weaving his way through the auditorium toward us was a tall man dressed in civilian clothes. Ted Hart was an older version of his son—grayish hair still slightly red, wearing chinos and a leather bomber jacket which he unzipped as he eased between the seats.

"Am I too late?" he inquired, taking a seat right next to me.

"Just finished, Dad."

"Damn! I'm sorry." He favored me with a grin. "And this must be Hannah. Am I right?"

I extended my hand. "Right."

"Dorothy says she doesn't know what she'd do without you."

"She'd be just fine, Admiral. The midshipmen do most of the work anyway. I mean, what I don't know about wing nuts and mitered corners could fill an encyclopedia. Paintbrushes I can handle."

"It's Ted, Hannah. Call me Ted." Even in the darkened theater his smile dazzled.

Kevin rolled his eyes and looked away.

"Ted, then." I stole a glance at his wife. "The work keeps us out of trouble and off the streets, in any case."

"It's fun seeing it all come together like this," Dorothy said, changing the subject.

"Is it still snowing?" I asked the admiral, thinking about the wet fat flakes that had been coming down earlier and about my cold walk home.

"Yes. Like Merry bloody Christmas."

The admiral's jacket, I noticed, was completely dry. But he was an admiral. Maybe it didn't *dare* snow on him.

When the mids broke for dinner, the Harts, Admiral and Mrs., left for home together, and I hustled onstage to finish up on Mrs. Lovett's harmonium. I spread a newspaper out to protect the floor and quickly sprayed the decorative scrollwork a bright gold. When I prepared to attach it to the front of her harmonium, though, I realized I'd left the box containing my hot glue gun wrapped up in my sweatshirt down in the Jabberwocky room.

By then the cast had reassembled on stage and the Pair-o-Docs was giving them notes, so I stepped between Mrs. Lovett's oven and the end of the body chute and trotted down the stairs to find it.

On the landing, I paused. Someone was in the Jabberwocky room, sitting on the sofa reading *Trident,* the Academy's good news newspaper. On the front page of that week's issue were two color pictures taken at last week's rehearsal. In one, Sweeney and Mrs. Lovett stood, arms locked, their razors and rolling pin held high, respectively. Emma was featured in another picture in all her ragged regalia, grinning toothsomely, with one of her incisors painted a disconcerting black.

"Oh, excuse me," I apologized brightly. "Forgot my glue gun."

The person reading the newspaper looked up. It was Jennifer Goodall.

I stared at her, my mouth ajar. She eyed me coolly, with disinterest, without the slightest spark of recognition in her eyes.

Although she had no reason to recognize me—our paths had never officially crossed—it made me furious that the woman responsible for very nearly wrecking my marriage didn't even know who I was. It seemed like only yesterday that deceptively innocent face had smiled out at me from the pages of too many newspapers, from behind too many microphones on too many broadcasts of the six o'clock news. Now, five years later, the face was leaner, the wrinkles around the eyes more pronounced, but Jennifer was still a very attractive young woman.

She was wearing the Naval Academy version of civilian clothes—chinos and a navy blue polo shirt—and no name tag.

I couldn't wait to get away from her. I retreated, facing down the flight of stairs that would take me to the dressing room. My hand rested lightly on the pipe that served as the handrail, and it felt icy and cold as my heart.

If not now, Hannah, when?

I wheeled around. "You're Jennifer Goodall, aren't you?"

"Who wants to know?" Her voice was flat, almost bored. I wondered where the "Yes ma'am" had gotten to, but figured she only trotted out the courtesy when she was in uniform.

"I'm Hannah Ives."

At the mention of my name, Jennifer said nothing. She didn't nod. She didn't even blink. She simply laid her newspaper aside.

"Perhaps you remember my husband, then." I clamped my teeth together, trying to keep a lid on my fury.

"Oh yes." A slow smile crept across her face and she relaxed into the cushions. "I remember Paul."

I wanted to smack that supercilious smile clean off her face, but I dug my fingernails—such as they were—into my palms. I didn't trust what might come out of my mouth next, so I stood there, staring at her like a dummy.

"I see him around," she continued with a maddening I-know-something-you-don't-know expression. "He hasn't changed a bit."

That smile again. She looked me up and down, taking in my paint-splattered jeans and T-shirt with a look of such distaste that I imagined her thinking: *What does a hunk like Paul see in a hag like you?*

Until Jennifer Goodall turned up to complicate my life,

there had been times that I could go for days without thinking about her and the damage she had caused. I realized I'd been carrying this woman around like an albatross, and I needed to rid myself of her once and for all.

"Tell me, Jennifer," I said at last. "Was it true?"

"A midshipman doesn't lie, cheat, or steal," she quoted.

"Neither does my husband, Lieutenant Goodall, so one of you has to be lying through their teeth."

Her smile didn't waver, but at least I made her blink.

"I'm just too tired to play games with you, Lieutenant. After all these years, the least you can do is tell me the truth." I drew a deep, steadying breath. "Did you have an affair with my husband?"

Jennifer Goodall fished a necklace up from her cleavage, hooked it with an index finger and ran her finger around the inside of the chain, back and forth, back and forth, idly toying with it and, it seemed, with me. "You *really* want to know?"

"Of course I want to know!" I shouted. "I wanted to know then, and I certainly want to know now! The truth, Miss Goodall! Did you sleep with Paul?" I spat it out, punching every word.

Jennifer studied me with cool, unblinking eyes, a technique she probably learned in terrorist boot camp.

"Oh, he was one of a kind, your Paul." She crossed one leg casually over the other and draped an arm languidly over the back of the sofa. "A real tiger in bed."

That wasn't the answer I expected, and I must have gasped. It took every ounce of control I could muster not to launch myself across the room, wrap both hands around her pudgy neck and squeeze and squeeze until her eyes rolled back and those fat, pink lips turned blue and she stopped breathing altogether.

"Paul likes it kinky. Did you know?" She tilted her head. "No, I can see that you don't. That time at Army-Navy? He just about wore me out, and that takes some doing." She smiled, as if remembering.

I swallowed hard, biting back the bile that was rising in my throat. Paul had attended that Army-Navy game alone when I'd been too sick to go along. Jennifer had testified that it happened in a Meadowlands hotel. That they'd met in the bar for a drink. That one thing had led to another.

Could it possibly be true? Had Paul been lying all along, to protect our marriage and his career?

I didn't want to hear it. Like Emily as a child, I wanted to press my palms hard against my ears and chant at the top of my lungs: *I'm not listening to you!*

Jennifer was studying me with morbid fascination, taking cruel pleasure at seeing my marriage and the trust I put in my husband erode, buried in an instant, like a home in the path of a California mudslide. One hot tear ran down my cheek, and I hated myself for it. This wasn't the time to show any weakness.

I could imagine why Jennifer would hate my husband enough to want to hurt *him*—she had been failing his course, and Paul refused to give in to her blackmail in exchange for a passing grade. But what did this young naval officer have against *me*?

"He said he was lonely," she elaborated. "He invited me up to his suite."

Suite! The word alone was a knife in my heart. Last time we'd stayed in a hotel it was the $69 special.

"Such an appetite!" she continued, twisting the knife for all she was worth. "He came for me on all fours, and he threw back his head and roared! Does he roar for you, Mrs. Ives?"

"What did you say?" I sputtered.

She opened her mouth to speak again, but I flapped my hand, waving her lies away. The last thing I needed was corroborative detail, particularly details on a jungle theme. Because now I knew, like a refreshing wave of water washing over me:

Jennifer Goodall was lying!

When he was seventeen, Paul had injured his back in a tractor accident on the family farm. As a result, several disks in his spine had been fused. He could no more crawl on his hands and knees, throw his head back and roar than he could fly from BWI to Heathrow without benefit of an airplane. Our lovemaking had always been special, but no acrobatics were involved. It's a good thing I didn't carry a gun, because I would have shot Jennifer then and there, square between her lying eyes.

And yet, I had to be sure. Not 99 and 44/100th percent sure, but 100 percent sure.

Fight fire with fire, to coin a phrase. If Jennifer could make up a pack of lies, so could I.

"You make me sick!" I screamed, so loudly that it made my throat ache. "You *both* make me sick!" I fell against the wall, sobbing. "We got matching tattoos, special, just for us. That's why Paul got it on his . . . his . . ." I choked, as if unable to continue.

"Paul is such a *generous* man," she said. "Would you like to see *my* tattoo?" She tugged at the corner of her shirt, which was tucked carefully into the waistband of her khakis, but I knew she was bluffing.

Why is there never a tape recorder around when you need it? I wanted our encounter on tape so I could play it back for Paul, so he could hear Jennifer Goodall damn herself in her own words. I couldn't imagine what Paul had done to her that would engender such hate, a hate that burned just as hotly now as it had half a decade earlier. I could only assume she was mentally ill.

I confronted her, my eyes like slits. "Paul doesn't have any tattoos, you lying bitch! I don't know why you're doing this, but I swear to God, I'll get even with you, even if it takes the rest of my life. I'm contacting my lawyer, you're going to retract everything, and if you ever make up baseless lies about my husband again, I'll . . . I'll . . ."

"Everything all right, Mrs. Ives?"

I spun around, both flustered and annoyed by the interruption. It was Midshipman Small, sweet, serious Gadget, standing on the stairway behind me.

The silence was heavy with unspoken words.

The auditorium above me was silent, too. No talking, no singing. No happy scrape of bow on string, no friendly trumpet blare. Rehearsal must be over.

"I heard shouting," Gadget said, moving closer. "Is there anything I can do?"

My hand dug into the handrail as I struggled for control. "No, thank you, Gadget. I was just leaving. Lieutenant Goodall and I were having a friendly disagreement, is all."

Jennifer stared at me placidly, still wearing that maddening smile.

"You sure?"

"I'm sure. Thanks."

Midshipman Small made way. I laid a light hand on his arm, then fled up the stairs, past Alice swimming up the wall, past the Dormouse, bursting out onto a stage filled with midshipmen.

Was everybody there? The whole blessed cast? Had everyone heard my argument with Lieutenant Goodall as it drifted upward from the Jabberwocky room?

I didn't give a damn.

Because Paul had been faithful!

I felt light-headed, my feet barely touching the ground as I found my coat where I had dumped it on a chair, waved good-night to the startled cast, and stepped out into the snowy night. I felt like shouting from the cupola on top of the chapel dome, loud enough for everyone in Anne Arundel County to hear. No, to the whole United States of America: Paul had been faithful.

And I ran the last block home, into his surprised but waiting arms.

The sun was pushing against the shutters, striping the duvet with light, when I came to the next morning. Paul lay beside me, already awake, his head propped up on the palm of his hand, smiling at me, his fingers playing idly with my hair.

"You roared," I said.

"Hmmmm," he replied, brushing his lips softly against mine.

"That was spectacular," I whispered, referring to the sex, not the roar.

Paul drew back, touched my cheek. "Only for you, sweetheart." He kissed my shoulder, my neck, my mouth.

Only later did I think to wonder: Who had Jennifer been waiting for?

CHAPTER 9

Two days before opening night, and panic set in. The cast had been banished to a rehearsal room in Alumni Hall so that the tech crew—working dangerously close to the deadline as usual—could finally hang the backdrop and wait for a last minute coat of paint to dry.

Opening night, minus one. Dorothy and I scrutinized the set and pronounced it as good as it gets. My fingers itched to touch up the red on the antique barber pole, but it was too late even for that; the cast was already straggling in. A few midshipmen at first, followed by a violinist, two flutes, and a drummer, then the Pair-o-Docs strolling side by side, conferring, shooing everyone along like mother hens.

Not much to do but find a seat and enjoy the show. We'd seen it, of course, but in pieces and bits, fits and starts, but this was dress rehearsal, the first complete run-through. We prayed it would come together—the costumes, the music, the dialogue, the sound effects, and the sets—like a jigsaw puzzle, complete at last.

Act One was a triumph. Sweeney's dark "Epiphany" and Mrs. Lovett's brilliant take on "A Little Priest" would bring the opening night audience to their feet.

Around six everyone broke for dinner, served buffet style on long tables set up in the lobby. Dorothy and I parked ourselves on a marble step, balanced our plates on our knees and worked our way through a passable beef stew served over egg noodles. Between the noodles and the carrot cake, I brought Dorothy up to date on my daughter and her family, fishing recent photos out of my bag of Chloe, now five, on her first day of kindergarten, and Jake, age two, posing with his stuffed chick, their top-knots standing in identical (and adorable!) spikes.

"I'm crazy about my daughter," I told my friend as she handed the photos back to me, "but my grandchildren? I'm certifiably nuts over *them.*" I shrugged. "How do you explain that?"

Dorothy thought for a moment. "Maybe because you can play with them for a while, then give them back. Let the parents deal with the dirty diapers, the runny noses, the bad report cards."

I had to laugh. "I guess it's a grandparent's prerogative to spoil them. It's part of the job description." Dorothy hadn't told me much about her home life, so I was curious. "Is Kevin your only child?"

She nodded. "I would have liked to have more kids, Hannah, but it wasn't in the cards."

I tried to draw her out about that, but she squirmed a bit uncomfortably and changed the subject. We ended up in safer territory, chatting about the latest installment of *Harry Potter* until the food went away and Act Two began.

"Fingers crossed," said Dorothy as we returned to our seats. I knew she was referring to Sweeney's chair. Would it work as we had planned?

The opening number, "God, That's Good," went off without a hitch, and I began to relax and enjoy the show. Several scenes later, while Mrs. Lovett distracted Tobias with one of her delectable pies, Perelli, upstairs, confronted Sweeney. Perelli swaggered to the washstand and picked up one of Sweeney's razors. "But I remember these . . . and you, Benjamin Barker," he sneered, blowing Sweeney's cover. In a carefully rehearsed move, Sweeney knocked the razor from his rival's hand.

"Ooooh, well done," said Dorothy.

The two men struggled. Advantage to Sweeney as he grabbed Pirelli by the throat and began to squeeze.

Suddenly, Tobias appeared on the stairs. Afraid of discovery, Sweeney dragged Pirelli—foot-dragging, arm-flopping limp—across the shop, tumbled him into the trunk and slammed the lid.

I held my breath. The next bit of shtick was my favorite.

Tobias rushed upstairs, adjusting his wig, looking for his boss. He's supposed to say, "Ow, he ain't here!" and sit down on the trunk with Pirelli's hand still dangling from it, but before Tobias could move, the trunk lid flew open, Perelli crawled out and sprawled on the floor.

I gasped, and looked at Dorothy. "That's not part of the script!"

"Maybe Sweeney got a little carried away with the strangling?"

On stage, the actor playing Perelli rose unsteadily to his feet and backed away from the trunk, wiping the palms of his hands on the trousers of his costume. We watched in silence as the lid of the trunk bounced back against the wall—once, twice—teetered, then slammed shut.

Perelli was wearing a body mike, so everyone heard what he said next. "Oh, Jesus. Jesus. Shit!"

"What's gotten into him?" I wondered aloud.

The music, which had been building steadily from *allegretto* to *poco accelerando* suddenly quit—*fermata*—as Professor Tracey cut the orchestra off with an impatient wave of his hand. He slapped both hands flat on top of the piano; the first violinist started, fumbled, and nearly dropped her bow. "What's going on, folks?" Professor Tracey yelled. "Have we got a train wreck up there?"

Mrs. Lovett, too, was aghast. She stood in her pie shop, hands on hips, gazing up.

Tobias and Sweeney exchanged glances and shrugged.

Medwin Black shot out of his seat, clapping his hands and bellowing, the glasses on his forehead like a second pair of eyes. "You're half dead, Perelli! You're supposed to *stay* in the trunk, not leap out of it like some demented jack-in-the-box!"

The midshipman playing Perelli didn't appear to be listening. He bowed, resting his hands on his knees, as exhausted as if he had just run a marathon. His panting came to us in ragged gasps, amplified a thousand times by the speakers.

Tobias stood to one side, whipped off his wig. He approached Perelli and laid a hand on his back. "You all right, man?"

Perelli waved at the trunk with a long index finger. "There's something in there! Jesus Christ, there's something already in there!"

Sweeney crossed to the trunk and threw back the lid. He bent, bobbled, then staggered backward. "Tim!" he shouted. "Give me a hand here!"

Tim/Tobias hurried over, his ridiculous wig forgotten. Together they reached into the trunk and pulled something out—it looked like a bundle of laundry—and laid it on the floor.

Medwin Black was already huffing his way up the steps to the stage, followed closely by John Tracey. I started to get up, but Dorothy grabbed my arm. "What is it?" she whispered, her breath hot against my cheek.

I pressed a hand to my chest, as if that would do anything to quiet my racing heart. "I think it's a *who*," I said, noticing that the bundle wore a blue and gold track suit and white Nikes.

"Cell phone! Who's got a cell phone?" someone yelled, nearly bursting our eardrums as his request blasted out over the speakers.

There wasn't a midshipman at the Academy who didn't own a cell phone—Sprint cut them a sweetheart deal—but after a mid took a call during rehearsal in the middle of "City on Fire," they'd been summarily banished from the set. The rule didn't apply to me, so I rushed to the stage, hauling my phone from its holster as I ran.

I held out the phone, then felt like an idiot when Professor Tracey just waved a hand and yelled, "Call 911, for heaven's sake."

I did as I was told.

While we waited for the paramedics, Tobias and Sweeney began CPR, Tobias doing compressions and Sweeney breathing into the victim's mouth. From the edge of the stage I could see only the victim's head, and it made my stomach churn. Blood covered the forehead and cheeks, and the eyes stared up, unblinking, into the spotlights in the fly gallery.

Sweeney checked for a pulse, shook his head, and the two began again, keeping up the rhythm until the paramedics clattered onto the stage and took over. It took less than five minutes for them to arrive, but I'm sure that to everyone—especially to Sweeney and Tobias—it must have seemed like hours.

It was, as I had suspected, too late. Their body language said it all. While one paramedic packed up their gear, two others lifted the body and laid it gently on the stretcher they'd brought with them. As the paramedics straightened the limbs, a twist of hair separated from the bloody mess that had once been a forehead and hung darkly down over one ear. Blond, I thought. The victim was a blonde. A blanket appeared from somewhere, and in the instant before the blanket covered the face, something clicked in my brain and I knew. The victim wasn't a midshipman at all.

It was Jennifer Goodall.

CHAPTER 10

Nothing—not my husband's embrace, nor a stiff shot of brandy, nor a half-dozen Paxil left over in the medicine cabinet from 1994—was going to take *this* misery away, not anytime soon.

When the investigators finally let us go, I trudged home alone through the deepening snow with the bitter wind tearing at my scarf, its icy fingers plucking at every seam in the fabric of my coat.

I'm glad she's dead.

There, I'd said it.

Just ahead of me, a man walked his beagle. When he stopped suddenly and turned, I feared I'd spoken out loud, but something in Dawson's Gallery had caught the man's attention. He paused for a moment, admiring, his nose pressed to the window while his dog stretched its leash to the limit and lifted its leg against a trash can. The pair moved on.

I'm glad she's dead. And if wishes had been arrows, Jennifer Goodall would have been dead years ago, an arrow from *my* bow shot straight through her callous heart.

Someone had solved my problem for me. Jennifer was gone for good.

My boots slithered along the treacherous sidewalk; I spread my arms for balance. I tried to dredge up sympathy for Jennifer's friends, her family, if only to prove that I wasn't as blackhearted as she. She had a mother somewhere who would grieve, I told myself, a mother who might have nothing now to cherish but a high school photo, a young girl's canopied bed, pencil marks on the kitchen door that marked young Jennifer's growth from child to woman.

It would be hours before the official identification, of course, before the police knocked on that mother's door in Kansas or Iowa or snowbound North Dakota, and the woman's grieving would begin. It would be days more before Jennifer's name hit the news. Paul would hear it first from me.

I turned left onto Prince George Street and slogged the half block to my door. I fumbled with my key and eased it into the lock. The welcoming blast of heat from a furnace working overtime hit my cheeks like a Caribbean breeze.

"Paul! I'm home!" I peeled off my gloves and arranged them to dry on top of the radiator. I kicked my boots underneath.

"Paul!"

Where the heck was he?

I hung my jacket on the hall tree my father had built, left with us when he moved to a smaller place in Snow Hill on Maryland's Eastern Shore, and padded in my stocking feet toward the kitchen. I stuck my head through the basement door. "Paul!"

"I'm in the office," he called. "Keeping the world safe from the Infidels!"

I should have known. Thursday night. Paul would be playing Civilization III.

I didn't go much for computer games. Emily had given me The Sims for Christmas, and even though it hogged the hard drive on my laptop, I'd installed it just to please her. Together we'd created families modeled on people we knew, and moved them into houses of our own design—a mother-daughter kind of thing. Then the Dennis character I'd named after my brother-in-law self-immolated in a kitchen fire, turning himself into a tombstone in the back garden, and I threw up my hands.

"Install a smoke detector," Emily had suggested, hanging over my shoulder, kibbitzing. "And make sure he studies cooking." Ever helpful, she downloaded a Sean Connery character from the Internet, Mel Gibson, too. I tried to hook Sean up with the freshly widowed Connie, but inexplicably, she refused. Little fool. Then characters started making decisions on their own—Mel wouldn't go to work, and while Mrs. Bromley's plumbing overflowed, a burglar broke in and stole her TV. I decided that real life was complicated enough without taking on a whole fictional community.

Life is real, life is earnest. I don't remember who said that, but the quote sprang to mind as I lingered at the top of the basement stairs and wondered how I would break the news about Jennifer Goodall to my husband. "Can you come up a minute, sweetheart?" I stammered. "There's something I need to tell you."

If my voice sounded strange to him, he didn't let on. "I can't leave now," he yelled back, "the Greeks are massacring the French. Give me a moment. Why don't you put on the kettle for tea."

Love and scandal are the best sweeteners of tea. At least I knew who said that: Fielding. The way my life was going lately, just like the British in times of trouble, I was always hauling out the tea.

The kettle was rumbling, nearing a boil by the time Paul finally joined me, sneaking up behind me where I stood at the stove, kissing the back of my neck. "Sorry, sweetie. The Zulus launched a nuclear attack on the Iroquois and I had to wait it out." He took me gently by the shoulders and turned me around, easing me gently back against the oven door. "Ummmm, you smell like—"

"Careful," I warned, worrying about the gas burner blazing merrily on high behind me, "or you'll set my butt on fire."

He kissed the tip of my nose. "You smell like turpentine!"

"Paul," I began, the teakettle quite forgotten. "Sit."

"What?" he asked.

"Just sit," I said.

I thought I'd cry. But standing at the stove studying the puzzled face of the man who had loved me unconditionally for more than twenty-five years, feeling secure in the comfort of my centuries-old kitchen with familiar objects all around me, I was dry-eyed, practically convinced that the whole horrible evening hadn't actually happened.

Paul backed himself into a chair, then patted the seat of the chair next to him. I sat down and with no preamble told my husband that Jennifer Goodall was dead.

Paul blinked once, slowly. A muscle twitched along his jaw. "Jesus," he said.

I folded my hands to keep them from shaking and rested my forearms on the table in front of me. I gave him the details, watching his face as I rattled on.

I told him how the paramedics gave way to campus security who locked all the doors and hustled everyone—actors, orchestra, directors, and crew—into seats in the auditorium. I described how they secured the scene, awaiting the arrival of the Naval Criminal Investigative Service, who took down our names and telephone numbers. Eventually NCIS kicked us out, one by one, and told us to go home. They'd be calling later for our statements.

"How . . . ?" Paul asked.

"A horrible head injury," I said. "What caused it, I don't know."

"I'm sorry," he said. Paul drew a long breath. "This'll be a major headache for the Academy, of course."

I nodded, hating the press corps that invariably materialized at the merest suspicion of a scandal, fully formed and hungry, out of Annapolis's cobblestones.

"Who . . . ?" Paul was working his way through the five Ws. We'd established the what, where, and when of it; but only time could answer the questions that were nagging at him now. "Who would do such a thing? And why?"

I shrugged, at a loss for words.

After a few moments he added, "When they know why, I suppose they'll know who."

"They'll be looking for people with motive," I said, following that train of thought to its logical conclusion.

Paul had been studying his thumbnail. He gazed up at me with a wistful smile. "Are you asking if I have an alibi, my dear?" The smile, such as it was, vanished. "It's not much of one, I'm afraid," he continued, not waiting for me to reply. "I've been home all afternoon, alone, playing with myself."

I smiled at his little joke, stalling for time. I had told Paul about speaking to Jennifer Goodall, of course, but I conveniently forgot to mention my blowup. I was ashamed of it, for one thing, embarrassed that I'd let her get under my skin like that. But my marriage wouldn't be worth a plugged nickel if I waited for the cops to come along and tell him about it first.

"Actually, I was thinking about *my* alibi," I told him.

Paul's eyebrows came together. "Oh?"

"That conversation Jennifer and I had the other day? The one where she made up that lie about you?"

"Go on."

"It wasn't exactly a conversation, Paul. It was an old-fashioned, back-stabbing, mud-slinging, your-mother-swims-after-troop-ships kind of shouting match." I flopped back in my chair, rested my head against the rungs. "Oh God, Paul, after what she said to me, I could have cheerfully drawn and quartered the witch."

"I've shouted at a lot of people, Hannah," Paul said, dismissing my confession, "but I've never killed any of them."

"Yes, but Jennifer's and my little tête-à-tête was overheard by Midshipman Small and practically everybody in the cast."

"I see." Paul squinted at the wall clock. "I suppose a lot will depend on exactly when she died."

I looked at the clock, too. Eleven forty-five? Nearly midnight. It felt like three in the morning. "She must have died shortly before her body was found. Tim told me her body was still warm." I shivered, remembering the young man's valiant but failed attempt at CPR.

A new thought occurred to me. "Jennifer could have been alive when the killer threw her into the trunk, Paul! She might have been lying in there unconscious, all through the first act. It might have taken hours for her to bleed to death." I remembered the blood covering her face, a dark glistening red.

I buried my face in my palms. "God, Paul, anyone could have done it."

The teakettle began to scream. Paul rose from his chair to shut it off. "But wait a minute, Hannah," he said gently. "I'm confused. I thought you told me that the set's been off-limits to anyone but the tech crew since last night's rehearsal."

I followed my husband to the stove, reached into a cupboard and selected two mugs. After I'd dropped the tea bags in, Paul filled the mugs with boiling water.

"That's true," I said, plunging my tea bag up and down. "But there's no security at all, really. The doors were not locked. Aside from the tech crew, anybody could have wandered into the auditorium, even a lost tourist."

I ran down a mental list of the tech crew. With the exception of me, I couldn't think of anybody who had a beef with Lieutenant Goodall. They probably didn't even know her.

As for the cast, the only midshipmen I'd seen talking to Jennifer Goodall had been Kevin and Emma. Had Kevin killed Jennifer to keep her from reporting him for harassing Emma? On the other had, if Emma had confided in Jennifer about her sexual orientation, and Jennifer had threatened to out her, that could have driven Emma to murder her, too.

"What happens now?" Paul wondered, taking his seat.

"We'll be interviewed, of course. NCIS told us to expect that."

"When?"

I shrugged. "I don't have the vaguest idea."

We finished our tea in silence, while variations on the theme of Kevin and Emma played themselves out in my head.

Paul finally coaxed me to bed, but I couldn't sleep. As he snored gently beside me, I lay in the dark, staring at the ceiling. The numbers on the digital clock clicked from three to four to five before I mumbled, "This is ridiculous," crawled out of bed and headed for the bathroom. I filled the tub with hot water, dumped in a quarter cup of lavender bath salts, added another tablespoon for good measure, and settled in for a good long soak.

I was standing at the sink, my head wrapped in a towel, brushing my teeth, when the telephone rang. It was 6:00 A.M.: way too early for someone to be calling. It had to be bad news.

I dove for the telephone, trying to silence it before it could ring a second time. "Hello?" I croaked, and braced myself for the worst.

It was Dorothy, her voice surprisingly bright. "Hannah, I'm sorry to be calling you so early, but I just had to let you know right away!"

"Let me know what?" I whispered, turning my back to my sleeping husband and sitting down carefully on the edge of the mattress.

Incredibly, the Academy had reached a decision about the show. "That woman had nothing to do with the musical," Dorothy reported. "They think it may be just a coincidence that her body was left there."

"And, so?"

"We're still on! They're finished collecting evidence," she continued. "We'll have to get a new trunk for Sweeney, of course, since they've taken ours away. Wasn't there one at Echos and Accents, that place off Chincoteague?"

Quite frankly, I couldn't remember.

"I'm sure that's the place!" Dorothy chugged on. "Could you pick it up for me, Hannah? You live so much closer than me."

Like a good little Do-Bee, I agreed even though I knew that the only way I'd fit that trunk in my LeBaron was on end, and I'd have to put the convertible top down. That would be an adventure in February.

"See you tonight," she chirped, and hung up without saying good-bye.

I stared at the receiver, too dumbfounded to speak. It was six in the ever-lovin' morning. How could she possibly know . . . ? Maybe it would make some sense after I'd had some coffee.

I rinsed out my toothbrush and had just hung it up to dry when Paul stumbled into the bathroom, bleary-eyed, his cheeks and chin dark with stubble. "To whom do I owe that wake-up call?"

"Dorothy Hart." I wrapped my arms around him and squeezed. "Sorry."

Paul rested his chin on the top of my head and hugged me back. "What did *she* want at this ungodly hour?"

"It was good news," I said, feeling a bit light-headed from the combination of heat, steam, and lack of sleep. "The Academy's decided." I took a step backward and waved my hand with a flourish. "In the best of theater traditions, sir, the show must go on."

CHAPTER 11

Sweeney Todd **was a smash, selling out from its** first night on. Standing room only, too. Morbid curiosity might have driven ticket sales into the stratosphere, of course, but each night after the curtain went down, no one could argue that the show wasn't worth the price of admission. The collective intake of breath, the seconds of stunned silence, followed by a standing ovation of *bravos* and *ooh-rah-ooh-rahs* that seemed to go on forever were proof enough of that.

The Naval Criminal Investigative Service had been busy, as well. Even before the post opening night congratulatory beers we'd downed at Ramshead Tavern on West Street had worked their way out of our systems, two NCIS agents had gathered up their notebooks, tape recorders, and video cameras, and moved from their permanent second floor offices in Halligan Hall to a small conference room in the Academy's Administration Building. There, in the shadow of the Naval Academy Chapel dome, they could conduct their interviews in neutral (and far more central) territory.

It was late in the second week of the show before Dorothy and I met to compare notes at Drydock, the snack bar in Dahlgren Hall. By then it seemed that everyone we knew had run the NCIS gauntlet.

"How'd they conduct the interviews?" I wondered

aloud as we merged into the end of the sandwich line. "A to Z? By rank?"

Dorothy shook her head. "I don't think so. I'm an H and they didn't get to me until today. Kevin says they talked to him on Monday, so I think midshipmen were the first priority."

I grabbed a plastic tray and a packet of potato chips and inched forward. "Makes sense, Goodall being the SAVI officer and all, although I hate to think of a midshipman being responsible. It was so . . ." I paused, involuntarily shivered. There were no words to describe the horror of what had been done to that poor woman's head. "There was so much *rage* in it."

Dorothy set her tray down on the tray track. Using both hands, she yanked open her packet of chips and offered me one. "I worried about you," she said just as I stuffed a chip into my mouth.

I chewed and swallowed quickly before answering, not wanting to deliver a shower of crumbs along with my reply. "Because of the argument, you mean?"

Dorothy nodded.

"I told NCIS about the fight right up front," I confessed, "so the interview wasn't too bad. They called my husband in at the same time, so I had Paul along for moral support. At least as far as the door," I added. "NCIS kept him cooling his heels in the hall while they interviewed me and vice versa."

"Next!" One of the servers behind the sandwich counter was looking up at me expectantly.

"Seafood salad sub," I said. "For here. Lettuce and tomato."

I watched quietly, remembering, while the server used an ice cream scoop to dip salad out of a huge plastic tub and heap it on a submarine roll. With gloved fingers she added a pale pink slice of tomato and a single frill of lettuce, before smashing the top down with the flat of her hand and skewering the whole thing together with a fringed toothpick.

That's how I'd felt, I thought, after I finally got out of that conference room—squashed and skewered. I'd dreaded the interview, of course, not least because of my very public argument with Lieutenant Goodall. But I'd been as forthcoming as I could, even going so far as to admit that I loathed the woman, figuring that NCIS would be up to speed on my checkered history with Jennifer Goodall anyway.

Describe what you did that afternoon.

I honestly couldn't remember. After lunch—had it been a cheese and garlic potato at Potato Valley, or had I skipped lunch that day?—I'd gone downtown shopping, but for what, I couldn't say. A greeting card, perhaps? Or a funky pair of socks at Goodies?

Around two I'd stopped in at Mother Earth, I knew that for sure, to check out the new feng shui paraphernalia my sister Ruth had for sale: five element aroma candles—water, earth, wood, metal, and fire!—and the glass and light "fogger" fountains that Ruth claimed would not only add beneficial moisture to the dry winter air in my home, but freshen, purify, and energize it by neutralizing free-roaming negative ions or some such nonsense. The agents' eyes had glazed over by that point, but I soldiered on, confessing that I found the fountains beautiful, though, like Chihuly glass bowls on tripods, wafting clouds of super-fine mist into the air, a far cry from the turquoise plastic humidifier I stored under the bathroom sink, I can tell you, and $200 more expensive, too. Frankly, I think they were glad to see me go.

I picked up my sandwich and set it on my tray. A tent card propped up on the counter advertised a COACH DENNIS JACKSON—a steak and cheese sub—and I watched as the server began assembling one for Dorothy.

"I wracked my brain trying to remember what I was doing that day," I commented to Dorothy as we pushed our trays farther on down the line.

"Me, too," Dorothy said. "In all the confusion, I nearly forgot that I was getting my nails done. And thank God for that," she added, reaching for her sandwich. "At least the manicurist can vouch for me." She curled her fingers loosely around her thumb and stared at her fingertips. "Damn. Look at that. I need to go back." Then she held her fingers out for my inspection. "Big Apple Red. Do you like it?"

I stared in silence at the spot where the glossy crimson enamel had chipped off her pinky. *Somebody's dead and she's worrying about her fingernails?* I was glad I kept mine short.

"I wonder what time they think Jennifer was attacked?" I said, trying to turn the conversation away from beauty tips and get it back on track.

"They did the autopsy at Bethesda," Dorothy told me. "They think maybe four in the afternoon."

I picked up my tray and headed for the drinks station, mulling over what Dorothy had just said. She seemed to be much more in-the-know than Paul and I, not that we hadn't tried. Our usual ace-in-the-hole had turned out to be a deuce. Paul had tried to worm information about the investigation out of his brother-in-law, Dennis Rutherford, with a singular lack of success. NCIS didn't share information with Chesapeake County police lieutenants, it turns out, or with anyone else, for that matter.

Admirals, apparently, were an exception.

"Ted made a few calls to Bethesda," Dorothy explained as she joined me in front of the ice tea machine. She pulled a plastic cup out of the dispenser and held it under the spigot, while I pushed down helpfully on the lever. "They know she died within an hour or two of being thrown into Sweeney's trunk, but they believe she may have been attacked somewhere else. They're still looking for where."

We paid for our food and found an empty table not far from the wall that separated the snack bar's dining area from the ice rink. A hockey game was going on behind the glass. Shouts, whistles, the *sloosh* of skates on ice and the persistent *thwack* of sticks against puck would punctuate our conversation over the next several minutes.

"Ted says there's high-level pressure from Washington to make an arrest in the case," Dorothy added as we set down our trays and settled into our chairs.

"I'll bet," I said. I stared at the salad oozing over the edges of my sandwich. "Whoops, forgot the napkins. Want one?"

Dorothy nodded.

In front of the napkin dispenser, I stopped to ponder. If Jennifer had been killed elsewhere, that meant the murderer had to carry her body from that elsewhere, up five steps to the stage and up another twelve steps—I helped build every one—that led to Sweeney's tonsorial parlor. *Why?* Why not leave the body where it lay?

Was the murderer trying to draw attention away from himself?

Or maybe he intended to discredit the musical, hoping to shut it down?

I'd put nothing past some of those right-wing nut jobs. One year they campaigned to shut down an Academy production of *Cabaret,* complaining in letters to the editor that the Nazis were "scary." I remembered Paul's dark eyes glowering over the top of the newspaper and his wry, "And their point might be?"

The second question was, *How?* Stuffing Jennifer's body into that trunk would require strength—she had been no lightweight. Kevin could have done it easily, I thought, but so could just about any midshipman, male or female. Mids were as fit as they come.

On my way back to the table with the napkins, I studied my friend. Dorothy's clothes hung loosely on her body, as if she'd bought them several sizes too large. At Goodwill.

No way could she have managed anything heavier than a bag of dirty laundry, I decided, and I wasn't even sure about that.

"How well did you know her?" I asked, settling into my chair once again.

"Who?"

"Jennifer Goodall, of course."

Dorothy shrugged. "I saw her hanging around the set is all. I didn't exactly *know* her."

"How about Kevin?" I ventured.

Using both hands, Dorothy lay her sandwich down on her plate. "Well, speak of the devil. . . ."

I turned to look. Emma Kirby was approaching from the direction of the soda dispenser carrying a large cup in each hand. Behind her came Dorothy's son, Kevin, balancing a pizza box on the flat of one hand. "May we join you?" Kevin asked, using his free hand to pull a chair out for Emma.

"Of course you may," Dorothy purred, patting the seat of the chair to her left, smiling proudly, as if to say, *See, my son knows the difference between* can *and* may.

Kevin took the seat his mother had designated. He lifted the lid on the pizza box to reveal a pie heaped so high with toppings that I wondered how he had had the strength to carry it from the kitchen to the table. He scooped up a slice tethered to the mother ship by a long string of cheese. Kevin caught the string with a finger, twisted it around until it broke, then slid the slice into his mouth, point first.

Dorothy observed this operation without comment. "You going to eat all that?"

Emma grinned. "I'm planning to help." She leaned forward and peered into the box. "Pineapple. Ick!"

Kevin studied the pizza like a surgeon about to make an incision. He plucked pineapple bits off several slices and piled them up in the space where the slice he had just inhaled had so recently lain. "Happy now?"

A look I couldn't read passed between the two midshipmen.

None of this was making any sense. One minute Emma's telling Kevin to get lost, the next he's her new best friend, even bowing to her preference in pizza toppings. Had they settled their differences?

"What's wrong, Kev? You look a bit down," commented his mother.

Emma licked tomato sauce off her fingers. "Kevin was hoping to step into the role of the Beadle this weekend," she said. "Adam's been S.I.R. for the past few days."

"S.I.R.?" I hadn't heard that expression before.

"Sick in room."

"Yeah, but at the last minute the S.O.B. rallied." Kevin's lips curled into a smile around his third slice of pizza. "Joke!" he added.

I wasn't so sure.

Emma shot out of her chair, waggling her fingers. "Gotta wash my hands."

I saw an opportunity to speak with Emma alone. "Me, too," I said. I pushed the remains of my sandwich aside and hustled off after her.

I caught up with Emma near the trophy case, stopping her with a light hand on her shoulder. "What is going *on*?" I whispered. "One minute you're talking about taking out a restraining order against Kevin, the next minute he's your best pal."

Keeping her greasy fingertips well clear of her uniform, Emma shrugged. "It's all right, Hannah. Kevin knows."

"He knows?

"Uh-huh."

"That you're gay?"

"Uh-huh."

Behind Emma's head a plaque the size of a turkey platter announced that in 1976 a midshipman named Ian Markwood had been named Most Valuable Player. I stared at the engraved bronze and wondered how one broke the news that you were gay to somebody who was sweet on you.

"How did Kevin react?"

Emma leaned back against the trophy case. "He didn't say anything at first, but then he smiled and said he understood."

"I would have thought he'd be crushed."

Emma shook her head. "It's an ego thing. Kevin said he couldn't figure out what he was doing wrong. Now he knows that it's not *his* fault I'm not attracted to him *that way*. To tell you the truth, Hannah, I think he was relieved. And now that all the sexual tension is gone from the relationship, we can be friends. You know?"

"Wasn't coming out to him a bit risky?" I asked, thinking how easily it could have gone the other way. Kevin could have taken his bruised ego straight to the Commandant of Midshipman and Emma's naval career would have been toast.

"I trust Kevin," she said. "We have this pact."

"Pact?"

"Sorry, Hannah, that's just between the two of us. But I can tell you this." Her dark eyes grew wide and serious. "Kevin is like a big brother to me now, and I couldn't be happier."

I'd always wanted a big brother—so he'd bring home his cute friends, for one thing—but my parents had been completely uncooperative and I'd ended up the middle child of three sisters. "Big brothers can come in handy," I said.

She winked. "Exactly."

I shivered, hoping that Kevin hadn't helped his "little sister" cover up a murder.

"Go wash your hands," I ordered, sensing that Emma had made her point and wouldn't be inclined to elaborate, at least not here in Dahlgren Hall with people to-ing and fro-ing past us on their way to the restrooms. "I'll see you back at the table."

When I rejoined Dorothy and her son, Dorothy seemed to be in the middle of bolstering Kevin's shattered ego. "Professor Black told me you're sure to get a lead next year," she said. "And there's still a chance that what's-his-name won't be able to go on."

"Adam. His name is Adam, Mother." Kevin selected another slice of pizza and raised it to his mouth. "I'm proud of what I'm doing with Jonas Fogg, Mother." He took a bite.

"Yes, but it's not a *singing* role, Kevin, now is it?"

Kevin's pale skin flushed. "Can't you leave it alone? Please?"

That was my cue to say *How about those Redskins?* but fortunately Emma rejoined us and the awkward moment passed.

"I'm so glad that you and Kevin are dating," Dorothy commented, addressing Emma.

Kevin glared at his mother, but she didn't appear to notice.

"When Sarah broke up with him," she forged on, "he seemed to lose interest in everything. If it weren't for you and the musical—"

"Mother!"

"No need to shout, Kevin."

"Come to dinner on Sunday," I interjected. "Let me tempt you with some decent food."

Emma's head shot up. "Will you make lasagna?"

"If you like."

Emma rolled her eyes. "Oh my gawd, Kevin, Hannah's lasagna is to *die* for. It's got meatballs."

"Dorothy?"

"Sunday?" Dorothy shook her head. "Sorry, Hannah, but Ted and I have a prior commitment."

I hoped my relief didn't show in my face. If I didn't have to play Hannah the Happy Hostess to Dorothy and the admiral, maybe I could get to the bottom of what was really going on between Kevin and Emma.

"How about you, Kevin? Around noon?"

"Sure thing, Mrs. Ives," Kevin mumbled around a mouthful of pepperoni, green pepper, mushrooms, and pineapple. "We'll look forward to it."

But that turned out to be an appointment none of us would be able to keep.

CHAPTER 12

It seemed as if my head had just hit the pillow when I dreamed I heard the doorbell ringing.

I rose up on one elbow, straining my ears. At first I heard nothing but the roar of the furnace kicking in, but then it came again, the muffled *brrring-brrring* of the ancient doorbell attached to our front door.

I squinted at the clock: 5:00. Who could be calling at such an ungodly hour?

I turned on the bedside lamp, swung my legs over the side of the mattress, and felt around for my slippers. As I slipped my toes into them, I turned to check on Paul. He lay on his side, one arm stuffed under his pillow, breathing deeply, sleeping the sleep of a man who'd drunk a bit too much beer with his brother-in-law the night before. I didn't have the heart to wake him. Paul didn't have early classes on Friday.

Still half asleep, I was shuffling across the hardwood floor, my feet half in and half out of my slippers, when the ringing turned to knocking. "Hold your darn horses!" I muttered to myself, feeling around in the dark for my bathrobe.

I flipped on the light at the top of the stairs and started down, knotting the sash around my waist as I went. In the front hall, I flipped the switch that turned on the porch light and peered out the window.

A short blonde dressed in a dark overcoat several sizes too big stood on the doorstep. Behind her stood four other individuals—three men and another woman—dressed in dark jackets. Struggling to remain calm, I raised my hand to the dead bolt. "Who is it?" I asked.

"FBI," the woman called through the door. "We have a warrant."

I was so relieved that the people clustered on my doorstep weren't state troopers calling to tell me that Emily and the children had been involved in a terrible accident that what she said didn't sink in. At least not right away. "A warrant?" I stammered. "A warrant for what?"

"To search the house," she shouted. "Open up, please, or we'll have to break the door down, and I'm sure you don't want that."

Next to the blonde-in-charge, a husky man shifted from one foot to the other, cradling a three-foot length of pipe about the diameter of a salad plate in the crook of his arm. As I watched through the window, hugging my arms and trying not to panic, one beefy hand moved to grasp the battering ram by a handle, and it looked like he was itching to use it. I decided not to give him the chance. Aside from a few unpaid bills, two overdue library books, and a 1998 federal income tax return that might have been a shade on the dicey side, Paul and I had absolutely nothing to hide.

I twisted the dead bolt and opened the door wide, holding my robe together over my nightgown as the cold morning air swept in.

The blonde didn't budge from her spot on my doorstop. "Hannah Ives?"

"Yes?"

"Hannah Ives, FBI. You're under arrest."

Blood roared in my ears. Dropping the end of the sash I was holding, I pressed a hand to my chest. "What did you say?"

"Step inside, please."

I was about to point out that I was already inside, when she pushed her way into my entrance hall, a pair of handcuffs dangling from her hand.

Instinctively, I backed away.

"Turn around, please. Hands behind your back."

I was outnumbered, so I turned obediently, knowing that the next thing I would feel would be cold hard steel closing around my wrists. "Paul!" I screamed. "Paul!"

Ignoring my cries, the blonde guided me toward a nearby chair. "I'm Special Agent Crisp," she informed me. "Please sit down."

I sat. I leaned forward when the back of the chair pressed uncomfortably against the handcuffs. I glared up at my captor as she quietly read me my rights—anything you say can and will be used against you . . . you have the right to an attorney . . . do you understand . . . ? Clearly, I was having a nightmare. Then the handcuffs pinched my wrists, and I knew it was no dream.

Slightly shorter than my five-foot-six, Agent Crisp's roundish face was framed by blond hair that curled gently under each ear. As she moved about the entrance hall issuing orders, her overcoat flapped open. Underneath, she wore a dark gray pantsuit and a crisp white shirt, and I realized that what I had at first taken for pleasing plumpness was, in fact, a bulletproof vest. I didn't know whether to be flattered or dismayed. Imagine! Donning a bulletproof vest for protection against . . . me!

"Is there anybody else here?" Agent Crisp asked.

"Of course there's somebody here!" I snapped. "My husband. He's upstairs in bed. It's not even light out yet!"

She nodded to a colleague who started upstairs to find Paul. A second agent headed in the direction of the kitchen. He must have let his buddies in the back door because before long there were seven FBI agents swarming around.

For her part, Agent Crisp was all business. "Are there any weapons in the house?"

"Of course not!" I snarled. I wondered if "weapons" included the Wilkinson presentation swords, crossed and hung on the wall in Paul's office, directly over his computer. I decided not to mention them.

"What the *hell* is going on?" Awakened by my screams, Paul thundered down the stairs wearing nothing but his Y-fronts, nearly trampling the agent who'd been sent upstairs to fetch him.

The agent grabbed the banister with one hand and raised the other. "Your wife is under arrest." Then seeing the rage on my husband's face, he quickly added, "Sir."

Paul swept the man's arm aside. "Under arrest? What the hell for?"

"For the murder of Jennifer Marie Goodall."

Paul's face grew dangerously red. "The hell she is!"

Murder! I doubled over, feeling like I'd been kicked in the stomach by a horse. Jennifer Goodall. I should have known. "This is a mistake," I moaned.

"Hannah." Paul took another step in my direction, but Agent Crisp's arm shot out like a toll booth barrier, blocking his way.

"Sir."

Paul froze. "I need to comfort my wife,"

"I think it's best if you wait in the kitchen, sir." Agent Crisp didn't smile, but her eyes seemed kind.

My cheeks burned with tears. I swiped at my eyes the best I could, using my shoulders, then turned my ruined face to Crisp. "I think I'm going to be sick."

Crisp nodded to one of her colleagues, who struck off in the direction of the kitchen, returning in less than a minute with a damp paper towel. He held it out in front of me helpfully, although what he expected me to do with it when my hands were cuffed behind my back, I hadn't a clue.

Paul snatched the towel from the agent's hand and quickly, before anyone had time to draw their weapon, used it to wipe my flaming cheeks.

"Oh God, Paul, I'm so sorry," I sobbed against his

hand. I couldn't look at him. Seeing the confusion in my husband's eyes would just set me off again.

In the meantime I could hear that Agent Crisp's intrepid colleagues had moved from my kitchen to my dining room, noisily opening and closing drawers and cupboards. Flashbulbs flashed. I heard the distinctive clanking of my mother's silverware as someone pulled open a drawer. Glassware in the china cabinet tinkled alarmingly.

"Paul," I bawled. "They're tearing the house apart. Please, make sure they don't break anything."

"Don't worry, ma'am." Agent Crisp was reassuring. "We're trained to be careful. We photograph the rooms both before and after we search. Everything will be left exactly the way we found it."

My head throbbed. *No, you're wrong! Nothing will ever be the same. You've invaded my home. I've been violated.*

But it was about to get worse.

"Stand up, please, ma'am. I'm going to search you now."

She was polite, Agent Crisp, and professional. There was a nurse at Anne Arundel Hospital Center like that, I remembered. No matter how terrifying the procedure I was about to undergo, she'd explain it to me carefully, as if I were a moron. "This is a pill. We're going to give it to you now. It's a sedative. It'll make you feel very sleepy."

I could have used one of those sedatives just then. Maybe a dozen. Maybe someone could wake me when it was all over.

With another officer and Paul observing, Agent Crisp removed my handcuffs just long enough for me to take off my bathrobe and step out of my slippers. Through my nightgown, she felt around my waist, then ran the backs of her hands along both sides of my legs, my upper body and arms. Finally, she checked my head. Some criminals hid weapons in their hairdos, I supposed, but considering my short bob, that additional step seemed rather ridiculous.

"You'll need to dress," Agent Crisp said. She tucked a wayward swath of bangs behind her left ear.

Still sobbing, I nodded.

"Where are you taking my wife?" Paul demanded.

"To the FBI Resident Agency here in Annapolis for processing, then up to the courthouse in Baltimore, where she'll be arraigned."

"On what charge?"

"The charge is murder, sir."

"But I didn't kill anybody!" I choked back fresh tears. "Why isn't anybody listening to me?"

Agent Crisp reached into her pocket and handed Paul a card that she'd already prepared. "Here's the name and number of the Assistant U.S. Attorney in charge of the case. Have your lawyer contact him."

"When can she come home?"

"That'll be up to the judge."

And with my hands still cuffed behind me, she marched me upstairs.

How many times had I stood in front of that very closet, trying to decide on an appropriate outfit for a wedding, or a funeral, or to dress the part of a trophy wife in order to trap a crooked insurance broker? What did I own that was suitable for going to jail?

Agent Crisp had planted me in the center of the bedroom, removed my handcuffs, and slid open my closet door. I felt ridiculously embarrassed by the mess inside. The clothes I'd worn the night—no, years!—before were heaped in a corner, and shoes I kicked off in a hurry lay scattered everywhere.

I realized Agent Crisp was waiting for me to say something. "What should I wear?" I asked, feeling helpless.

"Nothing expensive or tight," she suggested.

From five feet away I stared into the closet.

My jeans? Too tight.

My green wool skirt? Too new.

My black wool slacks from Talbots? Too expensive. They'd be ruined.

"That long skirt," I decided at last, pointing. "The one with the gored panels."

Crisp located the skirt and eased it off its hanger. Made by Ahni Salway, an Annapolis designer with a genius for fabric and color, the skirt was one of my favorites. Falling at mid-calf, it was smart but comfortable. Colorful geometric shapes swirled over one panel; Japanese courtesans lounged on another; ripe apples decorated a third. Usually it made me smile, but not that morning. "And a black sweater," I added. "I don't care which."

As Agent Crisp rummaged through my closet looking for a sweater, I tried to gather my wits. *They think I murdered Jennifer Goodall.* But I hadn't, of course, so what possible evidence could they have against me? The fight alone wouldn't have been enough to sustain an arrest warrant.

Maybe I was being framed!

Oh, God. What was going to happen to me? Would they lock me away forever? Send me to the electric chair?

Crisp interrupted my panic attack. "Where's your underwear?"

I gaped at her. *My God, I wasn't even going to be trusted with a pair of underpants!* "Top drawer," I told her, struggling to maintain control.

Agent Crisp opened the drawer I'd indicated and ran her hand around inside, checking, I supposed, for guns in my drawers. (Ha, ha!)

I asked for my black tights, but that wasn't allowed. *Were they afraid I might hang myself with them?* I would have to wear ankle socks instead.

Agent Crisp added the ankle socks to the neat pile she had made on top of my dresser. I knew I was supposed to get dressed, but I wasn't sure how. All the usual protocols had suddenly, drastically, changed.

I'd dressed in locker rooms before, of course, at summer camp and in college, but that was long before my mastectomy. It had taken me months after the surgery to gain enough confidence to show my body again, even to Paul. And Agent Crisp was a total stranger.

I stood there shivering in my nightgown, arms dangling at my sides, doing nothing.

Crisp seemed to sense my discomfort. She lifted the bra and panties from the top of the pile and held them out. "You can turn around, if you like," she suggested. "But don't go near any of the furniture."

I took the underwear from her outstretched hand, slipped the underpants on under my nightgown and then turned away. I eased my gown over my head and let it fall to the carpet. I fumbled for and dropped the bra. When I bent to retrieve it, I noticed Crisp flinch as she caught sight of my reconstructed breast. It wasn't bad, as reconstructed breasts go—the plastic surgeon had done a terrific job—but the nipple had migrated a little left of center. Clearly, it wasn't the breast I was originally issued.

I flushed, picked up the bra and put it on as quickly as I could, my back to her.

"I'm sorry," she said. "I know this must be difficult."

"I didn't do it, you know," I said as I struggled with the hooks. "I won't pretend that I'm sorry Jennifer Goodall's dead, but I didn't have anything to do with her ending up that way."

Agent Crisp slipped a sweater off its hanger, felt it over carefully, then handed it to me.

"And I can't be the only person in the world who hated her guts," I added as my head emerged from the neck of the sweater.

"I couldn't possibly comment on that, Mrs. Ives." Was it my imagination, or had Agent Crisp just suppressed a smile?

"My first name's Hannah," I told her, as if she didn't know. "What's yours?"

"Amanda," she said. "Amanda Crisp." She nodded toward her colleague, who at one point or another had joined us in the bedroom and now lounged tall against the door frame. "And that's Special Agent Elizabeth Taylor."

Taylor was a solid, sour-faced woman whose muscular arms and broad shoulders seemed custom-designed for blocking any attempt on my part to escape. She wore her dark hair in a ponytail tied low at the nape of her neck and not a speck of jewelry. Somehow I didn't find the knowledge that she shared a name—and little else—with a famous movie star reassuring. If we got into a Good Cop/Bad Cop situation, I knew which one of them would be the first to aim a five-thousand-watt klieg light in my face.

I touched my ears, then pointed at the dresser where my jewelry box sat. "Earrings?"

Amanda Crisp shook her head. "We don't recommend you wear jewelry."

I glanced at my engagement ring. The young Paul Ives had slaved all summer to earn the money for that ring, sweating from sunup to sundown in a South County tobacco field. It was only a third of a carat, but more precious to me than the Hope diamond.

Crisp noticed. "And you'd better leave that at home, too, Mrs. Ives. They're just going to take it away from you."

"They?" I croaked. "Who's they?"

"The U.S. Marshals at the Federal Courthouse in Baltimore. That's where you'll be arraigned."

I swayed on my feet, suddenly dizzy. "I need to sit down."

Crisp held up a hand, palm out. "Just a minute." While Agent Taylor kept her eagle eyes trained on me, Agent Crisp shook out the bedding and laid it aside. Using both hands, she tipped up the mattress and looked underneath, checking (I supposed) for any handguns I might have hidden in the box springs. Then she peered under the bed. "Okay. You can sit."

I plopped down on the edge of the mattress, inhaled deeply, and held my breath, as if by not breathing, I could stop time. It didn't work. I wrapped my right hand around my ring finger and considered what she'd just told me. "No," I said after a few minutes. "I'm not going to take my ring off. And if anybody tries to take it from me, I'm going to fight them for it!" I waved my hand in the air. "How can I possibly hurt myself with this?"

Crisp shrugged. "Your choice, but I think you're going to find that the U.S. Marshals are not particularly good 'people people,' if you know what I mean. They'll want to take it from you and put it in an envelope with your personal effects. Trust me. It'll be much safer with your husband."

Personal effects. They were talking about me as if I'd died.

Maybe I had, and instead of going to heaven, I'd ended up in hell. Maybe that's why my bladder was giving me fits all of a sudden. "Can I use the bathroom?" I asked.

Agent Crisp nodded. She gestured to Agent Taylor, who pushed herself away from the door frame and ambled into the bathroom. Taylor opened the medicine cabinet, ran her fingers over the items inside, removing a brown prescription bottle. I had no idea what it contained. She peered into the cabinet under the sink, lifted each towel. She peeked inside the toilet tank, too, checking for weapons there, also, I presumed.

Satisfied, she motioned me inside, then assumed a watchful position near the open bathroom door.

I stood by the toilet, waiting for her to leave, but she didn't move a single one of her oh-so-solid muscles. I needed to pee, but there was no way I could do it, not while Taylor was watching me. So I brushed my teeth. Made a production of washing and drying my face and my hands, anything to delay the inevitable.

Then I finished dressing and they escorted me downstairs.

"Where's your coat?" Crisp inquired when we reached the entrance hall.

Coat. I'd forgotten about a coat. It was February. It was cold outside. Why was I so hot?

Without any direction from me, Crisp located the closet, selected a black corduroy car coat with a fake leopard collar that used to belong to my daughter, and held it out. I was too exhausted to correct her.

Crisp patted down the pockets of Emily's coat before helping me into it. I was allowed to fasten the buttons, then we began what would become a ritual over the next several hours: coat on, handcuffs on, handcuffs off, coat off, handcuffs on. This time, though, the handcuffs went on in front.

While all this was going on, Paul stared at me forlornly from the chair in the entrance hall. "Hannah, Hannah," he crooned as the cuffs tightened around my wrists.

With a firm hand on my back, Crisp guided me toward the front door.

"Call your lawyer! Call Murray Simon," I yelled to Paul over my shoulder. "But please, don't tell Emily!"

Paul shot from the chair. "Don't worry, Hannah. Murray and I'll get you out of there. You'll be home for dinner. I promise."

"I know you will. And Paul? Don't *you* worry. I beat cancer, and I can beat this, too."

On the narrow one-way street outside our house an unmarked Ford Taurus idled, blocking traffic. Behind it, an irate motorist began backing up. I recognized the driver as one of my neighbors, Ray Flynt. As I watched Ray turn his car around near the William Paca House and drive the wrong way down Prince George Street, I prayed that he didn't recognize me, that none of my other neighbors were awake and peering out their windows.

Crisp opened the rear door on the passenger side of the Taurus and guided me inside with a gentle hand on my head, just like on TV. After I sat, she leaned inside the car and wove the seat belt through my handcuffs before inserting the buckle in the clip and clicking it shut. Then she slammed the door, walked around the other side of the car and climbed in next to me. With Agent Taylor behind the wheel, we rolled quietly away.

With tears streaming down my cheeks, I twisted in my seat to look over my shoulder. Paul stood framed in our doorway, barefoot, his bathrobe flapping open in the wind. Light snow had started to fall, each flake a sparkling diamond in the light from our porch lamp. Mother would have grabbed my hand, squeezed and said "Look, Hannah, it's a Winter Wonderland!"

Some Wonderland.

My husband standing half naked in a February snowstorm. And even in the lamplight, I could see he was crying.

CHAPTER 13

"What time is it?" I asked Amanda Crisp as Agent Taylor steered the Taurus through Annapolis's narrow streets, avoided the ever-present construction on Rowe Boulevard, and eased into the commuter traffic heading west on Route 50.

Agent Crisp stared straight ahead. "Seven."

Back in my cozy kitchen, the coffeepot would just be kicking into automatic, gurgling cheerfully, in the mistaken assumption that it was going to be just an ordinary day. At that moment I could have killed for a cup of coffee.

Except for the crackle of the police radio, it was quiet inside the car. I wanted to fill the silence with shouting: *I'm innocent! You're making a big mistake!* As if the FBI didn't hear those words twenty times every day.

Instead of heading north on I-97 to Baltimore, Taylor took the Riva Road exit, and I began to panic. "Where are you taking me?"

"The FBI Resident Agency."

"Oh, right." I remembered now. That's where they'd "process" me. Whatever the hell that meant.

"What happens there?" I asked.

"We have an automated booking process," she explained. "JABS. Saves having to do it up in Baltimore."

I remembered what Crisp had said earlier about the U.S. Marshals not being "people people" and began to relax.

We turned right on Truman Parkway. Just opposite the Farmers Market, Agent Taylor turned into the underground parking garage of an unremarkable brick office building I'd passed a hundred times before. My brain wasn't firing on all cylinders, especially without my usual shot of caffeine, but some questions were beginning to float to the surface.

"Why the FBI?" I asked as Crisp unbuckled my seat belt.

"Lieutenant Goodall was murdered on federal property," she explained. "That's where we come in."

"But it's a naval base," I said. "I thought the NCIS had jurisdiction."

Crisp stood outside the open car door, looking in. "They do, but we get involved, too, particularly whenever a civilian enters the equation."

Civilian. I thought for a moment. *That would be me.*

They marched me to the elevator.

A few minutes later I was seated in an ordinary office with ordinary desks and ordinary chairs arranged in ordinary cubicles, just like at Whitworth and Sullivan in Washington, D.C., and every other office where I'd ever worked. Ringing phones and clacking keyboards surrounded me with a familiar and strangely comforting cacophony. There were no bars on the windows to remind me that I was, after all, a prisoner.

But it was false security, I knew. The pounding in my head continued relentlessly.

Agent Crisp removed my handcuffs. I massaged my wrists and stared thirstily at a cup of coffee steaming on an adjoining desk.

Crisp noticed. "Would you like something to eat or drink?"

"Coffee, please."

"Special Agent Taylor?"

Agent Taylor grunted, and took off to fetch me a cup.

"Cream and sugar!" I called after her. "Please."

Meanwhile, Amanda Crisp began tapping at her keyboard. I couldn't see the monitor, but by the number of times she hit the Tab key, I figured she was filling out some sort of form.

"Okay," I said when she lifted her fingers from the keyboard for a moment. "I understand that you're only doing your job, but what possible evidence can you have against me?"

"After your lawyer talks to the Assistant U.S. Attorney assigned to your case, he'll have more information for you, Mrs. Ives. You should be able to see your lawyer later today."

"Aren't you going to ask me any questions?" I asked, gratefully sipping at the coffee Elizabeth Taylor had brought me.

"No, I'm not. You've asked for your attorney, and we're scrupulous about that."

Agent Crisp finished typing, then took me off to be fingerprinted. I'd expected them to smear ink all over my fingers, but the JABS system was fully automated.

"What's JABS stand for?" I asked as the technician helped me roll each finger on a glass plate.

"Joint Automated Booking System," he replied, his green eyes bright and serious behind his eyeglasses. "It eliminates the repetitive booking of offenders. All federal law enforcement agencies tap into it. We can collect up to seventy-five data elements about a case," he said, smiling with pride, as if he'd invented the system himself. "Mug shots, crime scene descriptions, photos of evidence, like that."

I watched as a bar of light panned across the glass plate like a miniature Xerox machine and he clicked on the button that would send digitized images of my fingertips off to AFIS. I knew what AFIS was: the FBI's automated fingerprint identification system. Then he scanned the four fingers of each of my hands together and sent those images off, too.

When the technician had finished, Amanda Crisp came

to collect me. By then my digestive system had processed the coffee and my bladder was sending out urgent messages. Privacy or no privacy, I knew I couldn't keep my legs crossed forever. "I need to pee," I told her.

Crisp grinned. "I'm taking Mrs. Ives to the restroom," she told Agent Taylor as we passed her desk. Together we walked down a long hall. "We don't have a private bathroom," Crisp explained. "Give me a minute." While I leaned against the wall, Crisp opened the door to the ladies' room and yelled, "I'm coming in with a prisoner!"

A chorus of toilets flushed in unison and Crisp stepped aside as three secretary types scurried out. I guess they didn't want to share the bathroom with a criminal.

Crisp checked the stalls, then nodded that it was okay for me to go in. She stood sideways holding the stall door open but not looking directly at me while I relieved myself.

My eyes filled with tears. Would I ever again be able to use the bathroom without an audience?

Of course you will, I told myself. *Murray will move heaven and earth to get you out. Paul will call in all his IOUs. Dennis will pull strings.* They knew I had nothing to do with Jennifer's death.

"We better hurry." Agent Taylor barged into the ladies' room. With a stubby finger she tapped her watch. "Shit, Amanda, we don't have time to get her up there for the ten o'clock arraignment."

I stood at the sink, thoroughly soaping my hands.

"We'll have to sit around that freaking courthouse until three," she complained.

I twisted the tap, adjusting the water temperature.

"Goes with the territory, Liz."

With the two FBI agents looking on, I rinsed my hands, then dried them carefully on a paper towel. I crumpled the towel into a ball and tossed it into the trash.

Then I smiled. "I'm ready for my close-up, Mr. DeMille."

"What?" Agent Taylor's eyes narrowed suspiciously.

Amanda grinned. "Never mind, Liz."

CHAPTER 14

Baltimore, Maryland. My second hometown. Druid Park Zoo, the National Aquarium, the Baltimore Museum of Art. The bliss of Friday nights in August, sitting on a folding chair in Little Italy watching *Casablanca* or *Life Is Beautiful* projected on the side of a building. Saturdays can be perfect, too. Strolling through Fells Point, grabbing the latest thriller from Mystery Loves Company and a cup of coffee from the Daily Grind. My sister Georgina lives in Baltimore, too, in Roland Park with her growing family.

But the feds? I wasn't sure where they hung out up Baltimore way, but when Agent Taylor made the left turn onto Pratt Street, I recognized the Garmatz Building and the statue of Thurgood Marshall, who'd been gazing out over the Inner Harbor for decades.

Regular citizens enter the building via a door behind Thurgood. Prisoners go around back, directly into an underground garage.

As I rode up in the freight elevator between the two agents, I felt strangely detached. Everything had taken on a surreal feeling, something I hadn't experienced since the last time I'd pulled back-to-back all-nighters at Oberlin or . . . well, since the last time I'd inhaled and enjoyed it. The Welcome to Baltimore sign where someone had painted in "Hon," Ravens Stadium, Camden Yards, even the battleship *Constellation* had looked strangely distorted, as if I were seeing them for the first time, or looking at them through the wrong end of a telescope.

Agent Crisp had called ahead. When the steel door slid open, two burly marshals were waiting, solid as trees. We were introduced, I feel sure, but if they had names, I've forgotten them. The big lug, I called Jesse. The shorter hunk, Arnold.

Arnold studied the paperwork Amanda Crisp handed him, raised one bushy eyebrow. "Her attorney's already here, raising hell. Demands to see her right away."

Jesse scowled. "Tell him to cool his jets. We haven't even searched her yet."

Her fingers still fastened to my upper arm, Crisp said, "We've already done that. She's clean."

Jesse puffed up. "You know the rules."

"We've already searched her, and she hasn't been out of custody." Crisp's fingers dug more tightly into my arm. A territorial squabble was going on, I was smack dab in the middle of it, and if Amanda Crisp didn't win, I'd be the loser, big-time. I'd be strip-searched: the ultimate humiliation.

While Arnold and Jesse conferred, the second hand on the wall clock jerked from five to six to seven. I decided to create my own distraction. "I *demand* to see my lawyer."

Jesse turned icy eyes on me, blinked, then looked at Arnold. "So what about her lawyer?"

"Some hot shot." Arnold was unimpressed. "Tell him she's being processed. Let him wait."

There was that word again: processed. I was being "processed" like meat or fish or plastic-wrapped squares of cheese food. But at least we'd moved on, and a strip search seemed to be off the agenda.

Crisp released my arm and said, "I'll see you later in

court, Mrs. Ives," before disappearing through the door we'd just come through. As the door slid shut, I stared after her like a lost friend, feeling completely abandoned.

Arnold took charge. My photo was taken, front and sides like the Unibomber, then transmitted to Washington as data element who-knows-what in the profile being built up on me in JABS.

Afterward, Jesse escorted me to a holding cell painted the color of mucous, handed me a white cardboard box, and slid the door shut behind me.

"What's this?" I asked, indicating the box.

"Lunch," he grunted.

I hadn't had anything to eat since dinner the previous night, but with acid gnawing at the lining of my stomach, just the thought of food made me want to barf.

I set the box unopened on the only furniture in the room—a bench molded into the wall—and paced out my temporary home—eight feet by eight feet. Was this miserable cell a preview of coming attractions? Would I spend the rest of my life pacing and pacing, staring at four blank walls? No, I corrected myself: three blank walls and a fourth wall with bars on it.

I slouched on the bench, with my back against the wall, my feet dangling, not even able to touch the floor.

I was finally, blessedly alone.

But instead of relaxing, I started to shake. My teeth chattered. I longed for my coat, but they'd taken that away. No scarves, no belts, no panty hose, either. If I wanted to end it all, my only hope was to roll off the bench and conk my head on the floor.

Breathe, Hannah, breathe!

I closed my eyes. Behind my eyelids a tropical island began to materialize: palm trees, frangipani, planter's punch on shaved ice with a tiny umbrella, waves gently licking a white sand beach.

Breathe! In through your nose, out through your mouth.

Warm breezes, sun sparkling on water clear as gin, snorkel and swim fins, a tropical reef with fishes darting in and out and . . .

Sharks!

My eyelids flew open. I'd have to tell Ruth that I tried, but visualized meditation simply didn't work in a jail cell. My shui was definitely all fenged up.

For lack of anything better to do, I opened the lunch box and sorted through the contents, laying each item out on the bench next to me. A ham sandwich. A packet of chips. A bottle of water. An apple that looked like it'd lost one too many rounds with a croquet mallet. Who had packed this mess? Prisoners? I leaned my head against the wall, fighting back tears. Would I spend the rest of my life eating crap like this? I had new respect for prisoners of war like Admirals Bill Lawrence and William Stockdale. I was going stir-crazy after only an hour; they'd been locked up and tortured by the North Vietnamese for more than six years.

"I want my lawyer!" I screamed to deaf walls. "I have a right to talk to my lawyer!"

It was probably only a coincidence, but several minutes later Arnold appeared. "Mrs. Ives? Your lawyer is here."

I could have kissed his scruffy cheek.

Arnold escorted me to a nearby room, where Murray sat at a table on the opposite side of a glass window. I hadn't seen Murray Simon since the grandchildren were born and Paul and I had updated our wills. Murray had the same round face, a little less sandy hair, and had switched from aviator glasses to a pair of trendy, narrow European-style frames.

As usual, Murray zeroed in on what was bothering me most. Before I could even say "Hi," Murray got right to the point. "Don't worry, Hannah, we'll get you out of here."

I folded my arms on the table and rested my forehead on them. "Thank God!"

I took a deep breath and gazed up at my attorney. I'd opened my mouth to ask the next question, but once again Murray was ahead of me. "You're going to be arraigned sometime after three o'clock. There's nothing I can do about that. You'll plead not guilty, of course, and we'll get you home by dinnertime."

"Not guilty to murder, you mean?" My mouth was dry, my throat so tight I could barely get the word out. *Murder.*

"No, you're being charged with manslaughter, Hannah." Murray paused, waiting for that information to sink in.

"Manslaughter? But what evidence does the FBI have against me?"

"Doesn't look good. They found the murder weapon."

I stared at him stupidly.

"It was a hammer, Hannah. They found it in the Dumpster behind Nimitz Library. And I'm afraid your fingerprints are all over it."

I fell back against the chair. "Of course my fingerprints are all over it, Murray! I was building sets with the damn thing!"

"It gets worse," Murray said.

"How could it *possibly* get any worse?"

"The hammer was wrapped in your sweatshirt."

I shuddered, suddenly remembering the sweatshirt and hot glue gun I'd left lying on a chair in the Jabberwocky room that night I'd fled from Jennifer Goodall's loathesome presence. "Oh, shit."

"And of course there was the argument."

I nodded. "Can't bother to deny that."

Murray whipped off his glasses and laid them on the table in front of him. He leaned forward, his mouth close to the glass. "Hannah, I need you to think carefully. What were you doing the afternoon Jennifer was murdered?"

"I don't remember exactly, but I know I went downtown to do some shopping."

"Were you hanging around Mahan auditorium at all, say between three and four in the afternoon?"

"Absolutely not."

Murray leaned back in his chair. "Then this is a tough one. NCIS has a witness who saw you leaving the auditorium about the time Jennifer was attacked, walking in the direction of the library."

"What witness?" My head reeled. I remembered the countless times I'd walked between Mahan and the set shop in Alumni Hall, waving to Nimitz staff as they lounged on the loading dock, smoking. I mentioned this to Murray. "Maybe the witness got the day wrong. I *know* I was shopping that afternoon. There must be credit card receipts somewhere!"

"Paul's looking into it, Hannah. He's checking your Amex and Visa card statements."

"Good." I relaxed just a fraction. "So, what can I expect?"

"The marshals will escort you into the courtroom. I'll be there, of course. You'll stand with me behind the defense table and listen quietly while they read the charges. You'll plead not guilty—that goes without saying—then the government will request bail."

"How much bail?" I interrupted.

"About $250,000 is usual in cases like this."

I gasped, seeing the door that had opened a crack slam shut behind me. "Where are we going to get that kind of money?"

"Don't worry. Paul and I are already making arrangements for a property bond."

"Uh-huh," I said dully, imagining our beautiful old house with a For Sale sign hanging in front of it.

"We'll counter with a reduced sum," Murray continued, "because you're a model citizen with a spotless record, family ties to the community, not a flight risk etcetera etcetera etcetera."

"Okay."

"And you'll have to surrender your passport, I'm afraid."

"My passport," I repeated numbly. Did they think I'd head for some South American country with no extradition treaty with the United States? Spend my life drifting aimlessly from one third world town to another? Visit my grandchildren only by video conferencing, assuming said third world country had broad band Internet access? No, I'd simply be a prisoner of another kind.

"But what if they find me guilty, Murray? What then?"

"They won't."

"But what if they do?"

"The federal sentencing guideline for manslaughter is ten years."

"Ten years!" I threw back my head and closed my eyes. Chloe and Jake would be in their teens. Paul would be planning his retirement without me.

Murray pressed an open palm against his side of the glass, his small way of comforting me. Deeply touched, I raised my hand to his, matching it finger for finger, and began to sob.

"Murray, please. I want to go home." The thought of clean towels, clean hair, and clean clothes made me ache with yearning.

"Hang in there, Hannah."

"Damn it!" I said, wiping my cheeks with the back of my hand. "I didn't survive breast cancer just so I could spend the next ten years stamping out license plates!"

"Trust me, Hannah. You won't have to."

"From your mouth to God's ears, Murray. To God's most merciful ears."

It happened just the way Murray had described. Arnold led me into the courtroom with my hands cuffed in front of me, past the empty jury box, depositing me behind the table with Murray. Agent Crisp was also there, standing at the prosecution table next to a tall dark-haired guy in a navy blue suit.

Murray leaned over and whispered, "That's Richard Knowles, the Assistant U.S. Attorney trying your case."

I took my time studying Knowles, sizing him up. He must have felt my gaze on him because he looked up, blinked twice, then went back to shuffling through the sheaf of papers he had laid out on the table in front of him. I caught Amanda Crisp's eye and smiled, but only her eyes smiled back.

After the judge read the charges and I'd looked him straight in the eye and said "Not guilty" in a strong, clear voice, bail was set at $200,000. Murray had said not to worry about bail. Hah! We were still playing catch-up with Emily's tuition payments to Bryn Mawr. Paul and I drove previously owned cars. The house needed painting. All that, apparently, was going to have to wait.

Finally the judge released me. The marshals removed my handcuffs and with Murray by my side, led us down a long hallway, where we checked in with pretrial services. On Murray's advice, I waived my right to a speedy trial so he'd have time to prepare my case.

I had every confidence in Murray Simon. The rape charges against a D.C. shock jock? Dismissed. The SEC bigwig charged with insider trading? Acquitted. And when a Naval Academy football player tested positive for cocaine, Murray'd gotten him off scot-free, too. Everybody knew *they'd* been guilty as hell.

Maybe there was a chance for me.

Paul was waiting for us in Murray's BMW out on Lombard Street. He grabbed me by the shoulders and folded me into his arms, crushing my nose against his chest. He kissed the top of my head, my forehead, my cheek.

Murray tossed his briefcase onto the backseat of the car. "Take Hannah away for the weekend, Paul." He handed my husband a set of keys. "These keys go to a cabin on Deep Creek Lake. It belongs to a client of mine. He won't be using it this weekend."

Paul curled his fingers around the keys and held his fist close to his chest, as if he were afraid they might disappear. "You sure?"

"Positive. He's doing three to five years for tax evasion at Allenwood."

I turned in Paul's arms to gape at my attorney. "Murray! I thought you'd never lost a case."

Murray shrugged. "Everyone thought he'd get ten."

Paul tucked the keys into his pocket, then pumped Murray's hand. "Thanks, Murray. I can't tell you how much this means to Hannah and me."

"Just don't take her out of the state, Paul, and make sure I know where to reach you."

Murray gave us directions to the cabin in the mountains of western Maryland. I gave Murray my cell phone number, and a great, big bear hug, too.

But it wasn't Murray who rang through on my cell phone at "Sweet Shelter," the lakefront cabin that securities fraud had built at the end of a winding dirt road just outside of McHenry, Maryland. It was my daughter, Emily.

"Jesus, Mary, and Joseph, Mother," Emily said without preamble.

"Hello to you, too, sweetheart."

"I just saw the *Washington Post.*"

I fell back on the pillows that formed a mound between my back and the solid oak headboard. We had known it was only a matter of time before the *Post* picked up the story, but I'd hoped for at least one, maybe two, days of peace. "What did it say?"

There was a rustling of paper. Emily cleared her throat. " 'Annapolis Woman Charged with Murder of Naval Officer.' "

The article was mercifully brief, but the reporter had found out about the hammer, and the sweatshirt, too. "Damn!" I said.

My daughter's voice rang with false cheerfulness. "You didn't do it."

"No."

In the background I could hear the cartoon channel going full blast. "Mom?" Emily's voice broke. "Are you okay? Really?"

"I'm fine. Your father is seeing to that."

She sniffed. "There's something I need to tell you, then. Dante said I shouldn't bother you with this, but I said you needed a diversion."

I could guess what was coming next. I'd heard that tone of voice before, whenever young Emily's allowance ran out, or she needed $500 for a skiing trip, or just a thousand, please, for a down payment on a car, I'll pay you back. I plumped up the pillow behind my head, hardened my heart, and said, "Yes?"

"Dante's put together enough investors to build his spa."

If I hadn't been firmly wedged on the bed between pillows, I would have fallen to the floor in shock.

"Emily, that's terrific news!"

She laughed. "It's so storybook, you won't believe it, Mom. Dante has this client? She's a widow from McLean? She put up thirty-five percent."

"Holy cow!"

"And you said there was no future in massage." Emily could never resist a good dig.

Paul chose that moment to wander in from the soaking tub wearing nothing but a goofy grin. He grabbed a piece of toast from the breakfast tray. "Who's on the phone?" he asked, munching.

I flapped a hand at him, urging him to be quiet.

"And that's not all," Emily continued. "Come August, you and Dad are going to be grandparents again."

Back in the soaking tub with my husband, nestled together like spoons, I learned that Emily's pregnancy was news to Paul. The spa, it turned out, wasn't. We were five percent shareholders.

"How can we afford—" I began, thinking of all the equity Paul had just tied up to spring me from jail.

Paul nibbled on my earlobe, cutting me off in mid-whine. "We won't lose the house," he said. "You're not going to skip town, are you?"

I turned in his arms and smiled up into his face. "Not unless you skip town with me."

He kissed me, softly at first with his tongue just tickling my lips in the way that makes me crazy. I responded, kissing him back harder, with more urgency.

"Everything's going to be all right, Hannah," he breathed against my lips. "You know that, don't you?"

I wrapped my legs around his waist. "I have to believe it, Paul, because life without you simply wouldn't be worth living."

Later, drowning in the luxury of the cabin's down bedding, with a fire crackling in the fireplace, we made love like newlyweds. And I fell asleep, at ten o'clock in the morning, with the reassuring beat of Paul's heart warm against my cheek.

CHAPTER 15

Sit tight. **Easy for Paul to say. I'd been sitting** tight all week with nothing but my paranoia for company.

On Thursday, Paul went out for a meeting, leaving me safely (or so he thought) kneading bread in the kitchen while watching *Dr. Phil* on the black and white TV on top of the refrigerator.

"Talk is cheap," said Dr. Phil. "Life rewards action."

I transferred the flour from my hands to my apron and adjusted the rabbit ears on the TV. "Taking action can be risky," he was telling some blonde with a severe overbite. "But *you* are worth that risk."

I covered the dough with a damp cloth and left it to rise, then turned my attention back to Dr. Phil. "It's what you *do* that determines the script of your life," the good doctor continued.

"Right on, Doctor," I said to the TV. I reminded myself to have a word with that playwright. The script I'd been given had been pretty shitty lately.

Monday, using an old recipe from *The Joy of Cooking,* I'd put up a batch of bread and butter pickles.

Tuesday, I made an angel food cake, from scratch.

Wednesday, I washed, starched, and ironed the kitchen curtains.

Today I was baking bread.

I might be earning points with Martha Stewart, I

thought, but not with Dr. Phil. "Life rewards action," he had said.

I shook a floury finger at the TV. "Okay. I hear you, Dr. Phil, but if that action gets me into any more trouble, I'm gonna throw up my hands and blame it all on you."

The only way I knew to achieve a happy ending lay right at the beginning, with Jennifer Goodall. And I was already one step ahead of the cops because I knew *I* hadn't killed her.

If so, who had?

I washed my hands, hauled out the phone book, and looked her up. Jennifer Goodall had lived at Chesapeake Harbour, an upscale waterfront community near Back Creek, a small tributary of the Severn River that ran into the Chesapeake Bay. I decided to check it out.

But I needed a disguise. For the past three days my picture had been all over the Annapolis paper; somebody was bound to recognize me. Nobody notices joggers, I decided, but the only jogging gear I owned was none too subtle: blue and gold with a big capital N on it.

If anybody deserved a little retail therapy, it was me. Leaving my bread to do its thing without me, I hopped into my orchid-colored LeBaron and drove to Annapolis Mall. I parked in the garage directly under Nordstrom and rode the escalator up to the second floor, where a sales associate in Juniors persuaded me to buy an outfit that would have made Emily proud—a bright turquoise Juicy Couture velour hoodie with matching pants. I might be $172 poorer, but Juicy's slogan was, "Be happy, wear Juicy." If it worked, I figured I'd be worth the money.

Back home, I squeezed into my new Juicy, reminding myself it was supposed to fit snugly, and checked myself out in the mirror. Hannah Ives, the turquoise sausage.

I clapped a ball hat on my head. A sausage wearing a hat.

I added dark glasses. I was a sausage wearing a hat with dark glasses, but with the addition of the sunglasses, even my sweet, sainted mother wouldn't have recognized me.

Wearing my disguise, I drove over the bridge into Eastport and out Forest Drive to Chesapeake Harbour, fully expecting to have to talk my way through the gate, but when I slowed at the guardhouse, the turnstile was up and the guardhouse abandoned. *Dear me*, I sighed. *Cutbacks everywhere.*

Once through the gate, I wound slowly around the complex, a labyrinth of three-story town houses with a numbering system clearly designed by a dyslexic builder. It took several circuits before I figured the system out and was able to pull into a visitor's space in front of Jennifer's building.

At the front door, I ran my finger down the buttons on the resident directory until I found the one labeled 3C. There was no answering buzz, of course, and I would have fainted dead if there'd been one.

I wandered back to my car and looked up, counting floors, trying to figure out which balcony belonged to Jennifer's apartment. Third floor, to the left, I guessed. I could see a hanging plant, a lounge chair. With my eyes still on the balcony, I backed up and crossed to the sidewalk opposite, where I stood on tiptoes. Through partially opened drapes I could see a floor lamp and a portion of a wing-back chair.

"Are you lost? Looking for someone?"

A woman had crept up behind me and was jogging quietly in place. She wore a pink fleece track suit, her brown hair tucked into an Orioles ball cap.

"Morbid curiosity, I guess." I flashed her a smile. "Isn't that Jennifer Goodall's apartment? The woman who was murdered at the Naval Academy?"

"I didn't know her very well," the jogger admitted. She poked at the frames of her round, gold-rimmed eyeglasses, pushing them farther up her nose. "But, yes, that's her apartment."

Suddenly she stopped jogging and studied me closely, her blue eyes enormous behind the thick lenses. "Who *are* you?"

"Emily Shemanski," I ad libbed, using my daughter's name and hoping the jogger didn't recognize me from my picture in the paper.

"Sorry, you just looked so familiar," she said. After a thoughtful pause, she added, "You live around here?"

I smiled. "Just jogging through. I live near Bembe Beach." I pointed in a vague northerly direction toward a neighboring community.

She smiled. "I'm Marisa Young. I live in the next building over."

I slipped my fingers into the pockets of my workout pants and smiled at her. "Jennifer and I were in the same book club," I improvised. "We met at her place a couple of times, but it was always at night." I turned to face Jennifer's building. "It's so strange seeing her apartment in the daytime. It doesn't look like anybody's touched anything, though, does it? Her furniture's still there."

"Oh, that's not Jennifer's stuff," Marisa confided. "They moved it all out at the end of the month. That hanging basket, barbecue, and stuff belong to the new tenants."

"Boy, they don't waste any time, do they?"

Marisa shrugged. "There's a huge waiting list for these condos. After the cops finished with her place . . ." Her voice trailed off.

"Who took Jennifer's stuff, do you know?"

"Dunno. Her parents, I imagine."

"She must have had a lot of friends in the neighborhood."

"No, I don't think so. Jennifer kept pretty much to herself. I sailed with her a couple of times, on the Academy boats, you know. We worked out together on occasion."

"Worked out? You mean you jogged together?"

"That, too," Marisa said. "But we usually worked out at Merritt Gym over on Moreland Parkway. We both signed up during one of those open houses. After the free month ran out, it got too expensive for me, but I think Jennifer is still a member." She swallowed hard. "Was."

After a thoughtful pause, Marisa patted a chunky thigh. "I should probably give the gym another try."

"Story of my life. I used to jog with a friend," I said, "but since she died. . . ." I turned my face toward the bay, fighting the tears that usually came whenever something reminded me of Valerie, who had died tragically, and too young, leaving a four-year-old daughter behind.

Marisa laid a hand lightly on my shoulder. "I'm sorry about your friend." She let her hand fall to her side and said, "I wonder if what they said in the paper is true?"

"About Jennifer?"

"No. About that terrible woman who killed her."

I tried to keep my face neutral. "But didn't Jennifer bring false charges against that woman's husband?"

"Uh-huh."

"And pick a big fight with her?"

Marisa nodded. "Still, that's no reason to kill somebody."

"I liked Jennifer and all," I lied glibly, "but she could be a bit *driven,* if you know what I mean."

"I think she was lonely," Marisa said in defense of her friend.

"But someone as attractive as Jennifer must have had boyfriends," I mused. "Did you ever meet them?"

"She mentioned someone in D.C. she was seeing from time to time, but I never met him." Marisa adjusted her eyeglasses more comfortably on the bridge of her nose, then began pumping her arms. "Well, it's been nice talking to you, but I better get back to my run." She jogged a few steps, turned, and jogged backward. "I just hope they lock up that horrible Ives person and throw away the key. Send her to the electric chair."

A chill ran along my spine. "I don't think Maryland has an electric chair," I told her.

"Lethal injection, then!" she shouted, and sprinted down the sidewalk in the direction of the community marina.

As I watched her go, something occurred to me and I jogged after her. "Marisa!"

"Yes?" she replied, not even breaking stride as I caught up with her.

"Did Jennifer keep anything at the gym, in a locker or something?"

"She did." As we pounded around the corner past the fuel dock, she added, "Jennifer usually went to the gym before work, so she kept her exercise clothes there."

"You don't know the locker number, by any chance?"

"They don't assign locker numbers at Merritt. You just take one that's available and slap a padlock on it."

"Jennifer had a padlock?"

"Yes, a combination lock, and if it's still there, you can't miss it. I had to laugh, because it looked so much like everyone else's that she tied it with a red ribbon."

"Thanks, Marisa," I panted.

"No problem," she said, then stopped. "Why do you want to know?"

"I loaned Jennifer a pedometer," I said, thinking quickly. "I thought maybe she might have left it there."

"Oh," said Marisa. "Well, I hope you find what you're looking for!"

"So do I, Marisa," I told her departing back. "So do I."

Merritt Gym was a long five miles from Chesapeake Harbour, down Forest Drive and across to West Street. The facilities were state-of-the-art, I would soon discover, but so were the Academy's. Why didn't Jennifer use them?

Maybe she decided that working out at the Academy would feel too much like going to work early. The Naval Academy was pretty intense. Maybe she needed a break from the place.

As a faculty wife, I was authorized to use the Academy's equipment, and I'd tried it once or twice, but all the testosterone sloshing about had been too much for me. Maybe it had been too much for Jennifer, too.

I turned off West Street at the used car dealership, drove past the turnoff for *The Capital* newspaper, wound down Moreland Parkway and found a place to park behind a convoy of moving vans.

Inside the gym, I stood for a moment, taking in the *ka-thwup, ka-thwup* emerging from the racket ball court and the *squeep* of tennis shoes on the composite floor, then I turned to the woman behind the reception desk, laid both hands on the counter and smiled what I hoped was a tragic, wistful smile. "Hi, I'm hoping you can help me. I'm here to pick up my neice's things? Jennifer Goodall?"

The receptionist looked up, her eyes wide and bright. Then her smile vanished. "Oh my gosh," she said. "I don't know. This has never happened before." She turned, her ponytail lashing her shoulders. "Pete!"

Across the lobby, a young hunk wearing white shorts and a blue polo shirt froze in mid-stride, pivoted and trotted over.

"This lady's Jennifer Goodall's aunt?" the receptionist explained. "Okay if she picks up her things?"

Pete winced. "Hey, that's tough." After an awkward silence, he led me past the reception desk, down a long hallway. "Here we go." Pete stood to one side and indicated the door marked Women. "Know where her locker is?"

I nodded. "Uh-huh. I was here with Jen a couple of times. She gave me the combination. Thanks, Pete." I smiled wanly and pushed through the door.

Wooden benches and walls of lockers surrounded me. I groaned. Even if I found Jennifer's distinctive lock, what would I do about the combination? As I scanned the ranks of lockers, I ran through the information I had gleaned about Jennifer from the Internet—her apartment number, her phone number, her Social Security number, her license plate, and her birth date. If one of those or a combination of them didn't work, I was doomed.

I found the lock easily enough, tied with a strand of red embroidery cotton. I nestled the lock in the palm of my hand, studying the three numbered tumblers, feeling unaccountably sad about that red embroidery cotton, wondering if Jennifer had been into needlepoint and how many projects had she left behind unfinished. I tugged on the lock, and to my utter amazement, it sprang open.

Jennifer hadn't even locked it.

And no wonder. There was nothing in the locker worth protecting. A pair of ripe athletic shoes, long past their sell-by date. Blue and gold jogging shorts. A white camisole top, clean and neatly folded.

I poked gingerly at the shoes with an index finger. Nothing was stuffed inside. I checked the pockets of the shorts and found two pink While You Were Out slips dated three weeks ago. One was from a Midshipman Lucas Judd. No phone number. The other had no name, just a number with the 443 prefix I usually associated with a cell phone. I shoved the slips into my own pocket, closed the locker, and replaced the lock.

I was about to slam the lock home when a flash-forward jerked me up short. Richard Knowles, the Assistant U.S. Attorney trying my case, standing before the judge saying: *And furthermore, Your Honor, Mrs. Ives was tampering with evidence!*

So I left the lock exactly as I had found it. Almost. Using the tail of my shirt, I wiped it clean of fingerprints.

When I emerged from the locker room, Pete, who had taken over at reception, appeared to notice my empty hands. "Find everything you need?"

"Yeah, thanks, Pete. Jen must have taken everything with her."

"Well, okay then. You take care, hear?"

I bowed my head theatrically and scuttled out the door.

"Nice outfit!" he called after me.

I was still smiling over the compliment when I jogged past a guy in a dark green Taurus reading a newspaper, a

FedEx delivery truck, and a moving van executing a three-point turn. Once inside my car, I grabbed my cell phone and dialed the 443 number. After three rings James Earl Jones cut it, telling me that my call had been forwarded to an automatic answering device and that somebody named Chris was not available to take my call. Would I care to leave a message after the tone? I certainly would—*Who the hell are you?*—but when I heard the beep, I chickened out and pressed End instead.

I tucked the pink slip of paper with Chris's phone number on it into my purse and headed out West Street toward Route 50. At the Rowe Boulevard exit I checked the rearview mirror for merging traffic and noticed a dark green Taurus dogging my tail. Was that the same car I'd seen outside of Merritt? Was I being followed?

Nonsense, I told myself. *There are hundreds of dark green Tauri. Don't be paranoid, Hannah.*

The Taurus stuck with me through the detour around the Spa Creek bridge construction, but when I turned left on Bladen Street, the driver continued straight on Northeast. I breathed a sigh of relief and headed home.

And just in time, too. The dough I'd left to rise had quadrupled in size, threatening to overwhelm the kitchen. I punched it down—thinking of Richard Knowles the whole time—then separated the dough into two loaves. By the time I'd had a cup of tea and shoved the loaves into the oven, I had formulated a plan to track down and have a word with the mysterious Chris.

CHAPTER 16

When Paul returned from his meeting, the seductive aroma of baking bread filled the house, and I was busily whipping up my famous turkey tetrazini casserole—turkey, mushrooms, heavy cream, gruyere and parmesan cheeses, linguini, and my secret ingredient, a dash of Marsala wine, not that paint thinner you get at the grocery store, but the real thing, Superiore Riserva, from Sicily.

I'd heard the front door slam, so it wasn't exactly a surprise when he crept up behind me, lifted my hair and kissed the nape of my neck. "Yum. You smell like cinnamon."

"You are hallucinating," I said.

"Faculty meetings can do that to you." He inhaled noisily. "God, that smells good. Will the bread be ready in time for dinner?" He leaned over my shoulder, snitched a noodle from the casserole I was stirring and lowered it into his mouth. "Staying home appears to agree with you."

I scowled. "That remark is so sexist that I'm not even going to dignify it with a response." I whacked Paul's hand with the back of my wooden spoon, then attacked the turkey noodle mixture savagely with it. "On second thought, I want to make it clear that although *you* appear to be the beneficiary of my staying home—in a culinary and domestic sense, that is—it has not agreed with me,

Mr. Paul Everett Ives. I can't tell you how much I hate being cooped up."

Paul's mischievous grin vanished. "Whenever you use all three of my names, I know I'm in trouble."

I waved the spoon, gloppy with cheese sauce. "They might as well have clapped me into an electronic ankle bracelet."

Paul eased the spoon out of my hand and laid it on the table, cupped my chin in his hand and tipped my face up to his. "Hannah, you must know that I was teasing."

"I guess my sense of humor has gone AWOL along with everything else."

He kissed my lower lip, which was protruding petulantly. "No need to ask what you've been doing all day, then."

"No."

I should have told him right then about my little expedition to Chesapeake Harbour, but I opened the fridge and pulled out a chilled bottle of Pinot Grigio instead. "Here," I said, handing him the bottle. "Make yourself useful."

While Paul coaxed the cork out of the bottle using a state-of-the-art corkscrew with ears like the Energizer Bunny, I popped my casserole into the oven, feeling more than a wee bit guilty. Paul and I had a relationship built on trust; I knew I should have consulted him before I went nosing about Goodall's apartment complex and her gym, but he would have been furious. I'd floated that balloon over the weekend, but he'd quickly shot it down. "Leave all that to Murray," he had cautioned. "He has an investigator working on it."

Paul had a point, I supposed. The last time I'd gone off half cocked, I'd ended up getting kidnapped, along with my eighty-something mystery writer friend, Nadine Gray, a.k.a. L. K. Bromley. But this time there were no high-speed chases, no broken bones, no harm done. I was home, safe and sound, Domestic Diva on Duty. No need to endure one of Paul's silent, wounded I-told-you-so looks.

After dinner, while Paul the Penitent cleaned up the kitchen, I carried my second glass of wine down to the basement office and powered up the computer. I checked my e-mail, but there was nothing but a Thinking of You e-card from Emily and the usual trash caught up in my spam filter.

After I emptied the trash, I clicked on Google, dug the While You Were Out slips out of my pocket and typed the 443 number that belonged to the caller named Chris on the query line. As I anticipated, there was no phonebook listing. If, as I suspected, the number was a cell phone, it wouldn't be listed in any telephone directory, AT&T, Google, or otherwise.

Surprisingly, however, Google found quite a few hits for the number on standard Web pages, some going back as far as three years. At one time the 443 number belonged to someone selling used cars on the Internet, but his name was Ed, not Chris. Maybe there had been a typo in the number; or perhaps the number had once belonged to Krazy Ed's Kleen Kars before it was reassigned to Chris. I moved on, paging through the truncated entries, clicking on each for details.

It's amazing what ends up on the Internet, I thought, as I Googled around. (I'd Googled myself once and found minutes of a meeting I'd attended years ago at Whitworth and Sullivan. In the year 3000, colonists on Mars, if they should care to do so, will be able to determine exactly how I felt about hiring a stress management consultant back on Earth in 1998.)

Chris's full name, I learned from Google, was Chris Donovan, and his 443 number showed up in the telephone lists of several church and gay rights organizations. If Google was correct, Chris Donovan attended St. George's Episcopal Church in Arlington, Virginia, served in a financial capacity on its fifteen member vestry, and in his spare time did volunteer work for Servicemembers Legal Defense Network and Lambda Legal Defense Fund.

Well, well, well, I thought. Maybe in her position as SAVI officer, Jennifer Goodall had contacted this Chris Donovan for help in advising Emma Kirby about issues related to her sexual orientation; perhaps she'd even arranged for Emma to talk to Chris Donovan or someone at SLDN or Lambda Legal.

I jumped from my chair and ran to the foot of the stairs. "Paul! Come here a minute! There's something I want to show you."

When Paul joined me, I filled him in briefly on Chris Donovan, telling him that I'd gotten Chris's name from one of Jennifer's neighbors, which was true, as far as it went.

"Marisa thought Chris might be a boyfriend," I told my husband, "but now I think he's someone Jennifer consulted with."

I pointed to the website for the Servicemembers Legal Defense Network. "It says here," I read, "that SLDN is a 'national, nonprofit legal services, watchdog, and policy organization dedicated to ending discrimination against and harassment of military personnel affected by Don't Ask, Don't Tell and related forms of intolerance.' "

"A noble endeavor," Paul commented, "but what does SLDN have to do with you, unless there's something you've been meaning to tell me?"

"I'm thinking," I said, backpedaling as fast as I could in an attempt to protect Emma's privacy, "that in her position as SAVI officer, Jennifer might have contacted this Chris person about one of her cases. If Jennifer had been advised to report someone up the chain of command for being homosexual, or for harassing a homosexual, that might have been a strong motive for that somebody to kill her. Other than me, I mean."

"But DOD has an antiharassment action plan." Paul flashed a crooked smile. "The faculty's had its consciousness raised several times about this plan since it first came out in 2000. As I recall, military chaplains and health care providers etcetera are given clear instructions not to 'out' service members who come to them for help."

"Tell that to Marine Lance Corporal Blessing," I said, tapping the monitor with my finger. "He was discharged for asking a military psychologist questions about sexual orientation. The psychologist, it says here somewhere, was just following the guidelines in the Navy's *General Medical Officer Manual*."

"That's the Marine Corps, Hannah, not the Naval Academy."

"I know that, but something *must* have been going on with Chris Donovan in relation to the Academy." I clicked the back button a few times. "Here it is: Donovan's also associated with—at least electronically—a group called USNA Out. It's a Naval Academy alumni group—not sanctioned by the Academy, no surprise—whose mission is to mentor gay midshipmen still bound by Don't Ask, Don't Tell.

"And this, too." I followed another link. "Someone named Chris Donovan is also loosely connected with an outfit called PlanetOut, which helps LGBT military personnel protect their online communications from Don't Ask, Don't Tell discharges."

Paul frowned. "What's LGBT?"

"Lesbian, Gay Men, Bisexual, and Transgendered People."

"Well, excepting for animal husbandry, that should about cover it."

"Paul, do be serious!"

"Sorry." He rested a hand lightly on my shoulder. "It's just that I can't tell you how much I don't care about someone's sexual orientation. It's simply not on my radar screen. And as for gays in the military, was it Barry Goldwater who said, 'You don't have to be straight to shoot straight.' "

"Couldn't agree with you more," I said. "Gay soldiers

are fighting and dying in Iraq right this minute, and keeping mum about their sexual orientation in order to do it."

I stared at the monitor for a moment, trying to organize the thoughts caroming around in my head. "But it's entirely possible that I'm barking up the wrong tree by pursuing the gay angle. Someone suggested to me that this fellow, Chris, is a friend or former colleague of Jennifer Goodall."

Paul scowled. "Someone?"

"Never mind, just wait!" I typed *St. George* and *Arlington* into Google and instantly found myself back at the Web page for St. George's Episcopal Church. A few clicks later I sat back and pointed to the monitor in triumph. "There!"

Paul leaned forward. His ear brushed my cheek and his breath blew warm across my neck as he read aloud from the brief bio Chris had posted when he ran for his position on the St. George vestry. Then he whistled. "So, when he's not working with gay rights organizations, Chris is a civilian personnel specialist working at the Pentagon."

"Interesting, no?"

"Very."

"So if Chris Donovan is, or was, a civilian working at the Pentagon about the same time as Jennifer Goodall, he might have known her."

"Hannah, the Pentagon is a huge place. I'll bet you twenty-five or twenty-six thousand people work there. That's bigger than half of the cities in America."

"Yes, but if you read that bio carefully, Mr. Ives, you'll see that at one time or another, both Chris Donovan and Jennifer Goodall appear to have worked in the Navy's office of Weapons Acquisition and Management, the same department that's now headed up by a certain Admiral Theodore E. Hart. From the dates, I'd guess that their time in that office didn't overlap, but still, I think that's interesting, don't you?"

Paul pulled up a chair and sat down on it, hard. I had him completely on board. "Type this in," he instructed. He gave me the URL for a Web page accessible to Academy staff and alumni only. I did as I was told and found myself at a page where I could type in the name and/or class year of any Naval Academy grad.

"We know Jennifer Goodall graduated with the class of 1999," Paul said. "So, type in 'Donovan.' "

My fingers flew over the keys, I hit Return, and in less than a second there he was, Lieutenant Chris Donovan, Class of 1999, near the bottom of a list of thirty-seven Donovans who had attended the Naval Academy since Robert Donovan graduated in 1877.

I fell back in my chair. "Holy moly! Jennifer Goodall and Chris Donovan were classmates!"

"Now that, I'd say, takes it completely out of the realm of coincidence," Paul said. "We must call Murray." He reached for the telephone.

"Do you have any connections at the Pentagon these days?" I forged on. "Someone I could talk to?"

"Hannah, as I told you this weekend, I think it's risky for you to go poking around." He started punching numbers. "Please, let's just make sure to pass on to Murray any information you turn up and let him and his highly trained staff handle it." He covered the mouthpiece of the receiver with his hand. "He's getting paid for this, remember."

As if I could forget. Our vacations for the next ten years were bankrolling Murray and his highly trained staff. Goodbye fifteenth century villas in the gently rolling hills of Tuscany. Hello to tours of Maryland's scenic Eastern Shore at the wheel of our Volvo.

"Good grief, Paul," I chided. "Nobody could be more involved than me. It's *my* life that's on the line. If Chris Donovan is a spurned boyfriend who murdered Jennifer, asking him questions will only put him on his guard. Or, consider this," I said as a new thought occurred to me.

"What if Chris Donovan is gay, and Jennifer was running true to form and threatened to 'out' him?"

Paul shook his head. "Donovan's a civilian, remember? He must have served the five years he owed the Navy, then got out. The Pentagon doesn't discriminate against gays, as long as they have the good sense to remain civilians."

"I'd still like to poke around and find out a little more about Donovan. I can ask Dorothy Hart about him, for one thing. If Chris Donovan worked for her husband, she might know something."

"I can see that I'm not going to change your mind." Paul reached out and squeezed my hand. "Talk to Dorothy, but for the love of God, Hannah, please, be careful."

I kissed the tip of his nose. "Of course I will."

While Paul left a message on Murray's home answering machine, I clicked the Print button and watched the printer spew out several pages of information about the Servicemembers Legal Defense Network and USNA Out.

After Paul hung up, I said, "But you didn't answer my question. Do you have any connections at the Pentagon?"

Paul leaned back in the chair with his hands behind his head. "Jack Turley might still be there."

"That gawky redhead who used to play basketball for Navy?"

Paul grinned. " 'That gawky redhead,' as you so eloquently put it, is now a captain in the United States Navy working for one of the Under Secretaries of the Navy for Something or Other. The last time I saw him was at Homecoming for his twentieth class reunion."

I groaned. "That makes me feel positively ancient."

Paul stood up and patted my head affectionately. "We *are* ancient, my dear." He bent down and kissed my cheek. "Jack gave me his business card at the game. I have it at the office somewhere. I'll try to reach him in the morning. Coming to bed?"

"In a minute. Your decrepit old wife needs to shut down her computer."

"No last minute games of solitaire?"

"No solitaire. Promise." I grinned up at him. "It's no fun playing with myself."

Paul's fingers trailed lightly down the length of my arm, lingering briefly on my fingertips. "That's just what I was hoping you'd say."

CHAPTER 17

The next day was Friday. While I waited for Paul to locate Captain Turley's business card and engineer an invitation from his former student for me to visit the Pentagon, I made it a point to track Dorothy down. I found her at the Academy, curled up in a chair in the Hart Room—no relation!—drinking coffee from a paper cup and reading a book.

I hadn't seen Dorothy since my arrest—hadn't seen much of anybody, really—so I was relieved when she shot out of her chair and embraced me like a long lost twin, separated at birth. "Hannah," she gushed. "I'm so, so sorry!"

"So am I!" I stepped back from her embrace and studied her face for any sign of suspicion or mistrust. "I didn't do it, you know."

Her cheeks flushed. "Of course you didn't, silly! Everyone knows that."

"Not the FBI, apparently."

She waved a hand dismissively. "They'll figure that out. Ted says that the evidence against you is circumstantial at best." She seized my hand and dragged me toward a chair. "Sit. Tell me about it."

I settled into the upholstered chair next to the one she had been sitting in and tucked my feet comfortably under me. The last thing I wanted was to relive the horror and embarrassment of the worst week, bar none, of my life to date, so I said, "I'll spare you the gory details. Suffice it to say that I'm out on bail and that my lawyer is, as we speak, working his tail off on my behalf."

"He's good?"

"Very good."

Dorothy sipped her coffee, her amber eyes serious over the plastic lid that covered her cup. "I just can't imagine what evidence they can have against you, Hannah."

"I only know what I read in the papers, Dorothy. The *Sun* said that Jennifer was killed with the hammer I'd been using to build the sets for *Sweeney Todd*. It did occur to the reporter, at least, that perhaps that would explain why my fingerprints were all over it."

"If that's all there is, it's pretty lame," Dorothy remarked.

I nodded. I considered telling my friend about the bloody sweatshirt and the witness who had supposedly seen me behind Mahan Hall on the day of the murder, but I could hear Murray Simon's voice rasping in my ear, cautioning me to trust no one, and for once I erred on the side of caution and listened. "My lawyer's talking to the U.S. Attorney in charge of my case," I explained. "Sooner or later they'll have to share whatever evidence they have against me, but I must say, they seem to be dragging their feet."

"Frankly," Dorothy said, "I didn't expect to see you here today."

"What else am I going to do? Stay at home and pull the covers over my head?" I paused and pressed my fingertips against my eyelids, suddenly overwhelmed by a strong wave of déjà vu.

"Hannah? Are you all right?" Dorothy's voice seemed to be spiraling down a long tunnel.

I opened my eyes. "I've never been arrested before, Dorothy, but I was just thinking that it doesn't feel that much different from being diagnosed with cancer."

Dorothy sucked in her lower lip and nodded. Clearly I was speaking a language that she could understand.

"What I mean is, in either case, there's the very real possibility that I'll lose my freedom at the end of it, by incarceration on the one hand, or death on the other."

Dorothy's eyes grew wide. "Cut it out, Hannah, you're scaring me."

"Sometimes I scare myself." I patted her knee reassuringly. "What I'm trying to say is that in both cases I feel such a lack of control, that I'm compelled . . ." I paused to reflect for a moment. ". . . no, I'm *driven* to do something, anything, because standing still is, at least for me, simply too frightening and painful." I forced a smile. "Usually I try to keep myself so busy solving other people's problems that I don't have time to worry about my own."

A single tear rolled down Dorothy's cheek. "I can't tell you how helpful you've been to me. The sets, the hats . . ." She waved her hand in a circular motion. "I don't know how I'll ever pay you back."

"Not necessary," I said, thinking that this was the time if ever there was one to call in that particular IOU, but I didn't want to jump on it too soon. Dorothy seemed particularly fragile that afternoon; she needed propping up. "I'm sure the time will come when you'll be a great help to me, too," I continued, "not to mention all the other breast cancer survivors you're bound to come into contact with. As an admiral's wife, you'll be able to play a particularly influential role in getting the word out about the importance of breast self-exams, early detection—"

Dorothy startled me by cutting me off in mid-sentence. "Why did you come this afternoon, Hannah?"

"I knew you had chemo tomorrow, so I wasn't sure if you'd be up to checking the set. I left a message on your cell phone—"

"Go home and relax, Hannah," she interrupted again, drawing on some inner strength hidden well within to pull herself upright. "I can take care of checking the set tonight."

"That's all I've been doing lately, sitting home and . . . well, not relaxing, exactly. Obsessing would be more like it. We can check the set together, then."

"Ted says . . . well, never mind what Ted says. Sometimes he's such a know-it-all that it makes me want to scream. I swear to God, if I said 'Knit one, purl two,' he'd say, 'No, Dorothy, think about it for a minute. It's " 'Knit two, purl one." ' And he doesn't know a goddamn thing about knitting."

Again, Dorothy had given me an opening to ask about her husband, and this time I leapt in with both feet. "It's actually your husband that I wanted to ask you a question about."

"Yes?"

"Were you aware that before she came to the Academy, Jennifer Goodall worked in the Pentagon for Navy Weapons Acquisition and Management?"

Dorothy's skin was already pale as a result of her chemotherapy. I didn't think it was possible for it to get any more so, but I was wrong. She collapsed into the upholstery, and whatever color remained in her face drained away, leaving it a chalky white, only serving to emphasize the bags, dark as bruises, under her eyes. The hand holding her coffee cup began to shake.

I took the cup and set it on the table. "Dorothy! I'm so sorry. I didn't mean to upset you."

She laced her fingers together, squeezing until the knuckles grew white, took a deep breath and let it out slowly. "I guess you're bound to find out anyway, you or that lawyer of yours."

"Find out what?"

"That Ted and Jennifer Goodall were having an affair."

"What?" Dorothy's news hit me like a two-by-four between the eyes. But as I sat there, trying to catch my breath, pieces of the puzzle began falling into place. Admiral Hart's unscheduled visits to the Academy, visits that surprised his wife as well as his son. Jennifer Goodall's persistent presence in Mahan Hall. I added the admiral's name to my growing list of suspects, right at the top of the list. I shivered, recalling the inside knowledge he seemed to have about my case. What was the sonofabitch up to, anyway? Was he planning to frame me?

"Had, actually," Dorothy continued, twisting her hands. "Ted had broken it off. He told me that Jennifer was too needy." She turned her wretched face to me. "As if I didn't have needs, too."

"Do you think that's why your husband kept showing up at the Academy?"

"He was trying to work it out," she sniffed, "but she wouldn't take no for an answer. She kept threatening to turn him in for conduct unbecoming." Using her fingertips, she massaged her temples in little circles. "Whatever some high-level government muckety-mucks have been able to get away with, I can tell you that the Navy still frowns on officers having sex with their subordinates."

"Even when it's consensual? You said they were having an affair."

"Well that's it, then, isn't it? Jennifer claimed it wasn't consensual."

Where had I heard that before?

I leaned forward, resting my elbows on my knees. "Dorothy, you read what the newspaper said about my case, didn't you?"

She nodded.

"Then you know that Jennifer has tried this trick before. With *my* husband!"

"Looks like we *both* had a reason to wish her dead." She dredged up a smile from somewhere and pasted it, lopsided, on her face.

"You and me, and how many others?" I wondered aloud.

Dorothy sat silently for a while, staring over my shoulder. "Ted, for instance," she said dreamily, still staring at the wall.

Ted, indeed. Interesting how often the good admiral's name kept coming up.

"Dorothy, look at me! You've been worrying about this, haven't you? Losing sleep over it?"

She nodded.

"Your job—your only job—is to concentrate on getting well."

"I know," she squeaked, meek as a kitten.

"As much as I'd like someone else to be in the frame for Jennifer's murder, if the FBI had evidence against Ted, surely they'd have arrested *him* by now, and not me."

A tear rolled down one cheek and dripped, unheeded, onto her sweater. "I suppose."

Hoping to steer the conversation in a less stressful direction, I said, "Dorothy, do you remember anybody who worked with your husband named Chris Donovan? A civilian?"

Dorothy had found a crumpled tissue in her pocket and was dabbing at her nose. "I don't think so," she said, giving her nose a good blow. "Why do you ask?"

"It's just someone whose name keeps coming up in connection with Jennifer Goodall," I told her.

A shadow passed over Dorothy's face, but just as quickly, it was gone. "No," she said, shaking her head. "Never heard of a Chris, but then, Ted works with hundreds and hundreds of people, all the world over."

"I know," I said. "And so did Lieutenant Jennifer Goodall, USN." I sighed. "Seems to me that our pool of suspects just keeps expanding. Pretty soon we'll need a stadium to hold them all."

Dorothy stuffed her used tissue into the liquid still remaining in her coffee cup, straightened her shoulders and smiled a crooked but unconvincing smile. "I'll ask Ted about Chris Donovan," she offered. "If I find out anything, I'll let you know. Deal?"

"Deal."

As we left the Hart Room together, my arm around her shoulders, Dorothy turned to ask, "Hannah, can you do me a favor?"

"Sure."

"Tomorrow I have my chemo, as you know, so I probably won't be up to much on Sunday. Could you check the sets before the matinee?"

"Of course," I said as we started down the elegant marble staircase, side by side. "Consider it done."

"Thanks."

At the bottom of the stairs I turned to face her. "Dorothy, go home. Get some rest."

She wrapped her arms around me in a brief hug. "Ditto ditto, Hannah."

CHAPTER 18

Paul is one of those professors former students go out of their way to visit whenever they return to Annapolis. It's the rare individual who can take a subject like advanced mathematics and make it interesting, let alone comprehensible, yet Paul manages to do it, year after year. His students have gone on to win Rhodes scholarships, reading "maths" at Oxford, where they dig into such fascinating topics as recursive Bayesian estimation or topological manifolds, none of which makes the least bit of sense to me, but then, I majored in French.

Paul's students are so grateful, some enormously so, that they donate money to the Academy in his name. One former student, now a honcho at Dell, endowed the Ives Prize in Mathematics, given to the graduate each year who makes the most significant use of computing in his or her work.

And there are name plates in Paul's honor, two affixed to chairs in Alumni Hall and one on a seat in the "Club Level" section of the refurbished Naval Academy stadium. Some grateful grad with a sense of humor even shelled out $1,000 to name a locker after Paul in the Roger Staubach Locker Room at Rickett's Hall. Paul, ever modest, takes it in stride. When I tease him about his memorial locker, he smiles. "In my *honor,* Hannah, in my honor. When they start giving money in my memory, that's when you start to worry."

Captain Jack Turley, it turned out, was one of these grateful students. Two decades ago, Paul had coached him to a solid A in Double E—Electrical Engineering—and there was nothing Turley wouldn't do for Paul, including inviting me to tour the Pentagon and allowing me to pick his brain, on short notice, too. Incredibly, we were on for Saturday, the following day. Naturally, Paul would be coming along, too. (Naturally.) And how about lunch? (How very kind.)

Since the senseless terrorist acts of September 11, parking at the Pentagon, always a problem, had become ill-advised, so we piled into the Volvo and drove to New Carrollton, where we planned to catch the Orange Line train into Washington, D.C. As Paul pulled into the long-term parking garage, I caught a flash of green in my side-view mirror. I gasped and squeezed Paul's arm. "Look! There's that green Taurus again. I swear he's been following me."

Paul glanced into the rearview mirror. "Where?"

I swiveled in my seat, but the Taurus had vanished. All I could see was a lineup of taxis at the Kiss-and-Ride and two Metro buses, spewing exhaust.

Paul rolled down his window, stuck out his arm for the ticket. "Do you know how many Ford Tauruses are being driven in the U.S. right now?"

I shook my head.

"I don't know, either," he chuckled as he steered the Volvo up the ramp that led to the second parking level, "but at the end of 2002, Ford celebrated the production of the five millionth Taurus."

"You're making that up just to make me feel better."

"No, I looked it up." He pulled into a parking space, hauled up on the emergency brake, and turned sideways in his seat to face me. He tapped my nose with the tip of his finger. "I'm not the only Googler around the house, you know, sweetheart."

As Paul turned off the ignition and released his seat belt, I studied his profile, strong, solid, familiar. I knew he was trying to be reassuring, but if so, the move had backfired. Why had Paul taken the trouble to look up information about Tauruses? I wondered. Had he been seeing phantom Tauri, too?

Inside the station, Paul handed me a five dollar bill. We stood side by side at adjoining ticket machines, waiting while the machines inhaled our money, judged it acceptable, and spit out our fare cards. Neither of us said anything as we joined the line of people climbing the escalator to the platform—D.C. subway riders wouldn't be caught dead simply standing to the right on the moving stairs—and scooted into seats on the train just as the doors were closing. Although I was sure they'd find it fascinating, I had no intention of sharing my run-in with the law with the other passengers, so Paul and I sat side by side, forearms mashed together, saying little, exchanging sections of the Baltimore *Sun* to pass the journey.

When the doors opened at L'Enfant Plaza, we hustled to the upper level, where we switched to the Yellow Line train that would head south through the city, briefly rise into the daylight as it crossed the Potomac, then dive back into the tunnel that would take us to the Pentagon.

"Have you ever been to the Pentagon before?" I asked Paul, breaking the silence as our train rolled into the underground Pentagon station.

"Never," he replied as the doors slid open and we stepped onto the platform. "After all these years, you'd think I'd have made it over here, but no. I'm looking forward to it."

On our way up the escalator, Paul explained that Captain Jack Turley served as the military assistant to one of several Under Secretaries of Defense whose offices were on the third floor of the labyrinthine building, in a VIP corridor only a few doors down from Donald Rumsfeld.

"But what does he *do*?" I asked as the escalator spit us out near the Pentagon bus stop.

"You'll have to ask Jack," Paul said, "but I imagine that

he does whatever the Secretary asks him to." He looped his arm through mine and led me around to the main entrance, where a line had formed in front of a kiosk. Security personnel sat at tables under an awning, inspecting handbags and briefcases. I was about to hand over my bag when somebody came pounding up behind us. "Sorry I'm late. Couldn't find a cab."

It was my lawyer, Murray Simon.

I hauled out my permagrin and arranged it across my face. "Murray, what a surprise." Then I aimed a scowl at my husband.

"Sorry, Hannah," Murray panted as he unbuttoned his overcoat. "I can tell from your expression how happy you are to see me, but Paul thought it was important for me to be here. You're in trouble, in case you've forgotten."

"How could I forget when you're always popping up to remind me, Murray."

"Hannah!" Paul hissed. "Murray's here to help. There's no need to be surly."

"Maybe if you told me he was coming," I hissed back, "I'd have been prepared." As a child, I'd never liked surprises. As an adult, I still don't.

After Security cleared my handbag and Murray's computer case, Paul used his cell phone to call Jack, who arranged to meet us in the lobby on the other side of the Pentagon's enormous stainless steel doors.

It was late February, so I'd expected service dress blues, but Jack was wearing khakis, the Navy's year-round working uniform. Ribbons marched in orderly rows across his heart: a Defense Meritorious Service Medal, a Meritorious Service Medal with one gold star, which meant he'd won it twice, and a green and white Navy Commendation Medal with two gold stars. There were others, too, like the blue ribbon with two thin green stripes that told me Jack was an expert shot with a pistol, but I didn't know what the others were, except one: the red, white, green, and black bar that meant he'd helped to liberate Kuwait. An impressive rack. Jack had certainly paid his dues.

Paul reached his former student in two strides, hand extended. "Jack! Good to see you, man!"

"Good to see you, too, sir." Jack pumped Paul's arm, then turned to me. "We met once, Mrs. Ives, at a tailgater one Homecoming game, ten, maybe fifteen years back. You probably don't remember."

"Surprisingly, I do," I said, squeezing his hand. "It's hard to forget that red hair."

"Or the freckles." He blushed, the tips of his ears turning pink. "Mother always swore I'd outgrow them." He leaned forward. "She lied," he whispered.

"And this is my attorney, Murray Simon," I said, sweet as molasses.

Jack beamed. "Pleased to meet you, sir. I followed the Ted Barber case in the *Post.* Brilliant work, sir, simply brilliant."

Ted Barber was a northern Virginia real-estate developer accused of murdering his wife, Melanie. Using Luminol, investigators had uncovered evidence of foul play in the stable of their Middleburg farm, but Melanie's body had never been found. Murray'd gotten Barber off scot free. *Keep your mouth shut, Hannah, and keep smiling, and maybe he'll do the same for you.*

Jack escorted us to Security and waited while a uniformed civilian peered at our drivers' licenses and asked us our business. When we successfully passed that hurdle, we were directed to X-marks-the-spot, where we were photographed and issued yellow plastic ID badges. I was impressed; the whole process took no more than thirty seconds. Good thing, too, as I'd been holding my breath, worried sick that my record in JABS would start alarms *whoop-whoop-whooping*, and that any second brusque, burly guards would materialize to haul my ass out of there. But either the Pentagon didn't share data with JABS or the data hadn't caught up with them yet, because the security guard simply smiled, handed me my photo ID badge and said, "Have a nice day, ma'am."

"Thanks so much for taking time to see us, Jack," I said as I clipped the badge onto the lapel of my jacket.

"My pleasure," he said.

Jack led us quickly through a maze of velvet ropes that in happier times had been used to control the tourists who flocked to the Pentagon like visitors to Disney World. There were plenty of military personnel and men in suits hanging around that morning, but I hadn't noticed anybody in sweats with cameras slung around their necks. Maybe February was a slow month. Either that or tour buses were taking those visitors to other Washington landmarks where security, especially for foreign visitors, was not nearly so tight.

As we followed Jack past the visitors' center and the nearly deserted gift shop toward the escalators, I was thinking about 9/11, feeling slightly queasy and desperately sad that just a short walk from where we were standing, terrorists had flown an airplane into the building and 184 people had died.

And then I saw it, completely covering the wall to my right, stretching so high that I had to throw my head back to see the top: a spectacular 9/11 quilt. From across the lobby it had looked like the American flag, but when we got closer, I could see that the flag was composed of thousands of four-by-four-inch squares, one for each individual who had perished in the nearly simultaneous terrorist attacks on New York, Pennsylvania, and Washington, D.C., that terrifying September day. Men and women, young and old, their faces smiled out at us. Christine Hanson of Groton, Massachusetts, who would never see her third birthday. Robert Grant Norton of Lubec, Maine, eighty-five, the oldest victim. White, black, Hispanic, Asian, Muslim, Jew—a cross section of America, land of the free, where their promising lives had been snuffed out in an instant. And for what? It broke my heart.

"Amazing, isn't it? Three thousand thirty-one squares altogether," Jack commented as he directed us to the turnstiles and showed us how to scan the bar codes printed on our badges. "The quilt was put together by quilters from more than forty states, honchoed by the Memorial Quilts group out in California. They toured it for a while, but I think it's home for good now." He clasped his hands behind his back and rocked back on his heels. "Frankly, I hope it stays forever. Not that anyone working here needs any reminding."

As we rode the escalator to the next level, I glanced up. A military guard dressed in camouflage gear stood on the landing, cradling a machine gun. In the corridor behind him was a shopping mall; I watched Pentagon workers scurrying from a dry cleaner to a card store, from a chocolate shop to one of several fast food stalls. "Expecting trouble at Burger King?" I asked with an uneasy eye on the cop in cammies with the gun.

"Regrettable, but necessary, I'm afraid. This is the main entrance," Jack explained. "If someone should barge in and jump the turnstiles . . ." His voice trailed off.

He didn't need to finish the sentence; I could see clearly what would happen. From his vantage point on the landing, that single guard controlled the entire lobby. Anyone attempting to charge up the escalator would be shot, easy as plugging a rat in a drainpipe.

"There's a river entrance, too." Jack waved a hand vaguely in the direction of the Potomac River just to the north. "But it's for the bigwigs."

Walking briskly, Jack led us up a gradual rampway into the Pentagon proper, past a more luxurious food court—KFC, Manchu Wok, Pizza Hut, Subway—with a common seating area furnished, to my surprise, with wooden tables and chairs and upholstered furniture that wouldn't look out of place in my own dining room.

Just past the ATM and the Navy Federal Credit Union, Jack paused before a glass case that housed a wooden model of the Pentagon. "You probably remember the structure of the building from the newspaper accounts of the crash," he said, "but this scale model shows it graphically. There are five levels to the complex." He tapped the glass with his finger, pointing out each feature of the building as he explained it to us. "Five levels, five sides and five rings. The A-ring is the inside ring, as you can see. The E-ring is the most desirable because it has windows that look out rather than looking in at other windows."

We had given the guy at Security Jack's room number when we registered, so it was still fresh in my mind. "So if your office is in room 3E844," I said, "that would be the third floor of the far outside ring, roughly in the middle of the eighth corridor."

Jack smiled. "Exactly. There are seventeen and a half miles of corridor in this building," he commented as he led us down one of them. "And they say it takes only seven minutes to get from any one point to another." He punched the button to call the elevator. "Tell that to me when I'm juggling coffee and a doughnut."

We rode up to the third floor, disembarking in a hallway that reminded me of a fine old hotel. Elegant dark wood paneling covered the walls beneath a chair rail, above which hung oil paintings of former Chairmen of the Joint Chiefs of Staff, the colors of the artwork vibrant in contrast to the creamy walls. On both sides of the hallway, dark paneled doors—some open, some closed—led to offices whose occupants, all high-level political appointees, were indicated by brass plaques bearing titles such as Secretary of Defense, Under Secretary of Defense for This and Under Secretary of Defense for That. Framed photographs of the incumbents and flags hung about everywhere.

As we strolled along the corridor, the large-scale oils gradually gave way to smaller works. Jack paused in front of one of them, an unassuming but competent landscape. "And this delightful little watercolor was painted by Dwight David Eisenhower," he told us.

Ah, yes, I thought, as I studied the pleasant fall scene and wondered if it was in Pennsylvania, where Ike had retired with Mamie. Eisenhower, like his friend, Winston Churchill, had enjoyed painting watercolors in his spare time.

We all need a hobby, I thought. Mine was knitting. Would they let me have knitting needles in jail? If not, I might never get back to that cable-knit sweater I'd started for Paul last Christmas.

Still worrying about the unfinished sweater, I hurried to catch up with the guys, who were standing in front of a massive wooden door, waiting for me. "This is where I hang out," Jack was saying to Paul when I approached.

The minute we entered the office, two well-trained secretaries leapt to their feet. Secretaries in the traditional sense—small *s*—they came out from behind their desks, greeted us warmly, took our coats and asked if we'd like coffee, which we politely declined.

Jack's office adjoined the Secretary's, capital *S*. It was smaller than I would have expected for a Navy captain, certainly small by Naval Academy standards, but large enough to accommodate his desk, a round conference table piled high with file folders, and several upholstered chairs, which we promptly settled into.

What is it they say? Location, location, location. Jack's office had it in spades. Prime real estate on the E-ring, with a window overlooking the Potomac.

"Paul told me over the phone what you're interested in," Jack was saying just as I was getting comfortable, "and I'm only too happy to oblige. You asked about Lieutenant Jennifer Goodall. She was stationed here for two years before being assigned to the Naval Academy. The last year she worked here, Goodall was Admiral Ted Hart's assistant."

"What would that entail?" I inquired.

"Well, she would keep his calendar, check his e-mail,

take his calls, sit in on all his meetings. In short, there wouldn't be anything she wouldn't know about the guy."

"It's my understanding," said Paul, "that Admiral Hart is still here, in charge of Weapons Acquisition and Management for the Navy."

"That's right. His office is just around the corner from us, in the tenth corridor."

"Hart's wife is convinced the two were having an affair," I cut in, "but I'm not so sure about that. When Goodall was at the Academy, she tried to hang an affair around Paul's neck, too." I caught Paul looking at me and smiled. "But she lied about that. At least she admitted that to me before she died."

Jack leaned forward, resting his forearms on his knees. "I remember reading about her accusations in *Navy Times*," he said, "but no one who really knew Professor Ives ever believed a word of it."

"That's gratifying," Paul said with a thin, grim smile.

"I did ask around as casually as I could about Goodall's sex life," Jack continued, "but there doesn't seem to be any scuttlebutt about that. If Goodall and Hart were an item, they played their cards very close to their chests."

"What about the possibility that Goodall was blackmailing Hart?" Murray asked, breaking what was, for him, an uncharacteristically long silence. "If not about sex, how about something else? Something job-related, for example."

"But wait a minute." I held up a hand. "If Hart were doing something dishonest, immoral, or illegal, wouldn't he try to hide it from his staff, just in case any of them were the whistle-blowing type?"

Jack raised a hand, the stone in his Naval Academy ring a flash of blue in the bright light streaming through the window. "Consider this scenario. As Hart's assistant, Goodall would normally sit in on all meetings. What if, all of a sudden, people started showing up who weren't on his calendar? What if she were excluded from certain meetings? She might get suspicious, put two and two together, start nosing around."

"My experience is mostly with the corporate world," Murray said, "so can you educate me a little? What sort of mischief could an admiral like Hart get into?"

Jack took a deep breath. "This is pure speculation, you understand, and completely off the record . . ." He paused. When Murray nodded in agreement, Jack leaned forward in his chair and continued. "Hart may be looking ahead to retirement, angling for a job at one of the biggies like Lockheed Martin, Boeing, General Dynamics, Raytheon, or Northrup/Grumman. It's possible he's steering business their way, in some sort of you-scratch-my-back-and-I'll-scratch-yours kind of scheme." Jack gazed at the ceiling, his green eyes completely innocent. "But you didn't hear that from me."

"Kickbacks?" I asked.

"Could be, but not necessarily. With that kind of arrangement, no money actually needs to exchange hands."

"That's drawing a pretty fine line," Murray snorted.

"But wouldn't there be safeguards in place to keep that from happening?" Paul wondered.

"Usually, yes, through a tightly controlled government contracting process," Jack continued. "But there's a war on in Iraq, and things need to get rushed through in the name of expedience, sometimes without the usual oversight. We call it fast-tracking."

I couldn't wait to put in my two cents worth. "Easier to explain why you let a government contract go to a crony than to explain to a grieving mother that her son died because he didn't have a bulletproof vest, right?"

"Right. And troops have to be fed and supplied from day one," Jack continued. "You simply can't afford to wait around for the usual contract procedures to run their course."

I'd dealt with government contracts before while working at Whitworth and Sullivan—writing a statement of work, advertising it in *Commerce Business Daily*, sending it out to perspective bidders, evaluating bids, awarding the contract, dealing with challenges from losing bidders who think they've been unfairly excluded. It could take years before the actual product showed up on your loading dock.

"But aren't the fast-track vendors prequalified in some way," I wondered, "like the blanket purchase order agreements I remember from back in the old days?"

"Many are, particularly for goods and services that we anticipated a need for, but now we're dealing with companies capable of providing expertise to quickly gear up and handle critical large-scale public works projects like water, sewer, electricity, housing, transportation. It's a whole new ball game."

"But still, even with fast-tracking," I said, "surely there are safeguards to keep DOD employees from playing fast and loose with the contract regulations?"

"Of course there are, but it's ridiculously easy for things to slip through the cracks. Governmentwide, we're still dealing with largely a paper system. It's stunning how much time we waste faxing paperwork back and forth and making phone calls."

As if it knew we were talking about it, the telephone on Jack's desk warbled once. Jack ignored it. "Besides, a lot of the fast-track contracts are set up for projects that fall under a certain amount, say fifty thousand dollars. Nobody really looks too hard at them."

"Are there a lot of contracts in that category?" Murray asked.

"Thousands upon thousands."

"It could add up," Paul commented dryly.

"It could."

One of the secretaries to whom we had been introduced earlier rapped once on the door frame and stuck her head into the room. "You asked to be reminded when it was time for lunch."

"Thanks, Sue. We'll just be a minute." Jack smiled and turned to me. "Now, about that other name you asked me about, Chris Donovan?"

"Yes?"

"I checked for you. She's a civilian, working in Personnel."

"She?" Paul and I said it at the same time.

Jack shrugged. "Short for Christine, I suppose, but she always goes by Chris. I thought you knew."

"Well, that's very different," I quipped, quoting Miss Emily Latella of *Saturday Night Live* fame. What an ignoramus I'd been! Chris was a woman. That could change everything.

"In her present capacity, Donovan probably wouldn't have worked with Goodall," Jack continued. "But before she got out of the Navy, Donovan also worked in Weapons Acquisitions and Management. I'm sure you'll want to ask her about it."

I was absolutely certain of that, too.

"Donovan's not here on Saturday," he added. "I checked. Her office says she'll be in on Monday. You can call back then." Jack handed me a slip of paper on which he'd written Chris Donovan's telephone number. I tucked it into my purse for safekeeping, but I had no intention of waiting until Monday to check back with Chris Donovan at her office. Now that I knew Chris was a business associate of the dead woman and not an ex-boyfriend with murder on his mind, I'd call her on my cell phone using the number I'd filched from Jennifer's locker.

With the memory of Marisa Young's recent tongue-lashing still fresh in my mind, I decided that whatever it took—fibs, fairy tales, flim-flam, or farrago—I'd figure out a way to get Chris Donovan to open up and talk to me.

"Lunch?" Jack asked, rising from his chair.

Like hungry little ducklings, we followed.

Lunch was served in the oh-so-elegant Pentagon Executive Dining Room, where crystal, china, and heavy silverware graced tables covered by thick white linen cloths. In the days since my shattering box lunch experience in Baltimore, every meal had been a treat. Tuna noodle casserole, Triscuit and gouda, even the cheeseburger at the drive-through McDonald's on I-68 outside of Frostburg on our way back from Deep Creek Lake had been, for me at least, a gourmet delight. So when I sat down and checked the dining room menu, I thought I'd died and gone to heaven.

We ordered Caesar salads all around, and by some sort of silent consensus, possibly engineered by Paul, talked about everything but my awkward situation vis-à-vis the law.

By the time the waiter brought our apple pie, we'd come to an uneasy agreement over the 2004 elections and the war in Iraq (with a good deal of overlap between the two). Over coffee, we discussed the proper role of the U.N. in world politics, but hadn't reached a conclusion by the time the waiter brought the check.

After the waiter bowed and left with his tip, Jack stood, laid down his napkin and said, "Before you go, there's something else that I want to show you."

Five minutes later the four of us were standing silently before a marble memorial on the first floor of E-ring: AMERICA'S HEROES: A GRATEFUL NATION REMEMBERS. On our right, the name of each civilian lost when a terrorist flew American Airlines Flight 77 into the Pentagon had been incised in a marble slab, black and smooth as satin. On an identical slab to the left, the names of the military victims were carved. Stubby pencils and oblongs of tissue paper had been provided for friends and family to trace the names of their loved ones.

The Naval Academy, I remembered all too well, had lost eleven of its sons in the Pentagon attacks.

I ran my hand over the cool stone, feeling each letter beneath my fingertips. Chic Burlingame, captain of the ill-fated Boeing 757, had been a Navy Top Gun. He died one day shy of his fifty-second birthday. Gerald DeConto, class of 1979. We'd known him as "Fish." Pat Dunn, class of '85, whose wife Stephanie had been two month's pregnant when the doomed airplane smashed into her husband's office. At one time or another we'd known them all.

Behind us, yellow film covered the windows that faced Arlington Cemetery at the exact point where Flight 77 slammed into the building.

"I'll leave you here," Jack whispered after a while. "I've got another meeting. You know the way out?"

We nodded silently.

To my right a double door opened into a memorial chapel. Signaling to Paul and Murray my intention, I went in and sat down on one of the straight-backed chairs, upholstered in a mottled rose and blue. At the front of the chapel, just behind a small wooden altar, was a brilliant five-sided stained-glass window featuring the head of a bald eagle, the image of the Pentagon, a flowing U.S. flag, and the words UNITED IN MEMORY, SEPTEMBER 11, 2001. The window was fabricated, according to the brochure I'd picked up outside, from five hundred pieces of inch-thick, faceted glass called Dalle de Verre. One hundred eighty-four of them were crimson, arranged in a double ring.

I bowed my head, studying my shoes against the red carpet. Then I closed my eyes and prayed. I prayed for those gone too soon before their time—the victims, my mother, my friends Valerie and Gail—and I even prayed for the troubled soul of Jennifer Goodall.

And while I was at it, I said a little prayer for myself.

Then I stood up, squared my shoulders, and went out to face whatever fate might send my way.

CHAPTER 19

Late Saturday afternoon when Chris Donovan returned my call, I did what anybody with her fingerprints on file in JABS would do. I lied. Using my daughter's name, I told Chris that I was a naval officer in imminent danger of being outed by my louse of an ex-husband, and she agreed to see me in Fairfax, Virginia, after church services the following day.

I briefly considered resurrecting my disguise, but even in this day and age, jogging attire—no matter how upscale—didn't seem appropriate for Sunday-go-to-meeting, so I decided on a black and white herringbone pantsuit and a black V-neck sweater over a crisp, white, open-collared shirt.

There was a chance I'd be recognized. The Baltimore paper had unearthed a ghastly old photo from their archives and splashed it above the fold of Thursday's Anne Arundel section, but the Washington papers had left me mercifully alone. I was betting that Chris didn't read the *Sun* and decided to risk it.

Why anyone chooses to live in the northern Virginia suburbs, paying grossly inflated prices for the privilege, is completely beyond me. Even on weekends the highways are snarled with traffic any normal human being would count as rush hour, and I've never driven to Tysons Corner without getting hopelessly lost. To avoid all this, I take the Metro.

One hundred years ago, when the corner of Oakland and Ninth was probably just a cow pasture, someone—God bless 'em—had the good sense to build St. George's Episcopal Church practically smack dab on the site of a future Orange Line Metro station. To get to the church where I'd meet Chris Donovan, I didn't even need to switch trains. I'd timed my journey perfectly, too, emerging into the daylight at the Virginia Square/George Mason University stop at 10:15 A.M.

Aside from an apartment tower and a number of lofty office buildings, practically the first thing I saw was the church. The Episcopal Church of St. George and San José took up the entire block. On my right, a large brick sanctuary dominated the complex. Centered over a pair of tall wooden doors, a stained-glass window of Gothic style and proportions sparkled in the afternoon sun. A modern parish hall extended back to the left, and more modern still, two stakes had been pounded into the lawn and a banner stretched between them announcing St. George's URL. As if acknowledging the parish's Spanish heritage, an alternate entrance, much older, was constructed of stone. A single bell was suspended in an open, Spanish mission-style tower over its door.

Keeping one eye out for Chris Donovan—she told me she'd be wearing a pink suit—I stepped into the nave, smiled at one of the greeters, accepted a church bulletin, and sat down in a pew near the back of the sanctuary, trying as hard as I could to fade into the woodwork.

I studied the bulletin. The church's official seal featured St. George jousting with a dragon, but his mount was a bicycle instead of a horse. I smiled, hoping that the service wouldn't be as laid back as their logo.

I turned to the program for the morning service, and was disappointed to read that while the Holy Eucharist was taken from the Book of Common Prayer, that morning, at least, they were following the more modern Rite 2. I preferred Rite 1, the version that more or less maintained the majestic beauty of the language of King James. Back in 1979, when the BCP was revised, not even the Lord's Prayer had escaped the commission's tinkering, and "lead us not into temptation" became "save us from the time of trial." I stared at the fur hat sitting lopsidedly on the head of the woman in the pew in front of me and thought: *Time of trial. Thanks for reminding me, Lord.*

As the pews around me began to fill, I gazed east toward the altar. A large red cross was mounted over a brass, open-worked altar screen behind which some sort of tapestry had been hung. On the wall above that, near the apex of the roof, a stained-glass window bloomed like a flower: a five-petaled flower. Five petals, like the Pentagon. I closed my eyes. Was the entire world becoming a place of symbols, each one serving to remind me of the late, unlamented Jennifer Goodall?

During the organ prelude ("*Durch Adams Fall ist Ganz Verderbt*," by Johann Sebastian Bach) I listened quietly. The Bach was definitely a good sign that the service itself wouldn't be too happy-clappy or the hymns so "relevant" that the ink was barely dry. As the organist wrapped up the prelude and made a clever little segue into the first hymn, I wondered idly what the Standing Commission on Liturgy and Music would come up with in 2012, the next time the prayer and hymn books were due for revision. Back in 1979 nobody'd had laptops or forty gigabytes of anything, so it wouldn't surprise me if future prayer books came in the form of customizable PowerPoint programs, designed to be projected on huge screens hanging over the altar.

But I needn't have worried about St. George's, at least not that day. The prelude was glorious, the hymns traditional—a little Ralph Vaughan Williams makes my heart soar—the choir small, but excellent, and the sermon inspirational, delivered as an extra bonus by a twinkly priest with a neat, slightly graying beard. I relaxed, even enjoying the inspired goofiness of Eucharistic Prayer C: "At your command all things came to be: the vast expanse of interstellar space, galaxies, suns, the planets in their courses, and this fragile earth, our island home."

Island home? My mind wandered, I couldn't help it. Palm trees, gentle ocean breezes, a little Parrot Head music on the steel drums. Now *that* was symbolism I could live with.

During the Prayers of the People, I offered up a proper prayer for my speedy delivery from whatever evils might be lurking in the cold, hard hearts of the FBI, reiterated my request during the post-Communion prayer, and in the time it took to play the postlude, I sat, head bowed, praying for the wisdom to know what to do.

After the service, everyone streamed in the direction of the parish hall, but Chris had said she'd skip the fellowship hour and meet me on the steps of the church. I waited there, as instructed, leaning against the iron railing of the handicapped ramp, my eyes fastened on the massive wooden doors.

When Chris came out, I recognized her at once: the tall, reed-thin soprano who had been singing in the back row of the choir. The pink suit, which was actually a particularly violent shade of fuchsia, had been covered by her choir robe. Chris's blond hair tumbled about her ears in a tousled bob that must have cost big bucks to achieve that casual, just-slept-in look. She'd draped a paisley scarf over one shoulder and secured it with a jeweled safety pin. In unrelieved checkerboard, I looked comparatively dowdy, like a black and white movie. Chris, however, was in dazzling Technicolor.

I'd told her I would be carrying a copy of *Newsweek* magazine, so I held it up. She noticed, caught my eye, smiled and hurried over. "Emily?"

I nodded, feeling like the world's biggest fraud by answering to my daughter's name. I hated to con the woman, but other than sending a surrogate, I was running out of options.

"Let's go someplace quiet where we can talk," Chris said. "There's a Starbucks by the Metro station, near the clock tower? Do you know it?"

"Yes, I noticed when I got off."

"Right. I have some loose ends to clear up here, then I'll pick up my coat and join you in about ten minutes. I'll have a regular coffee, black."

When Chris found me, I was still standing at the Starbucks fixings bar, sprinkling vanilla powder on my cappuccino. "Here's your coffee," I said, handing it to her. "Chocolate chip cookie, too," I said, pointing to the counter where I'd set down a cookie the size of a salad plate, wrapped in waxed paper.

She peeled the lid off her cup and took a sip. "Thanks. Where do you want to sit?"

I shrugged. "Anywhere is fine with me."

With Chris in the lead, we migrated toward a table in front of the floor-to-ceiling windows. Chris slipped her arms out of her coat and turned the shoulders inside out over the back of her chair. I kept my coat on. In the first place, I felt cold. In the second place, I figured I might need it if I had to blow the joint once she found out who I really was.

"Where did you get my name, Emily?" she asked before I could even make a dent in the foam on top of my coffee.

"Jennifer Goodall," I said, watching her face carefully for any sign of a reaction.

Chris blinked twice, then set her coffee down, using both hands to steady it. "She's—"

"I know," I said. "It was a terrible thing."

Chris stared over my shoulder at something so far away that even the Hubble telescope couldn't bring it into focus. After a long silence she said, "So, how did you know Jennifer?"

"We met when she came to the Academy." That was the truth, at least.

"Jen and I were classmates at Annapolis," Chris volunteered. "After graduation, we went our separate ways, but we met up again at the Pentagon."

"I'm so sorry," I said. "Were you close?"

"At one time, yes, very, but not since she went back to Annapolis."

"Still, it must have been a shock."

Chris shuddered. "It's not something I care to think about." She stared into her cup for a few seconds, then took a sip. It seemed to fortify her. "So, Emily, tell me. How can I help you?"

"Well, first I need to be honest with you. My name's not Emily Shemanski. I was afraid if I told you my real name, you wouldn't agree to see me."

"In my line of work," Chris said with a small smile, "I'm used to dealing with people who are reluctant to use their real names. With 'Don't Ask Don't Tell,' secrecy is the name of the game. Let me assure you that anything you tell me stays with me, *Emily.* So, tell me, what's the problem?"

I took a deep, steadying breath. "My problem is . . ." I paused, backtracking a little. "First, promise me you'll hear me out, no matter what."

"Of course I will. I wouldn't have agreed to meet you otherwise."

I studied my thumbs for a minute, then looked up. "After I finish, I will understand perfectly if you want to throw your coffee in my face and walk out, but I don't know who else to turn to."

"For heaven's sake, Emily, relax. I don't bite."

Taking her at her word, I squared my shoulders and said, "My real name is Hannah Ives, and my problem is that I've been arrested for a murder I didn't commit."

Chris studied me with pale, almost translucent blue eyes. "Hannah Ives? My God, you're the woman—"

I reached out and grabbed her hand, squeezing hard, holding on to keep her from bolting. "I'm sorry for giving you a false name, but I couldn't take the chance that you'd refuse to see me."

For what seemed like an eternity, she stared at me, her eyes hard as winter ice. "Okay, then, *Hannah*." She slung my name back at me like an epithet. "Tell me why I should give you the freaking time of day."

"Because I came all the way from Annapolis to see you, hoping you could tell me something, *anything*, that might help me figure out who really killed your friend and get me off this great big hook."

"Seems to me that's your lawyer's job," she said, gently extracting her hand from my grasp.

"Of course it's my lawyer's job, but he can't be everywhere at once."

"Ives . . . Ives . . ." Chris laced her fingers together and rested her chin on the tips of her thumbs. "Didn't Jen claim that your husband—"

I cut her off. "Yes, but that was lies from one end to the other."

Suddenly Chris was no longer looking at me, but studying a poster on the wall. "I know," she said in a voice so soft that I almost missed it.

"What do you mean, you know?" Every muscle in my body clenched. "You were at the Academy then. If you knew the truth, how could you have kept silent? My husband's reputation was on the line! His job was in jeopardy!"

She raised her hands, palms out. "Sorry. So very sorry. I didn't mean to imply that I knew about it at the time. It was several years after the fact before Jennifer hinted to me—just *hinted*, mind you—that there might not have been anything really going on between her and Professor Ives, and by then the charges against your husband had long been dropped. Jen had moved on with her life."

Moved on. And with absolutely no concern over the boats that got swamped in her wake. The little bitch.

Chris's face softened, and almost as if she had read my thoughts, she said, "Jen was putting pressure on your husband, wasn't she?"

"Uh-huh. For a diploma. She was flunking his course." I shifted awkwardly in my chair. "Look, Chris, I know that Jennifer was your friend, and I don't mean to imply that she was in the *habit* of blackmailing people, but—"

Chris didn't let me finish. "You wouldn't be talking to me if you didn't believe that."

I felt my face flush. "Well, it did occur to me that if she'd tried it once, she might try it again. And if she tried it on with the wrong person, they might have wanted her dead."

"Your husband, for example?"

I shook my head vigorously. "If that were the case, Jennifer would have been dead six years ago."

I took a sip of coffee before moving on. "No, I was thinking that it had to be somebody she was working with recently. Admiral Hart, for example?"

"Look, Mrs. Ives . . ." She paused, as if deciding how forthcoming she was prepared to be with someone she had just met. "Jennifer and I got reacquainted when we were both working at the Pentagon." Chris had pinched off a piece of cookie the size of a silver dollar, but instead of eating it, she laid it on her napkin. "She worked for Admiral Hart and I was in Personnel, so we might never have seen one another. But one day I ran into her in the food court." She paused. "We became very close."

There was an awkward silence. "I'm sorry for your loss," I said.

She stared at me, no trace of emotion on her face. "Thank you."

"I know you're very much involved with the Servicemembers Legal Defense Network," I said, pinching off a bit of cookie for myself. Then I took a giant leap. "Was Jennifer involved in the group, too?"

One platinum eyebrow shot up. "Yes, but not actively. It

wouldn't have been particularly career-enhancing, would it?" Chris smiled grimly. "But Jennifer referred midshipmen to us from time to time."

"I know. That's how I really got your name, from one of the mids we were sponsoring." Another fib. I was turning into a career criminal.

We drank our coffee silently for a few moments. "Do you mind if I ask you a personal question, Chris?"

Chris shrugged. "Go ahead."

"Why did you get out of the Navy?"

"I think that's obvious, don't you?"

"You're gay?"

"Right."

I leaned across the table and followed that admission to its logical conclusion. "So, you and Jennifer were lovers," I whispered. "Weren't you?"

Chris lowered her cup from her lips and nodded. "Until very recently. I issued an ultimatum." She smiled miserably. "Never do that unless you're sure you can live with the outcome."

"An ultimatum? Do you mind telling me what it was?"

"Two of them, really. First, I wanted her to get out and come out. Jen had put in the five years she owed the Navy for her Academy education, so she could have resigned her commission at any time. But she told me she was committed to her Navy career and didn't want to give it up, not even for me." She buried her head in her hands, and I thought she might be crying, but when she looked up again, her eyes were dry. "If it weren't for that ludicrous Don't Ask, Don't Tell policy, Jen and I could have made a life together. It was either me or the Navy. She made her choice."

"You said two reasons. What was the other one?"

"As I said, I didn't approve of what Jennifer was doing vis-à-vis the admiral." Chris spread her fingers and swiped them through her hair. "Jen told me she'd uncovered evidence that the admiral's been running his office like a supermarket for weapons manufacturers, soaking up bribes, divvying up multibillion-dollar contracts and diverting work to firms he secretly controls with his partners. Before I left the Navy, I used to work up in WAM, but that was long before Hart took over. I've got enough experience with it, though, to see how easily that sort of thing can happen."

I stared at her for a few moments, collecting my thoughts. If what Chris was saying were true, the situation was far worse than anything Jack Turley had suggested might be going on, hypothetically or otherwise.

"But how is Hart getting away with it? Isn't there oversight of government contracts anymore?" I remembered my days working at Whitworth and Sullivan, where we kept an archive of all the "blue cover" reports published by the United States Government Accountability Office, the government agency chartered by Congress to track down instances of waste, fraud, and abuse within the government. Congress commissioned some fifteen hundred GAO reports a year, holding up for ridicule such government expenses as $1,118 spent on plastic caps for stool legs or $2,548 for a pair of duckbill pliers. "GAO even looks into things like standards for bottled water," I ranted. "Surely they must have some idea of what's going on with the Raytheons and Halliburtons of the world."

"You would think," Chris said. "But when the U.S. is at war, all bets are off."

"But if Jennifer knew about it and *you* know about it, surely someone else does, too?"

"Jennifer talked big," Chris explained, "but she never shared any of her evidence with me."

"What about watchdog groups and FOIA?" I continued. "Surely contractors are required to respond to Freedom of Information Act requests."

"They are and they aren't," she said. "Contractors can claim that specific financial data falls under the heading of a trade secret and that making it public would give their competitors unfair advantage. There's often months and months of legal wrangling before a report finally arrives, and when it does, the cost figures have often been redacted."

"Good grief."

"Jen hinted that Hart had always been very clever about keeping his activities under the radar, but she claimed she finally had the goods on the guy and was going to blow the whistle. After separating him from a chunk of his money first, I'm afraid. Seeing all those unaccounted-for millions pass over her desk every day, the temptation must have been enormous."

"But I still don't understand. Knowing all this, how come *you* didn't turn Admiral Hart in?"

"I loved her."

Three simple, one-syllable words that explained everything.

"I hated her methods," Chris continued after a moment of silence, "but I couldn't stop loving her. I thought I'd talked her around at last. Forget the money, I told her, turn the son of a bitch in."

"But now that Jennifer's gone?"

"You must think I'm some sort of monster, sitting on information like this, but I'm not. I don't have a speck of proof, and working in Personnel, there's really no way I'd have access to it. But just so you don't think I'm totally beyond redemption, I can tell you that I made a few phone calls to Arianna Huffington's office, and to the Center for Public Integrity. They have much better connections than I do."

"I wouldn't trust Hart any farther than I could throw him," I snorted, "which, considering his size, isn't very far!"

Chris started. "How do *you* know Hart?"

"His son is a midshipman. The kid has a role in the

Glee Club musical, and I was working with his wife helping to build sets. Hart came to the Academy several times, to see his son perform in *Sweeney Todd*, or so I thought. But Jennifer always seemed to be hanging around at the time. Eventually I put two and two together."

"I see." Chris sighed. "Do they still do the musicals in Mahan Hall?"

"Yup."

"I remember Mahan," she commented wistfully. "Lots of nooks and crannies where a mid can hide out, far from the prying eyes of Mother B."

Mother B—Mother Bancroft—was the midshipman equivalent of Big Brother.

"Or two mids," I amended.

She grinned. "That, too."

"That's probably why Jennifer arranged to meet Hart there. Anyplace else, even in downtown Annapolis, they were very likely to be noticed." I paused, staring at the reflection of the overhead light shimmering on the surface of my coffee.

"Did Jen actually get money from the admiral?" I asked. "Do you know?"

"No." A look of absolute misery stole across her face. "Hart found out about us, you see."

"I see." Jennifer and the admiral had reached a stalemate.

Chris twirled her empty coffee cup around on the tabletop. "Jen enjoyed playing with fire, but this was the first time she got burned."

As I watched the cup go round and round, for the first time in weeks I thought I could see light at the end of the tunnel. "Chris, will you tell my lawyer what you just told me?"

To my surprise, she smiled mischievously. "I've not been quite honest with you, either, Hannah. Your lawyer came to see me late last week. Everything you know, he knows."

Even though I wanted to snatch him bald-headed for not sharing this bit of critical information with me, my rating of Murray went up several notches. "But how did he find you?"

Chris shrugged. "Maybe he learned that I'd already been contacted by NCIS and the Navy I.G.?"

"Oh." What a blockhead I was! Here I thought I'd been on the bleeding edge, but the foot soldiers for both the prosecution and the defense had gone charging ahead, leaving me to wander in the darkened woods, picking up bread crumbs.

Chris stood and lifted her coat off the back of the chair. "I've got to go, but if it means anything, I want you to know that I don't hold you responsible for Jennifer's death."

"Thank you. It means a lot."

"Call me again, any time." She slipped a business card out of her wallet and handed the card to me. "Good luck, Mrs. Ives. I'll be praying for you."

•

CHAPTER 20

I watched through the window as the back of Chris's dark blue coat disappeared west down Ninth Street. I fumed a bit, too, wondering why Murray hadn't mentioned Chris Donovan yesterday, why he pretended that all the information Jack Turley told us about Chris was news to him. And if he'd interviewed the woman, he had to know that *he* was a *she*. Murray, I decided, was sometimes a class-A jerk.

As I mined for foam at the bottom of my cup with a plastic spoon, I amused myself by dreaming up punishments for an attorney who withheld critical information from a client, information that could have prevented her from making a proper fool of herself by pretending to be her own daughter. A *New Yorker* cartoon came to mind, a dominatrix, with a lawyer groveling at her feet:

—So, worm, shall I tie you up in litigation?

—Yes, please, and make it lengthy and expensive.

I smiled. Maybe I should listen to Paul and let the professionals handle this.

I decided a brisk walk might clear my head, so before heading back to the Metro, I called Paul on my cell phone, leaving a message that I'd be home around six and that if he didn't want to wait for supper, there was leftover Chinese food in the fridge.

Just the mention of the Chinese food made my stomach

rumble. Except for the coffee and crumbs of chocolate chip cookie I'd shared with Chris, I hadn't had anything to eat since dinner the night before. I needed a snack to fortify me for the long ride home, but one that wasn't fifty percent sugar. I was already so wired, another cookie might send me into orbit. I tossed my paper cup into the trash and went out the door to forage.

Perched on a doughnut-shaped planter in front of the coffee shop, the concrete chilling my buns, I looked around me and decided that the Virginia Square/GMU Metro stop was a misnomer. As far as I could tell, no square existed, and the GMU of the title turned out to be only a small branch of George Mason University in Fairfax, farther to the west. I hadn't remembered seeing any restaurants in the vicinity, so I bopped back into Starbucks to quiz the barista who was cleaning off the milk foamer with a damp rag.

"Are there any places to eat around here?"

"There's Pica Deli, just across from the Giant." She checked her watch. "But you better hurry, because they close at three on Sundays."

I followed the directions she gave me—north on Monroe and right on Washington Boulevard—looking for the "building with the cool murals." It would have been impossible to miss. Pica Deli was a box-shaped, two-story building with a wide-eyed marmalade cat, a slice of Italian bread, and a fruit bowl painted hundreds of times larger than life on one side of the building, covering the siding all the way from roof to foundation. But the muralist hadn't contented himself with that. I entered the restaurant through double glass doors to the left of a giant strawberry pie.

Pica Deli was the perfect spot for grazing. I strolled past gleaming glass and chrome cases containing salads and pasta, meats and cheeses. Pegs of chips, wooden bins of wine, and shelf after shelf of gourmet items filled the shop almost to overflowing. A seven-seat wine bar provided a place for those who preferred their snacks in liquid form.

At the deli case, I ordered a Velveteen Rabbit—cucumber, tomato, red onion, dill havarti, and sprouts on thick farm bread—grabbed a lemonade from the cold case and sat down at a table.

So, Chris and Jennifer had been an item. I chewed thoughtfully, wondering if Admiral Hart had figured that out, how many other people had, too. But so what? Would somebody have murdered Jennifer simply for being gay?

Yes, I decided. Such things had happened before. PFC Barry Winchell had been beaten to death with a baseball bat at Fort Campbell, Kentucky. Allen Schindler was stomped to death on shipboard near Japan. Jennifer had died violently, too. A hate crime could not be entirely discounted.

When the sandwich was gone and I'd cleaned every last crumb from the plate, I decided I'd better get on home. I was eager to log onto the Internet to see if *I* could find any evidence that Hart had been diddling with the government contracts under his jurisdiction.

I left Pica Deli, looked both ways to orient myself, then headed off in the direction of the Ballston Metro, which, according to the little advertising map I'd picked up in the store, seemed to be the closest station to the restaurant. As I walked, the sun began to set in a lavender sky and darkness was just beginning to steal over Washington Street, a tree-lined avenue that ran through a residential neighborhood of family homes punctuated by small businesses like bakeries, thrift shops, and dry cleaners.

At Nelson, I crossed Washington to stroll along the boundary of Quincy Park, with its playgrounds, playing fields, and picnic tables. As I skirted the park, I counted off the names of people who probably weren't crying into their pillows now that Jennifer Goodall was gone.

Me because of Paul.

Paul because Jennifer had tried to ruin him.

Dorothy because she thought Ted was screwing Jennifer.

Ted because Jennifer was going to spill the beans.

Emma, to keep from being outed.

Chris, for being jilted.

Maybe even Kevin, but I couldn't think why. With every step I took, the list grew longer and longer.

To my left, leaves rustled. I glanced over my shoulder, but nobody was there. The park, in fact, was practically deserted. It was late on Sunday; Arlington residents were all in their homes, and the city workers wouldn't arrive until morning. And yet, as I continued to walk, more quickly now, I couldn't shake the feeling that I was being followed. I began to regret taking so much time for my meal. It would have been much wiser to start home before dark.

As I turned south on Quincy Street, I heard footsteps again, echoing hollowly off the concrete walls of the Montessori House. I spun around to took. Nothing. Maybe I was losing my mind. Nevertheless, I hustled in the direction of a lighted parking lot, hoping to reach it before the bogeyman got me.

A twig snapped, and this time when I turned, I caught sight of a shadowy figure among the trees. Heart pounding, I bolted toward the lights, instantly regretting the high-heeled shoes I'd chosen to wear that morning. They looked smashing with my outfit, but pinched unmercifully and were completely unsuitable for jogging. Ten steps, twenty, my feet pounded the pavement, each jarring step driving my leg bones painfully into my hip sockets.

Chest heaving, I clattered up the steps and into the welcoming arms of the Arlington Public Library. I burst through the door, leaned against the lobby wall for a moment, panting. After several minutes, when no homicidal maniac had crashed into the lobby to rape me, my heart rate returned to a reasonable facsimile of normal. I decided that my imagination (or the caffeine) was definitely working overtime. Yet, overactive imagination or not, I was reluctant to go back outside, into the dark unfamiliar streets, particularly not while the staff and resources of the Arlington Public Library System were waiting inside to welcome me. I called Paul and told him to definitely eat the leftover mushi pork and steamed dumplings. I was at the library and there was something I needed to do.

Arlington Library, bless 'em, had a Cyber Center, open until 9:00 P.M. on Sundays. Claiming that I was staying with a sister in the area, I produced my Naval Academy library card and used it to apply for one of Arlington's own cards. Using the new card, I went to the automated sign-in station to request a terminal. Fortunately, one was available almost right away.

First, I checked my e-mail. Paul sent a silly animated card from BlueMountain, saying he hoped it would cheer me up. It did.

Moving on to Google, I was still smiling when I typed in *fast tracking* and learned that there was something called the Iraq Reconstruction Office, which processed thousands of fast-tracking contracts worth billions by holding what the website described as "hold-onto-your-hats" job fairs for prospective contractors in Washington, D.C. and London. What fun for them.

The General Services Administration had a "get it right" plan that purported to secure the best value for federal agencies and American taxpayers through an efficient and effective acquisition process, while ensuring full and open competition, and instilling integrity and transparency in the use of GSA contracting vehicles—blah blah blah—but that was for federal agencies, not Department of Defense.

Several clicks later I landed at http://www.defenselink.mil/contracts, where Army, Air Force, Navy, and Coast Guard contracts—if it was military, they had it—valued at five million dollars or more were announced each business day.

Now that was more like it.

A button to the right invited me to do a DOD Search, so I obliged. I typed in the largest company I could think of, *Megatron Industries,* and learned that the corporation had been awarded more than one thousand contracts with DOD, most of them in billions, not millions, of dollars. If I had been a slot machine, my eyeballs would have been spinning, eventually turning—*ka-ching, ka-ching*—into double dollar signs.

Hart's office—Navy Weapons Acquisitions and Management—was not mentioned in the database specifically, but I could determine what was being done and for what price, where the work would be performed and by whom, the projected completion date and whether or not the contract was competitively procured. Many of the contracts, I noticed, were not. The list of projects went on and on: parachute deployment sequences, diesel engine noise suppression, midair collision avoidance systems. Who knew how many of the "contracting activities" might actually be divisions that reported to the admiral? It would take someone more knowledgeable than I, holding a copy of DICNAVAC, to sort through all the acronyms and figure it out.

I could have spent hours playing with the sophisticated DOD search engine, experimenting with various combinations of search terms—how many contracts were awarded to the Megatron subdivision in Providence, Rhode Island, in 2001, for example—but people were waiting in line to use the terminals, and Paul was waiting patiently for me at home. I jotted down the URL of the DOD website and signed off.

It wasn't until I reached the front door that the heebie-jeebies returned. Was my stalker still out there? I loitered by the front entrance, casually reading the community notices, until a young couple joined at the hip breezed past.

I fell into step behind them and followed them onto the sidewalk. "Nice evening," I said, thinking just the opposite.

"Yeah."

"You students at GMU?"

They quickened their pace. "No."

I had to hustle to keep up. "Going to the Metro?"

"No."

Even though I was fairly well dressed, they probably thought I was one of those creepy bag ladies who seem to be drawn to public libraries the way my sister Ruth is drawn to garage sales. I dogged their tail until, with a quick glance at me chugging along behind them, they turned into the park, the guy's arm looped around his girlfriend's waist, guiding her along with a thumb hooked through a belt loop on her jeans. I watched until they disappeared into the shadows. No way *I* was going into that park, or back down the deserted street to the Virginia Square Metro station, either.

I pulled the little map out of my purse, checked it, then reversed direction and headed south. With one ear cocked for the sound of anyone on my tail, I made my way to the corner of Fairfax and Quincy, where someone, I swear, had built the next building just to creep me out: the Arlington funeral home, a two-story brick mansion with a pillared entrance and an American flag flapping away under a spotlight. I veered away from it, heading right on Fairfax, and hustled straight to the Ballston Metro Center and the welcoming lights of the Hilton Hotel.

I couldn't get down the escalator fast enough.

Then the turnstile rejected my fare card. I swore softly and trotted back to the solemn rank of fare card machines, where I slipped it into the "Trade in Used Fare Card" slot. The card's value—a buck twenty-five—flashed up on a tiny screen. It was off-peak hours, so I'd need to add a dollar ten before I could get me and my aching feet back to New Carollton. Still standing in front of the machine, I rummaged in my purse, but only managed to come up with two quarters, a nickel, and a Canadian dime. Why hadn't I saved my cash by paying for my sandwich with a credit card? I was such a moron!

I rode the escalator up to street level and made my way to the Hilton, looking around for an ATM. I found one tucked away in a corner of the lobby, but it kept spitting out my ATM card. "Something wrong with this machine?" I asked a passing bellman.

"Out of order, ma'am."

"Damnit!" I looked around until I found the tiny surveillance camera mounted in the ATM, faced it bravely and mouthed, "Why don't you fix your damn machine?"

I turned back to the bellman. "Know of any other ATMs around here?"

He squinted up at the ceiling as if the answer was written there. "Over to Ballston Mall."

"Thanks."

Following, his directions, I made my way to the glass-covered pedestrian bridge that spanned Ninth Street, wound through the atrium of the National Science Foundation building at treetop level, and trotted across another bridge with colored glass insets that would have caught the sunlight in the daytime but now reflected the headlights from cars driving on Wilson Boulevard some thirty feet below.

At the mall, I found an ATM that accepted my card, whirred for a moment considering it, decided I wasn't a deadbeat, and spit out two crisp twenty dollar bills. "Thank you!" I kissed the bills, tucked them into my purse, and headed back in the direction of the Metro.

I had almost forgotten about being followed until I heard the footsteps again, directly behind me. I stopped. The footsteps stopped.

I hurried along to the National Science Foundation, where I pretended to be fascinated by the sculptures and palm trees in the tropical wonderland below. Without turning my head, I skewed my eyes to the right. If someone had been behind me, they were gone now.

Walking quickly, I entered the next pedestrian bridge, at the end of which was an elevator that would take me down to Metro level. Suddenly, the footsteps were back, echoing hollowly along the glass walls, moving quickly and coming closer.

At the other end of the bridge a couple emerged from the Hilton, arms linked and laughing. Witnesses! It came back in a flash, something I'd learned in a self-defense class many moons ago. I spun around, raised both arms and confronted my pursuer. "*Kee-yah!* It's an attack! Call the cops!" I screamed.

"I am the cops."

It was Special Agent Amanda Crisp, dressed in blue jeans, a hooded gray sweatshirt, and well-worn tennis shoes.

I bent over, rested my hands on my knees, trying to catch my breath. "What the *hell*?" I panted. I squinted up at her through a fringe of damp hair. "You've been following me for days, haven't you? Why?"

"You have a certain reputation," she said. "We know about your background. We were afraid you'd go off on your own like V.I. Warshawski."

"Afraid or hoping?" I snapped.

We stood on the darkened bridge, staring each other down.

"You okay?" The male half of the couple that had been coming out of the Hilton had arrived, cell phone at the ready. "I've dialed 911."

"No, it's okay," I said. "A misunderstanding."

Crisp flipped open her Nextel, identified herself and cancelled the 911 while the young man looked on, curiosity all over his face.

"Thanks for coming to my rescue," I said, leaning against the wall. "Tell me your name?"

"Mick."

"Thanks, Mick."

"No problem." He stole a quick glance at his date, who hadn't budged from the protection of the Hilton. "If you're sure . . ."

I nodded. "I'm sure."

When they'd passed on, I turned on Special Agent Crisp. "So, why were you tailing me? You scared me half to death."

"We wanted to keep an eye on you, and—"

I cut in. "Afraid I'll skip town?"

She raised a hand. "Let me finish. Because of some new information we've received."

"What? You think I'm in danger?"

"Maybe. Maybe not. Best if you stayed home and let us run the investigation, Mrs. Ives."

I had the childish urge to say, "Make me," but counted silently to ten before answering instead. "I don't intend to spend one more minute in a jail cell, thank you very much, so I want to go on record right now that I'll do whatever it takes to find out who really killed Jennifer Goodall."

"We want you to go home and stay put. Stop talking to people. You're just going to screw things up."

"How can I get any more screwed than I already am?"

Crisp sighed and seemed to be weighing her words. "Because you've just come very close to blowing a carefully orchestrated, multiagency sting operation."

I stared at Crisp, my mouth hanging open. Literally. "You've got to be kidding me."

"Jennifer Goodall had been cooperating with us and with the Navy I.G. to bring the admiral and his accomplices down."

"The I.G.," I repeated, stunned by this information.

"Inspector General."

"I know what the I.G. is," I snapped. "So, you think one of *them*—whoever them is—killed Jennifer Goodall?"

"It's certainly possible."

The gaze I sent Special Agent Amanda Crisp was shot straight out of the gates of hell. "Let me get this straight. The NCIS and the FBI and the Navy I.G. have conspired to frame me for a murder I didn't commit just so you can divert attention from the real target of your investigation, some rogue admiral?" I was shouting now, and I didn't care who heard me.

"You clapped me in handcuffs, sent me off to that horrible place in Baltimore, you *humiliated* me. . . ." I sputtered. My temper rose like mercury on a hot summer day. I could practically feel my red blood cells congealing. Any minute, I was going to have a heart attack. "You may have taken years off my life. How *dare* you?"

I spun on my heels and headed for the elevator. "That's it. I'm out of here."

By pure dumb luck, the elevator door opened the minute I pushed the button, and to my enormous satisfaction, it slid shut in Agent Crisp's astonished face.

She caught up with me by the fare card machine. "We arrested you in good faith, Mrs. Ives. You have to admit there was probable cause."

Sounding like a win at Dover Downs Slots, the change from my twenty—all quarters—tumbled down the chute. I stooped to gather it up. "I don't believe you," I said.

"Look, Mrs. Ives. Go home. Now. Chill out. You need to trust me. Trust that I'm doing everything I can to get you off the hook with the feds." She paused. "*All* of them."

"That's not good enough."

"It will have to do. It's all I have to offer."

I folded my arms and scowled at her. "So, what exactly are you doing to clear my name, Agent Crisp, tell me that? Aside from putting a tag-team tail on me." I remembered some unexplained static on my landline and added, "And tapping my telephone, too, for all I know.

"And speaking of telephones, I haven't had any phone calls from my lawyer telling me that the FBI has called to tell him that it's all been a big mistake and that the charges against me have been dropped. For me, that's the only acceptable outcome."

"We know about your involvement with the Dunbar, Vorhees, and Tinsley cases," Crisp said. "But I need you to back off now. This investigation could have serious, international repercussions."

"Frankly, Agent Crisp, I couldn't care less about international repercussions. I just want to be able to hold my head high in public again."

"This case is much broader than little cases of domestic violence," she continued.

"Little cases of domestic violence?" I repeated. "Little?" I didn't realize I had been shouting until a woman standing at the fare card machine grabbed her daughter by the hand and, with a nervous glance in my direction, scurried off in the opposite direction. "Explain that to Mr. and Mrs. Dunbar! That little case of domestic violence, as you so crudely put it, cost them the lives of both their daughters."

Amanda Crisp raised a cautionary hand. "I certainly don't mean to trivialize those tragedies, Mrs. Ives, but I think it's fair to say that if government contracts are compromised, particularly in wartime, thousands of soldiers and innocent civilians could die. We've spent over a year setting this up and I'm not asking you to go home, I'm ordering you to."

I studied her face in the harsh Metro station lights and decided that in spite of myself, I believed her, but I was too angry to give her the satisfaction.

"You're a long way from Annapolis," she said. "Give you a ride home?"

I shook my head. "No thanks. I'd rather not." I didn't want to spend one more second in a police vehicle, even if I were sitting up front in the passenger seat holding a doughnut in one hand and a cup of coffee in the other.

I fed my fare card into the machine and pushed through the turnstile. As I headed for the train, I turned and called back over my shoulder. "And it's Kinsey Millhone."

"What?"

"Kinsey Millhone, not V.I. Warshawski. Nicer wardrobe. Cooler car."

CHAPTER 21

By the time I got home, it was after eight. I tossed my keys on the table in the entrance hall, peeled off my coat and scarf and called out the proverbial, "Hello, honey, I'm home!"

Paul returned my greeting from the living room, where I found him reading the latest Robert Parker crime novel. He'd propped his stocking feet up on an ottoman and aimed them at a fire that flickered in the fireplace, more for ambience than for warmth. He closed the book and let it drop from his fingers to the carpet, then patted the arm of his chair, inviting me to join him. "Successful day?"

I crossed the room, kicking off my shoes as I went. I perched on the chair next to him, kissed the top of his head. "You won't believe it when I tell you."

"Try me."

"Chris Donovan tells me that Jennifer was blackmailing the admiral. She'd discovered some gross irregularities in the contracts coming out of his office and she was using that information to get money out of him. But then, he discovered—how, I don't know, Chris didn't say—that Jennifer Goodall is, or was, gay, so there went Jennifer's leverage."

Paul's eyebrows shot up. "Gay? Now that's a surprise."

"I got it straight from Chris Donovan, and she had no

reason to lie about it. At one time she and Jennifer were lovers."

"I never would have guessed, not with the way she came on to me." Paul captured my hand in both of his and squeezed it reassuringly. "I wasn't the only faculty member she singled out for special attention, of course."

"That's because you're so devilishly handsome," I quipped. After a moment of silence, I added, "Of course, it's perfectly possible that Jennifer swung both ways."

An equal opportunity sexual predator, I thought maliciously.

"We need to call Murray." Paul reached for the portable phone sitting on the end table.

I took the receiver from his hand. "No need, he already knows. Chris said he'd interviewed her about it."

Paul's eyes narrowed. "Funny he didn't mention it."

"My thoughts exactly," I said. "But then I ran into Special Agent Crisp at the Metro."

Paul turned in the chair to face me. "Ran into? As in 'What a coincidence seeing you here, Special Agent Crisp?' "

He had such a goofy grin on his face that I had to laugh. "More like, 'Agent Crisp, we can't go on meeting this way.' " Skipping the part about my embarrassing karate demonstration, I forged on. "That phantom Taurus we've been seeing lately? I think it's for real. The FBI has been keeping tabs on me, it seems, and Crisp wanted to rap my knuckles for messing about in her investigation."

"If you won't listen to me, Hannah, and you won't listen to your lawyer, I don't know why she thinks you'll listen to the FBI."

"But Paul, that's just it! It's not *my* case she's afraid I'm messing with. The FBI is part of some multiagency sting operation that's focused on Admiral Hart."

"Damn!"

"And it gets better. In warning me off, Crisp practically

admitted that she doesn't think I had anything to do with Jennifer Goodall's murder."

"Now we definitely call Murray."

I handed him the phone. "You dial," I said.

We got Murray out of the bath. After Paul had passed on what I'd told him about the sting operation, he handed the phone to me. "Agent Crisp is right, Hannah, you need to stay out of it. Let me and my staff do the work."

I asked Murray why he hadn't told us about his interview with Chris Donovan, but he brushed me off with a simple, "I'm interviewing dozens of people, Hannah. When I know what's important and what's not, then I tell you. That's what you pay me for."

On the other end of the phone, I heard water running and realized that Murray must still be in the tub. No wonder he was being crabby. "And leave the government watchdogs alone," he was saying. "It could very well turn out that Hart's activities are directly related to whomever killed Jennifer Goodall. If so, the last thing we need is for you to stick your nose in and blow the case they're carefully building against him. Let the feds do their job."

I scowled into the phone. "If we leave it to the feds, Murray, I might never have my name cleared. Bureaucracies move with the speed of a glacier."

But as I handed the phone back to Paul, I had to admit there was logic in what he was telling me, so I decided that like B'rer Fox, I'd lay low.

Sunday night I slept more soundly than I had in weeks. Paul awoke early. While he puttered quietly around our bedroom dressing for his Monday morning class and humming off-tune, I lay absolutely still, with my eyes closed, thinking how much I loved him.

After he left, I fell into an uneasy sleep. I dreamed I was riding on a merry-go-round with Agents Crisp and Taylor seated on the horses just behind. Next to me, Paul rode a swan—up and down, up and down—turning to grin at me from time to time as he leaned out, hand extended, to snag one ring, then two, then three. Ted Hart was there, too. Framed by lightbulbs that flashed in sequence like a Times Square marquee, the admiral stood at the carousel's center, dazzling in his dress whites, one hand on the stick, pushing it forward, laughing, as we revolved. I looked around, calling frantically, "Dorothy, Dorothy," knowing she must be there, but not seeing her anywhere. Faster and faster we whirled, until the scenery became a blur. Faster still, with Hart pushing on the stick, laughing maniacally, until I spun off my horse and went flying, flying over the bumper cars, over the Ferris wheel . . . and awoke, heart racing and out of breath.

I lay in bed with the covers up to my chin, quietly fuming. I certainly didn't need Sigmund Freud to tell me the meaning of that.

Even after two cups of coffee I was still steaming. Something about the database search I had begun the previous day at the Arlington Library was nagging at me. I trotted down to the basement and powered up the computer.

I was back at Defenselink, engrossed in a complicated Boolean search strategy, when a voice from the top of the stairs called, "Hannah?"

I got up from my chair and stuck my head around the door frame. Emma Kirby stood there, neat, fresh-faced, and cheerful, each crease in her black uniform pants and long-sleeve shirt perfectly aligned.

"Emma! Come on down."

She clumped down the stairs, her black shoes so well-polished that they flashed even in the subdued lighting of my basement hallway. She was carrying a small bag that I recognized. It contained her dirty laundry. "Sorry to bother you, Hannah. I rang and rang but nobody answered, so I just let myself in. I put the key back."

"Thanks, Emma." All my midshipmen knew where we kept the spare house key, in a secret compartment in a fairly convincing plastic rock that I'd tucked into the flower bed to the left of our front stoop.

Emma dropped her laundry bag in the hallway, then made a pit stop at the basement refrigerator, where she helped herself to a Diet Coke. "I just came over to see how you were doing," she called over the *pfssssst* of the tab being popped.

"I'm fine, more or less. Thanks."

Emma wandered into my office, swigging from the soda as she came. She leaned over my shoulder and studied the monitor. "Government contracts. *Ugh!* I thought I'd find you relaxing. Reading or watching TV or something."

"I'm still trying to recover from last week," I told her.

Emma plopped down on a tufted bean bag chair that had once been in our daughter Emily's room. "Nobody believes you killed Lieutenant Goodall, Hannah. Nobody!" She split the word into two syllables—No Body—and I had to smile.

"That's reassuring, Emma, my dear, but I may be a very old woman before the FBI calls to tell me they've made a terrible mistake." I pointed at the computer. "That's what I'm working on here. I'm looking for people other than me who might have wanted to make Jennifer disappear permanently."

"But why government contracts?" Emma wanted to know.

"My husband and I talked to a former mid, one of his students, who used to know Jennifer." I was purposely vague, not wanting to mention Kevin's father. "This guy told us that before Goodall came to the Academy, she was working at the Pentagon in an office that handles big Navy contracts. I'm probably just spinning my wheels," I continued, "but I thought if I could connect the particular office she worked in with contracts—particularly large ones—that were awarded disproportionately to one company over another—"

"Jeeze, Hannah, that'll take forever. Do you have any

proof that she was fiddling around with the contracts she was supposed to be working on?"

"Not really. Just speculation."

"If you ask me—which you didn't, but I'll tell you anyway—it's a big waste of time."

"You're probably right," I said, thinking so many contracts, so many databases, so little time. "But you know what, Emma, at least I'm doing *something*!"

"I should have figured you wouldn't sit still and wait around for other people to do the legwork."

While Emma was talking, I moused over to Start and shut the computer down. "I did find out something interesting yesterday," I told her as the blue screen on the monitor turned to black.

"What was that?"

I swiveled my desk chair around, wondering whether I should tell Emma or not, but figured that it couldn't be a sin to out a dead person. "Lieutenant Goodall was gay."

Emma smiled. "I know."

"You know?"

"Uh-huh. She came out to me maybe the second or third time I went to see her for help about the harassment."

I felt like I'd gone out for popcorn and missed part of the movie. "Emma! What harassment? You didn't tell me you were being harassed."

Emma lobbed her empty soda can into the trash can. "Some firstie in Sixteenth Company. I think. Can't be one hundred percent sure. Anyway, this guy, he kept asking me out and I kept turning him down. I guess he couldn't figure out why I kept rejecting such a burning, burning hunk of love as him, so he started a rumor that I was a lesbian."

"That's despicable."

Emma puffed air out through her lips. "If not dating is proof positive of homosexuality, then fifty percent of the brigade must be gay."

"So, what did this guy do?"

"I'd get hate mails from anonymous Yahoo and Hotmail accounts. And I'd come back from PT to find notes on my bed, like go home dyke. D-I-K-E. Jackass couldn't even spell."

"Did Lieutenant Goodall put you in contact with anybody who could help?"

"Oh, sure. She got me with an outfit called the Servicemembers Legal Defense Network."

I nodded, thinking five points for Jennifer for hooking Emma up with Chris Donovan, one of the few people in all this mess who I felt I could trust.

"And?" I prodded.

"One of their counselors explained that harassment of gays is not allowed and that the Pentagon even put out regs about it. Problem is, nobody in the Navy's ever heard of the regs, at least not so far as I can discover, so nobody knows what to do. And there sure as hell hasn't been any training."

"It seems to me that harassment of any kind shouldn't be tolerated, it doesn't matter what that harassment is about."

"Well, right."

"Can't you complain about the harassment without admitting anything about your sexual preference?"

"Well, sure, but who's gonna believe *that*?" She scrunched farther down into the doughnut-shaped cushion. "'Where there's smoke, there's fire,'" she singsonged. "That's what they'll think."

I wanted to reassure the young woman, but I knew, too well, that what she was saying was true. People in the military were notoriously hard to turn. See an opening, they'd drive a wedge into it, and keep pounding and pounding and pounding until you broke, or simply gave up and went away. I'd seen it too many times before.

Then Emma surprised me again. "Lieutenant Goodall wanted me to be some sort of test case about the whole harassment issue, but I didn't want to rock the boat any more than it'd already been rocked. I told her to forget it."

Emma drew her legs up, wrapped her arms around them and rested her chin on her knees. "So, I decided to create a diversion. That's where Kevin came in." She looked up at me and beamed. "You know what he did?"

I shook my head.

"He cornered the firstie in the basement of Bancroft and beat the shit out of him. Told him to leave his girlfriend alone or else he'd cut off his balls and . . . well, never mind. It was pretty graphic."

Normally I don't condone resorting to violence to solve problems, but the way things were going for me lately, violence was looking like an attractive alternative. "Good for Kevin," I said with some conviction.

"Now Kevin is stuck with taking me to the Ring Dance." She smiled. "But I told him I'd step aside if the right girl came along. That goes for me, too, of course."

I laughed, then helped Emma load her laundry into the washing machine. Shortly afterward, I sent her back to Bancroft Hall with a Ziploc bag full of cookies.

After she left, I began to wonder. Had the seed Chris Donovan planted in Jennifer's mind taken root, grown and blossomed? If Jennifer Goodall had been on a mission, looking for cases to test the military's Don't Ask, Don't Tell policy, perhaps another one of her clients hadn't been so sanguine about it.

In his landmark study, Alfred Kinsey claimed that homosexuals make up ten percent of the population. The Academy has four thousand students. If we believe Alfred Kinsey—and who am I to argue with an expert?—the list of suspects in Jennifer Goodall's murder had just grown by another four hundred. Pretty soon we'd need Alumni Hall to hold them all.

CHAPTER 22

I have no way of knowing for sure, but I suspect Paul and our daughter, Emily, are in cahoots. How else—other than the most unlikely of coincidences—to explain her phone call on Monday evening.

Plans for the spa were proceeding apace, Emily said. Dante and Phyllis Strother, the woman who was his major investor, were meeting on Wednesday, along with an architect and a platoon of lawyers. They had found a piece of property. Would I care to come see it?

"I'm supposed to be laying low," I reminded my daughter.

"I can really use your help, Mom. I feel like shit in the morning."

"Pregnancy can do that to you," I offered helpfully.

Emily groaned.

It would have been nice to see my grandchildren, of course, but I didn't feel like driving for hours and hours to Virginia just to pat Chloe and Jake on the head, turn right around and come back.

That wasn't going to be a problem, Emily said, because Phyllis was footing the bill. Food, hotel rooms. There'd be a separate room for Grandma, too.

It was tempting, but I was already in enough trouble with the law. "Emily, I'd love to, but I'm out on bail. I'm not supposed to leave the state."

"Oh pooh, Mother. They'll never know."

"Oh, yes they will," I said, and told her about my Sunday adventure, caught red-handed by the FBI, hot-footing around northern Virginia.

Emily listened, oh-ing and ah-ing and laughing at all the right places. Then the little scamp played her trump card. "Well, you're not off the hook yet, ha-ha-ha, because the property we're looking at is in Maryland, so you just can't say no. Pleeeeeeease?"

I'd heard that tone of voice before. When Emily *just* wanted to go to a rave. When she *only* needed $150 for a ski trip. When *all* her friends were spending the weekend in Ocean City and I was the meanest mommy in the world.

And then I did what mommies down through the centuries have done. I weakened. "Tell me about it."

Emily knew she had me. "Oh, thank you!" she gushed. "It's in a development called Charlesmeade, down in Indian Head, Maryland. The realtor says it was built as a country club for one of those golf course housing developments. The developer built the club first, to attract buyers for his homes, I suppose. But then his company went belly up."

Indian Head is a charming waterfront community in southern Maryland, about twenty-five miles south of the Capital Beltway, where Mattawoman Creek meets the Potomac River. I'd visited several times, most recently when my father—a retired naval officer with decades of experience in the aerospace industry—had been considering a job at NAVSEA. "How come nobody's bought the developer out?" I asked.

"Phyllis says there have been a number of interested parties, but nobody's come up with the money so far. The realtor thinks they may be willing to sell the club in a separate parcel. Oh, Mom, it's perfect!" she raved. "It's twenty-five acres, and right on the water! You should see the pictures!" Emily was in full exclamation mark mode.

Truthfully, I loved to look at model homes and homes

under construction. And visiting with the grandkids was an added incentive.

Once I had agreed to go, Emily got serious. "Mom, do me a favor."

"What's that?"

"Now don't take this wrong."

Don't take this wrong. I knew for *sure* that I wasn't going to like what was coming.

"Phyllis doesn't know anything about your present, um, predicament, so I'd appreciate your not mentioning it."

I felt as if I'd been slapped, and considered reneging on the spot. "You think I'm *proud* of being arrested, Emily?" I sputtered. "What do you think I'd say? 'Good morning, Mrs. Strother. So pleased to meet you. I'll very much look forward to having tea with you after I get out on parole.' "

"Moooootherr!"

"Well?" There was a long silence during which I was left to fill in the blanks.

"Okay. Maybe I'm being silly, but I don't want anything to jeopardize this deal. Dante has worked soooooo hard to put it together, and Phyllis is soooooo enthusiastic."

I bet. Even the name Phyllis Strother sounded like it belonged to an astute businesswoman who recognized a good thing when she saw it. Whatever else you may say about my son-in-law, Daniel Shemanski, Haverford College dropout, from shiatsu to rolfing, the man knew his massage. New Life Spa had hired him away from the Broadmoor in Colorado Springs, one of the most prestigious spas in the country. At New Life, nestled in the Blue Ridge mountains of Virginia, he'd gone on to make himself quite a reputation, attracting a regular Who's Who of clients, including Exhibit A, Phyllis Strother.

I had no idea what went into running a health spa. My only qualifying experience was the occasional massage that I managed to squeeze in while on vacation.

Thinking about Indian Head, I said, "Emily, southern

Maryland is kind of provincial. Do you think there'll be enough customers who are willing to pay—"

Emily cut me off. "I know what you're thinking, but the place is growing by leaps and bounds. And the Navy's got all kinds of things in the vicinity."

"But what if Congress cuts Navy funding?"

"Not going to happen. NAVSEA's been there for over a century. Besides, there's Pax River, and the Weapons Center Testing Facility, and the Naval Electronic Systems Engineering Activity . . ." She ticked them off so skillfully that I suspected she was reading from a brochure.

"But think about the kids. How about the schools?"

"Charles County has great schools," Emily claimed. "But for heaven's sake, Mom, we're just looking. It's not a done deal." She lowered her voice. "Besides, if Phyllis doesn't like it, the deal's dead."

So, early Wednesday morning, I packed an overnight bag, tossed it into the backseat of my LeBaron, and two hours later found myself checking into the only motel in town, a Super 8 on Indian Head Highway, with my grandchildren for roommates. The roommates were my idea.

The green Taurus had followed me as far as the Capital Beltway, but when I turned south on 210, I was handed over to a dark blue Crown Vic. I smiled when I noticed the switch in my rearview mirror. Smooth as clockwork—the Taurus continuing straight across the Wilson Bridge into Virginia, the Crown Vic easing into traffic from the breakdown lane.

After a potty break at the Super 8, we lunched at McDonald's while the Crown Vic idled in the parking lot, envying us our french fries, no doubt. Then we piled into my son-in-law's SUV and drove to Charlesmeade with the Crown Vic staying a discreet twenty car lengths behind.

Dante glanced in the rearview mirror. "Who's that following us?"

"My bodyguards," I said. "They won't let me out of their sight."

Emily turned her head so suddenly I feared she'd get whiplash. "Mother! I thought you were kidding about being tailed."

"Not kidding. Frankly," I added, with a casual wave to whomever was keeping tabs on me from the comfort of the Crown Vic, "I'm kinda flattered by the attention."

"Well," commented Emily matter-of-factly, "at least nobody will be kidnapping you, not while the FBI is on the job."

With my shadow bumping along behind, we turned right onto a narrow one-lane country road and rattled along for about half a mile before Dante brought the SUV to a stop in front of a sign, still bright with new paint. I rolled my window down for a better look. CHARLESMEADE GOLF CLUB AND COUNTRY ESTATES, the sign said, 250 SINGLE-FAMILY HOMES. LOTS STILL AVAILABLE! LAND, WATER AND GOLF. IF YOU LIVED HERE, YOU'D BE HOME NOW.

"This is it!" he announced. After Emily had read the entire sign out loud to Chloe, Dante eased his foot off the brake and accelerated up the winding drive that led to the club, a sprawling one-story colonial-style building, painted white. The driveway was edged with boxwood alternating with saplings that had been so recently planted, they were still supported by stakes. Dante pulled under the pillared portico behind a black Lincoln town car and a Honda Civic. It didn't take much detective work to figure out which vehicle belonged to Phyllis Strother.

The minute the emergency brake went on, Chloe unfastened her seat belt and was hot to trot. As I struggled to extract Jake from his car seat, Dante slid open my door and offered me his hand. I hopped out, plucked Jake from his seat, and stood beside the van, holding the children's hands while Dante helped his wife out of the passenger side. The Crown Vic, I noticed, was idling at the bottom of the hill.

We found our realtor, Guy Winebarger, just inside the club, behind revolving glass doors that had been beautifully etched with sketches of Chesapeake Bay flora and fauna. He was dressed in dark blue chinos, a blue oxford shirt, and a yellow power tie, but in spite of the cold weather, wore no jacket. I hoped he'd left it in his car.

Phyllis Strother, on the other hand, was sensibly dressed for late February. As she approached from the end of a long hallway, I took in her gray A-line skirt, white blouse, and gray and pink boucle jacket under a Burberry raincoat that flapped open as she chugged our way. From her knees down, Phyllis wore dark gray tights and a pair of no-nonsense stacked heels.

"Dante!" she exclaimed. She grabbed his hand, her bronze-colored page boy swinging from side to side with the vigorousness of the handshake. "And this must be your family." Under her bangs, her green eyes twinkled as she smiled at me, then turned to Emily and shook her hand, too.

"Phyllis, this is my mother, Hannah Alexander."

Alexander? Emily had used my maiden name. For a moment I stood there speechless, amazed that nobody heard my molars grinding. Was Emily afraid that Phyllis would recognize my name? Call the deal off? If she hadn't been my only child, the mother of my grandchildren, I'd have flattened her on the spot. Instead, I shot her a look—*we'll talk about this later*—and stuck out my hand. "I'm so pleased to meet you, Mrs. Strother," I managed, dredging up some of the southern charm I'd inherited from my mother.

"Oh, do call me Phyllis," she boomed in a voice so robust that I thought it'd be accompanied by a vigorous *whump* on my back.

"And I'd be pleased if you'd call me Hannah, Phyllis."

"My pleasure, Hannah. And these must the grandchildren."

Jake chose that moment to go down on all fours on the inlaid marble, while Chloe cowered behind me, grasping my leg, as if not sure what to make of this other grandmother-type who loomed over her.

"Come on, children," Emily chirped. "Let's go look at the big house!" With the ease of experience, she grabbed each child's hand, swung Jake into her arms, and marched off in the direction Phyllis had just come from, with Chloe skipping happily by her side.

The four of us followed at a more leisurely pace. I listened while Guy Winebarger droned on about title abstracts, conveyances, escrow and points, but tuned out sometime during the discussion of how the seller proposed to prorate the property taxes and utility bill. Instead, I concentrated on what might soon be the place where my daughter and her family would be spending most of their time.

Although the floor where we stood had been covered with alternating squares of black and white marble, and several of the rooms that led off the lobby had been carpeted, there was not a speck of furniture anywhere. As we walked and talked, our voices and footsteps echoed hollowly off tile floors and ricocheted off the empty walls.

Dante turned to me and said, "You see what I mean, Hannah? The place has real possibilities."

My son-in-law was right. But as far as I could figure out, those possibilities all depended upon the largesse of a certain Phyllis Strother of Charlottesville, Virginia. After listening to her for a while, I hoped her pocketbook was as grand as her ideas. "The lobby, of course, will be the central reception area. The receptionists will sign you in, discuss treatments, arrange for payment, and so on, then escort you to the appropriate dressing room."

"There'll be a men's wing and a women's wing," Dante explained as we moved down the hallway of what would become the women's wing.

"The locker rooms already exist," Guy Winebarger informed me. "They were intended for the golfers, of course. Perfect, huh?"

In each wing, I learned, there'd be a hot tub to accommodate ten, each with its own lounge chairs, fresh towel cabinets, and refreshment centers. A sauna room and a steam room would be adjoining.

As we stood in the future hot tub area for women, Phyllis waxed almost poetic about it. "You'll wait here," she mused, "tubbing, reading, sipping a fruit smoothie, whatever, and when it's time for your appointment, a uniformed attendant will appear to fetch you and take you to a private cubicle—I see walnut paneling, don't you, Dante?—and you'll have your massage, or facial."

"Botox, too?" I asked as we passed through a set of double doors and stepped into the dining room. I had noticed Phyllis's smooth, seamless forehead and was feeling frisky.

"Botox, too," she said, not skipping a beat. "And when you're ready to face the world again, you can take a plunge in the indoor/outdoor pool." She waved an arm, indicating an expanse of glass that had been intended, I felt sure, to give the dining room a panoramic view of the Potomac River. "The pool will have to be built, of course," she hastened to add, "but I see it starting here and ending . . ." She waved a hand toward the river. ". . . there."

"With a vanishing edge, right?" I asked. If money were to be no object, might as well go for broke.

"Of course."

The former club room and its thirty-foot bar, I soon learned, would become the spa's dining room, where nutritious, low-carb lunches would be served, prepared by a master chef—Dante already had somebody in mind. "We won't serve alcohol, of course, only a full range of designer waters and approved fruit juices."

"If you want a blended drink," Phyllis chortled, "it had better be a smoothie!"

At the end of the men's wing, in a large room Winebarger said had been intended for a pro shop, we caught up with Emily and the children. When we pushed through the double doors, Emily spread her arms and spun around like Julie Andrews on the mountaintop in *Sound of Music*. She wound to a stop and grinned. "And this is going to be the day care center. I'm going to run it! Won't it be wonderful?"

Chloe, who had been imitating her mother, kept spinning around the room like a dervish until she collided with a pillar and fell over. Jake pounced on his sister, and in a tangle of arms and legs, the two children giggled until they got hiccups. Just watching them made me laugh, too.

"But you'll have to have a gift shop, right?" I pictured ball caps and bathrobes and T-shirts emblazoned with the spa's logo; gift baskets of health care products; designer sunglasses; self-help books.

"That will be off the main entrance, where the developer's office used to be," Dante said.

They seemed to have it all worked out. And if Phyllis Strother's check had cleared, there didn't seem to be any financial impediments, either.

"Do you think Dad will approve?" Emily wanted to know.

"I don't know why not." I smiled, thinking of Paul's measly five percent share. Looking around the building now, I figured we might end up owning the coat check room, or perhaps a restroom or two.

"Aunt Ruth is going to help with the decor."

Why was I not surprised? Emily and my sister Ruth were soulmates. I could see it all now: banzai, meditation gardens, fountains, and wind chimes all over the place. With Ruth involved, everything would be perfectly feng shuied.

While Dante huddled with Phyllis and Guy, discussing what offer they were prepared to make on the property, I, "Hannah Alexander," wandered the facility with Emily and the children. Outside the dining room windows, snow began to fall, dusting the tufts of brown winter grass with white.

"Emily, what are you going to name the spa?"

" 'Paradiso,' " she told me. "Dante's Paradiso. Do you like it?"

"Yes," I said truthfully. "I really do."

Leaving Emily to play tag with the kids, I opened the door and stepped out on the patio. The future spa was set high on the riverbank, with no trees to break the wind that came roaring across the creek, tossing my hair about my ears. I pulled my coat more tightly around me. In addition to the renovations, the place would need serious landscaping.

I circled the building, making a mental list of all the work that needed to be done before the golf club became a spa. I grew discouraged, and more and more concerned that Emily and Dante might be overextending themselves, both physically and financially.

I'd forgotten about the Crown Vic until I heard its engine rev. I turned in the direction of the noise just in time to catch sight of the vehicle as it roared down the road, spewing slush and gravel in its wake, emergency lights flashing.

What's that all about? Had the FBI lost interest in me?

"Paradiso." I closed my eyes and lifted my face to the sky. Plump snowflakes fell on my cheeks, lingered there for a brief second before melting away. *Paradiso.*

O Lord, I prayed. *Let it be so.*

Paradise, after all, sometimes had a way of turning into hell.

After dinner at the Golden Star, where Chloe pronounced the shrimp with snow peas "yummy" and Jake worked the fried rice thoroughly into his hair, we returned to the Super 8 for baths and bed. With the children asleep in the queen-size bed next to me, I nestled under the covers and had just turned the channel to HBO when my cell phone rang.

I picked up, thinking it'd be Paul, but according to the Caller ID, it was Dorothy.

"Dorothy. Hi," I whispered, not wanting to wake the children.

"Oh, Hannah, I just had to talk to somebody!" Dorothy was weeping so copiously I could barely understand her.

"What's wrong?"

"It's Ted," she wailed. "He's being investigated. People are crawling all over his office and he's being transferred!"

I leaned back against my pillows. It was happening. At long last it was happening. The feds had closed in on Ted Hart. If all went well, the spotlight would be trained on him now, not on me. A weight had been lifted from my shoulders, but it had been placed squarely on Dorothy's. With her health so precarious, I worried she'd not be strong enough to support it.

Dorothy was saying something about Norfolk.

"Norfolk?"

"Ted's going to Norfolk, Virginia. They're assigning him as Special Assistant to the Commander, Fleet Forces Command. You know what that means."

I did. It meant that the Navy was kicking him out of Washington, D.C. with a rocket tied to his tail. While they investigated the allegations against him, Admiral Hart would drive a desk. He'd plan menus, address invitations, and write place cards for Navy Relief balls. As much as I wanted the Navy to dress Theodore Hart in cammies and drop him off in downtown Falujah with a target strapped to his back, there was no way they'd give the man anything important to do.

"Oh, Dorothy, I'm so sorry." And I was sorry, too, but for her, not for the admiral. He'd made his bed and would have to lie in it. Eventually, there'd be a courtmartial. Chances are, Hart would do hard time in Leavenworth.

Dorothy wept quietly into the phone and I waited her out. "I have a migraine like you wouldn't believe," she sobbed.

"Don't worry about checking the set this week," I told her. "You just stay home and get well."

"But I want to stay involved," she choked. "What else am I going to do now that—that—"

"Does Kevin know?" I asked.

My question set off another crying jag. It was over a minute before Dorothy was able to speak to me again. "Kevin's so angry, I thought he was going to kill his father."

"Is Kevin with you?"

"No."

So Kevin was laying low, too. I wasn't surprised. Until this happened, he'd been the pampered son of an admiral, cocky, behaving as if the stars his father wore were his own. When the news broke, it'd be payback time. The brigade would not treat him kindly.

"Dorothy? I'll call you later, okay?"

Snuffle.

"If you need anything, you just let me know."

Sniff. Sniff.

As I hung up the phone, I realized that Dorothy's worst fears had come true. Except for me, she was utterly, completely alone.

CHAPTER 23

I checked in with Dorothy every day after that. On Friday her headache was better, so she'd gone ahead with her chemo. The next day, however, the migraine came back with a vengeance, affecting her vision. Ted Hart, at home on leave before departing for Norfolk, called the doctor, who prescribed Imitrex for the pain. Kevin talked to his mother on the telephone, expressing concern, but refused to visit while his father was present.

It seemed like years had passed since opening night, but *Sweeney* was winding down at last. Friday's show ran smoothly, Saturday's was a triumph. Only the Sunday matinee to go, and the show would go down in Academy history.

On Sunday morning I telephoned Dorothy to say I'd check the set before the final performance, but Dorothy didn't pick up. Never mind, I thought. She's either too sick to answer the phone or she's already on her way to the Academy. Better to err on the side of having two people show up to check the mechanisms rather than nobody.

The snow that had fallen midweek had begun to melt in one of those warm snaps that often comes to Annapolis in late February, fooling the crocuses into sending out green shoots and hopeful yellow blossoms in the mistaken assumption that it's spring. I pulled into a parking spot in front of Mahan, where the piles of snow thrown up by the snow plow had begun to melt, sending rivulets of water trickling across the pavement.

Although it was nearly noon, few people were around. At the chapel, the Protestant service was still in session. Back in Bancroft Hall, midshipmen were probably catching a few last minute z's before Noon Formation, sleeping off the excesses of a Saturday night away from the Yard.

In the auditorium, everything looked as we had left it the night before. The curtains stood open but the house lights were off so I couldn't see very well, just the gray outlines of a set that I'd come to know so well—Sweeney's tonsorial parlor, Mrs. Lovett's pie shop, the hulking rectangle of her diabolical oven. It was so quiet I could hear my own breathing.

Or was it?

The breathing became a whimper, the whimper a moan, and I realized I was not alone.

"Hello?" I called out. "Anybody there?"

I drew closer to the stage. "Hello?"

The moaning seemed to be coming from the area around Mrs. Lovett's oven, so I climbed the steps to the stage and crossed over to it. Someone was slumped on the floor, bent over a plastic waste basket, violently retching. "Dorothy?" I rushed over and knelt next to my friend, lifting her chin so I could look into her eyes. "My God, Dorothy, what's wrong?"

"Oh, Hannah, I think I'm losing my mind! I had chemo yesterday, but this whole business about Ted and the investigation has got me so spun up that I forgot to take my antinausea medication. Oh, God, I feel like hell." She ducked her face into the wastepaper basket again, her body jackknifing in its futile attempt to vomit up something, anything.

"Dorothy, how long have you been like this?"

With her face still in the basket, Dorothy shook her head. "I don't know, maybe an hour." She curled up like a leaf in autumn, and the horrible dry heaving continued.

When the retching subsided, I gathered her into my arms, gently rocking. I straightened her wig, which had tipped over her forehead and was in danger of falling off the next time she dove for the wastebasket. "Dorothy, this is way past the point where it's going to get better by itself. You need to see a doctor. I'm going to take you to the emergency room."

Dorothy lay limply in my arms and moaned.

One arm at a time, I shrugged out of my coat and folded it like a pillow, using it to prop Dorothy into a sitting position against the oven. "Wait here. I'll be right back."

Dorothy raised a hand, then let it drop to her side. "Hannah, don't leave me."

"I'll be right back. A minute, no more."

I dashed off stage left and ran down a short flight of stairs that led to a little vestibule. On my left a spiral staircase went up and up, first to the balcony, then to rooms at various levels in the clock tower. In the other direction was a janitor's closet, and just beyond, on the other side of the door, I remembered seeing a water fountain. I wrenched open the closet door, grabbed a handful of paper towels, and wet them thoroughly at the water fountain. Then I hurried back to Dorothy.

"Here," I said, handing her a paper towel dripping with water. "Suck on this. You're dehydrated."

"I'm going to *die!*" she moaned.

"Trust me. You're not going to die." With one of the towels, I swabbed her forehead and cheeks. "You're going to the hospital where they'll give you something that will stop the nausea." I tugged on her shoulders, urging her to muster what resources she had and stand up, but she was dead weight in my arms. "Come on, Dorothy," I urged. "Work with me here."

"Oh, oh, oh, oh, I *am* going to die," she whimpered.

"You're going to be fine, but not unless you stand up and let me take you out of here." I tugged on her again. "Dorothy!"

"I don't want to go to the hospital! Kevin's coming!"

I checked my watch. Twelve-fifteen. Kevin would be arriving in about an hour, along with the rest of the cast of *Sweeney Todd,* ready for costumes and makeup.

"What do you plan to do? Sit in the audience holding a wastebasket on your lap? Think! If you don't come with me now, you won't be well enough to see the performance, so there's no use complaining about it." I shifted my position until I was kneeling in front of her. I thrust my hands under her armpits and eased her into an upright position.

Dorothy's hand began roving erratically over the floor. "Where's my purse?"

"There you go!" I teased. "Barfing up major body parts and the woman still wants her purse."

At that, Dorothy managed a laugh, but it quickly turned into a moan.

I felt around in the semidarkness until my hand touched the strap of her handbag. "I've got it," I said, looping the strap around my neck. Then I persuaded Dorothy to wrap her arms around my neck, too. With Dorothy and her handbag hanging from my neck, I staggered to my feet. I eased an arm around her waist and shuffled her off the stage, into the lobby, and down the front steps of the building, where I opened the door of my car and pretty much shoved her in. "Lie back. We'll be out of here in a minute." I elevated her legs on a stack of overdue books, then covered her with my coat, tucking it snugly around her. In spite of the coat and the warmth of my car, she began to shiver.

After running the mini obstacle course of Jersey barriers that surrounded the sentry post at Gate 8, I turned left at the light and broke all kinds of land speed records getting to Rowe Boulevard. At Route 50, Rowe turns into Bestgate and it's pretty much a straight shot to Anne Arundel Medical Center, if you know the back way in. After passing the Wawa, I turned left onto Medical Drive, ran the orange light at the next intersection, and veered left, winding around the Clatinoff Pavillion to the front of the building where EMERGENCY glowed in red neon from the top of the roof that sheltered the entryway.

I pulled in, set the emergency brake and left Dorothy in the car with the engine running. I waited—come on, come *on*!—for the glass doors to *whoosh* open ahead of me, then barged into the emergency room and looked around, feeling frantic.

With the exception of a receptionist, there wasn't a nurse or an aide in sight.

Damn! Just when you need them, they disappear. Every time I'd been to Anne Arundel before, pink-shirted volunteers kept sprouting up like weeds, pushing gurneys, magazine carts, and empty wheelchairs, causing traffic jams all over the place. I rushed the information desk, where an aide was busily attaching a form to a clipboard. "Excuse me, but I've got a very sick woman in my car." I waved my hand toward the wall of windows that separated me from my sick friend.

The aide looked up from her work, her face grave. "Tylene, give this lady a hand, will you?"

From behind a partition, Tylene appeared, dressed in turquoise scrubs in a cheerful ice cream cone print. Within seconds she'd located a wheelchair and followed me outside to help Dorothy get into it.

With Dorothy sagging like a cooked noodle, Tylene pushed the chair up to the information desk, where I explained Dorothy's problem to the aide, who handed me a clipboard and asked me to have Dorothy fill it out. "She's so sick," I replied, "that I don't even think she can remember who she is, let alone hold a pen."

"I've got to get the roast into the oven," Dorothy muttered, pretty much proving my point. "It's just sitting out on the counter. And the potatoes need peeling. But I suppose I could make rice." On and on she babbled, leaping from dinner preparations to movies she forgot to TiVo to plans for an addition to their Davidsonville home.

"Do the best you can, then," the aide said with a sympathetic smile. "We'll fine-tune it later."

In the end, I filled out the form as best I could by rummaging around in Dorothy's purse for her driver's license, military dependent's ID, and her Tricare health insurance card. "Here," I said, handing the card over the counter along with the clipboard. "Over to you."

The aide scanned the form, photocopied Dorothy's insurance card, then, apparently satisfied, handed me a square pager made of black plastic with a blinking red light like the kind you get when you go to dinner at Outback Steakhouse. I showed it to Dorothy, whose eyes were now hovering at half mast. "Look, they'll call us when our table is ready."

Dorothy's eyes flew open. "How long do I have to wait?"

Earlier, I'd noticed a sign prominently displayed on the information desk: approximate wait time for non-life-threatening emergencies. Underneath the notice was a selection of flip cards hanging on pegs. The flip card said: < 1 HOUR.

I read the sign aloud. "Less than one hour."

"Okay." Dorothy managed a weak smile, then grabbed the hem of her sweatshirt and began retching into it.

Almost instantly, Tyrene materialized like a guardian angel, carrying a kidney-shaped basin and a wet cloth. "Here you go, sweetheart," she soothed, wiping Dorothy's face with the cloth. "They're kinda busy back there right now, but we'll be getting to you right soon."

Dorothy nodded, and using both hands, pressed the wet cloth against her eyes.

"Can't we get her something to drink?" I asked.

Tyrene shook her head. "Not till the doctor takes a look at her." She pushed Dorothy's chair out of the traffic and eased it into position next to an upholstered chair, which I plopped down in immediately.

And we did what you do in waiting rooms. We waited.

At the far end of the room, a huge, flat-screen TV was tuned to CNN and some Army brigadier general (retired) was pontificating about the war in Iraq. Next to us a bearded man in a plaid shirt dozed under a ficus tree, his head thrown back and his mouth yawning open, a black pager balanced precariously on one knee. Every time somebody wandered in the vicinity of the doors, they would *whoosh* open, letting cold air in. After five minutes of that, I moved Dorothy over several rows to keep her out of the draft. Tyrene must have noticed because she reappeard bearing a flannel blanket, fresh from the ER blanket-warmer, which she helped me tuck around Dorothy's shoulders.

Eventually our pager started flashing like an alien spaceship and someone appeared to roll Dorothy away. I offered to go with her, but in three or four rambling sentences, Dorothy refused. Trying not to feel miffed, I watched TV, read two old *National Geographics* from cover to cover, telephoned Paul to tell him where I was, left a message for Admiral Hart on his home phone, and filed my nails, not necessarily in that order.

Three hours later Dorothy was back, smiling bravely. "That's it?" I asked Tyrene.

"That's it. You can take her home." She handed me a sheaf of papers. "These are for her primary care physician. She'll need to follow up with him in three days."

"What did they do?" I asked Dorothy.

"Blood and urine tests. Then they started an IV and put something in it. I felt better almost right away."

Tyrene looked down at her patient. "Now you take it easy for a couple of days, you hear me, Dorothy?"

Dorothy nodded mutely.

I set the hospital forms on Dorothy's lap, went around to the back of the chair and started pushing. "Home again, home again, jiggidy jig."

Dorothy twisted in her chair. "Oh, no! My car's at the Academy!"

"We can pick it up later. You shouldn't be driving anyway."

She checked her watch. "I'm missing it, I'm missing it!"

"Missing what?" I asked.

"Kevin's final performance!" Her eyes glistened with tears. She grabbed my hand where it rested on the handlebar of the wheelchair. "Please, Hannah, take me back to Mahan."

After everything that had happened in the past several hours, I'd completely forgotten about the musical until she reminded me. "You have been to every rehearsal. And you haven't missed a single one of Kevin's performances," I reminded her. "He'll understand if you miss just this one."

"I need to go back to Mahan."

"Well, then you'll have to push yourself down Route 50 in this wheelchair, because I am going to take you home."

"There won't be anybody there," she pouted. "Ted has to report to Norfolk in the morning. He's already gone."

"That's all right. If nobody's home, I'll just stay with you until we're sure you're all right. End of story."

With Dorothy muttering mild curses under her breath, I pushed her chair in the direction of the sliding glass doors, but had to pull to one side to make way for an emergency. An ambulance had roared up, siren *whoop-whoop-whooping*, and a pair of EMTs had opened its rear doors, preparing to off-load some poor soul on a stretcher.

Five seconds later the EMTs eased through the door with the stretcher, followed by someone I recognized: Professor Medwin Black. Before I could even begin to wonder what he was doing at the hospital instead of overseeing the musical at Mahan Hall, Dorothy screamed. I turned my head and watched as her eyes rolled back in their sockets and she fainted dead away. "Dorothy? What the hell?"

The form on the stretcher stirred. The left side of his face was covered by a bandage that wrapped completely around his head, and his neck was encased in a brace. "Mother? What are you doing here?" he slurred, before he, too, lost consciousness.

The casualty was Midshipman Kevin Hart.

CHAPTER 24

How we all fit into the private treatment room without a shoehorn, I'll never know.

Kevin lay on the gurney, woozy but conscious, and Dorothy sat in a chair—a regular one, without wheels—appearing more alert than I'd seen her in weeks.

"How are you feeling, Kev? Can I get you anything?" Dorothy shot up and down from her chair like a jack-in-a-box, with Medwin Black and me running interference to keep her from actually climbing up onto the gurney with her son.

Kevin's left eye was turning black and he'd been X-rayed. No broken bones, thank heaven. We were awaiting the arrival of a plastic surgeon who'd been called in for consultation about the nasty gash on his cheek.

"What happened?" I asked Kevin after doctor number one came and went.

"I crashed my car," he replied, squinting at me through his one good eye. "I was moving it from in front of Mahan to a space along the seawall." He paused, as if trying to piece it all together. "I remember feeling groggy. Then *wham*!"

"He missed the ninety-degree turn at the end of McNair and drove head-on into the seawall," Professor Black explained. "He was driving slowly, thank goodness, but the air bag deployed, hitting him square in the face."

"Oh, his face, his poor face," Dorothy crooned. "It'll be all right, Kev. Of course it will be all right. Don't you worry about a thing."

To my way of thinking, Kevin had plenty to worry about. The results of his blood test, for one thing, if, as I suspected, he'd been driving under the influence. The penalties for that are severe, especially on a federal reservation.

His eye, for another. I cringed at the sight of the bruise that was blossoming around his eye socket. Hopefully it was simple, just a humdinger of a shiner. If Kevin's vision were impaired, that would shelve any plans he had of becoming a pilot.

He turned his head, and winced in pain. "I tried to call you, Mom. I didn't want you to miss me."

"Miss you? What do you mean?"

Medwin Black smiled. "Adam Monroe, our Beadle, was just diagnosed with infectious mononucleosis. The doctors grew concerned about his liver, so Kevin was slated to go on." Professor Black turned to his student. "But you'll get your chance next year, Kevin. I'm sure of it."

"Tough break, Kevin," I said with a smile. I turned to Professor Black. "So who ended up playing the Beadle?"

"And someone had to sub for Jonas Fogg, too." Professor Black twiddled with his beard. "Never happened before, to be two actors down. It was a bit of musical chairs," he said, finally getting around to answering my question, "but we got it covered. One of the grave diggers had played Beadle Bamford in high school, and we sent Dean Kelchner in for Fogg."

"Kelchner?" Kevin erupted, groaned, pressed his palm flat against his temple. "Kelchner couldn't act his way out of a wet paper bag."

Professor Black grinned mischievously. "There is that," he said. "But we wrote his speech down and pinned it to the back of one of the lunatics. Kelchner managed fairly well."

"The show must go on," Dorothy said in a small, sad

voice just as the plastic surgeon blew into the room, his lab coat flapping. He shooed everyone out except Kevin and his mother.

"Just a few stitches," Kevin told us after the surgeon was done and the nurse allowed us back into the treatment room. A small, neat bandage covered the wound under Kevin's impressively bruised eye.

Dorothy hunched in a corner, arms folded across her chest. "You need to see a specialist."

"They have fine plastic surgeons at Bethesda, Mother. Some of the best in the country."

"They just don't want to pay for proper specialists, is all. Damn the military."

I could understand her point of view. First her husband, now her son, was getting, in her words, royally screwed by the military.

A few minutes later doctor number one returned and cleared us all out again. I leaned against the wall outside the door to Kevin's room, engaged in some serious multitasking. With my right ear, I listened to Medwin Black tell about the cruise he took to the Greek isles the previous summer. My left ear stayed glued to the door, trying to overhear what the doctor inside the treatment room was saying.

"What were you taking, young man?"

There was a pause, during which time Medwin was dancing to the music of bouzoukis on Rhodes late into the summer night; meanwhile, I imagined Kevin's brows lifting in surprise. "Taking? I wasn't taking anything! Glucosamine for my knee. That's all I can think of."

"Were you nervous? Stressed out? You exhibit all the symptoms of an overdose of tranquilizers."

"Kev?" Dorothy again, playing the mother card. "Did you drink anything before the show?"

"Jeeze! I ate lunch. Drank milk with that. When I got to Mahan, I had a Dr Pepper. That's it. Say, Doc, you don't think I was *drinking*, do you?"

Next to me Medwin snorted, and I realized he had finished his travelogue and was listening to the conversation, too. "Hah!" he grunted. "I've seen midshipmen go on stage so pickled that even if you shot them, they wouldn't fall down."

"No, no," the doctor on the other side of the door hastened to add. "There's absolutely no trace of alcohol in your blood."

"Of course there isn't," Dorothy chimed in. "He's an actor. He had a show to do."

"Did you find traces of tranquilizers, then?" Kevin asked with a tinge of panic.

"No, and I wouldn't expect to. Most tranquilizers are completely metabolized by the body."

"I can't explain it, then," Kevin said.

"A mistake," said his mother.

Ten minutes later Kevin was released. Over the tearful protestations of his mother, Professor Black drove the midshipman back to the Academy.

I chauffeured Dorothy to her home in Davidsonville, settled her into a chair in front of the TV, fixed her a cup of tea and a bowl of hot oatmeal with butter and brown sugar, and waited with her until I was sure she would keep it down.

It was nearly seven before I returned home to Paul. He'd gone ahead and fixed dinner, the sweetheart, although about the only good thing you can say about Paul's five-alarm chili is that it clears your sinuses.

I was applying a medicinal glass of red wine directly to the inferno raging in my stomach when Murray Simon called. "Paul, pick up!" I yelled.

When Paul joined us on the line, Murray said, "Hannah, I have good news and bad news."

"Oh for heaven's sake, Murray, get on with it! Please!"

"The good news is that the FBI is dropping the case against you," Murray said. "Seems they picked it up under pressure from NCIS, and now that the sting operation is over, they don't think there's enough evidence to convict you."

"I'm so relieved." I could actually feel my blood pressure going down.

"The bad news is that NCIS isn't similarly inclined. They may be taking the case forward on their own."

I was speechless, gasping for air.

Paul filled in the blank. "If there isn't enough evidence for the FBI, why is there enough for NCIS?"

"Well, there is that other matter."

"Murray!" I'd found my voice at last. I actually screamed into the phone. "Sometimes you can be the most *infuriating* man!"

"What other matter?" Paul was spitting nails.

"We know who NCIS's key witness is, the person who saw Hannah leaving Mahan Hall the day Jennifer Goodall was murdered."

I gripped the arm of my chair so tightly that I must have left my fingerprints embedded in the varnish. "Who?"

"Are you sitting down?"

"I'm sitting down."

Murray cleared his throat. "It was Dorothy Hart."

CHAPTER 25

That night I lay in bed, numbly studying the shifting shadows cast on the wall by the light of the full moon shining through the branches of the tree outside my window.

For a long while Paul lay awake beside me, trying out possible scenarios, but after a particularly lengthy lull in the conversation, followed by regular snuffling sounds, I turned my head to find that he'd drifted off to sleep.

I'd thought Dorothy was my friend. We'd worked together, laughed together, cried together. How could she betray me with such a monstrous lie?

I knew I had been nowhere near the back of Nimitz Library on the day Jennifer Goodall died. Dorothy had to know it, too.

Was she simply mistaken? That hardly seemed likely.

Was she purposely trying to frame me? As strange as her behavior had been in recent days, I couldn't believe that either.

My bet, after staring at the ceiling for quite some time, was that in pointing the finger at me, Dorothy believed she was diverting suspicion from somebody else, somebody far more important to her than I was.

There were only two people on that list: her husband and her son.

Kevin, I knew from Emma, had an ironclad alibi. He'd been doing a Physical Readiness Test at the time of the crime. The PRT was a killer of another kind: sixty-five sit-ups, forty push-ups, run a mile and a half in ten minutes or less, or a midshipman doesn't graduate. Kevin's PRT had been monitored by a couple of straight-arrow firsties.

Ted Hart had an ironclad alibi, too. He'd been briefing the Joint Chiefs.

When I asked him to, Murray Simon had confirmed both alibis.

For a change of scenery, I turned over in bed and watched the digital clock cycle from 12:01 to 12:02 to . . .

Three!

Hannah, you idiot! There were *three* people on Dorothy's short list. Her husband, her son, and *herself*.

I'd always discounted Dorothy as a suspect. She was too frail to overpower a healthy young woman like Jennifer Goodall. Besides, Jennifer's body had been found in Sweeney Todd's trunk. There was no way Dorothy, in her weakened condition, could have moved her body from . . .

I sat up straight in bed. I switched on the bedside lamp. I pounded Paul on the back until he groaned and opened one bleary eye.

"Dorothy did it!" I shouted, slapping him lightly on the thigh to emphasize each syllable. "I'm not sure how, but she did it. She got Jennifer to come to Mahan Hall on some pretext, lured her up to Sweeney's tonsorial parlor, then clobbered her with the hammer and pushed her into the trunk."

I folded my arms across my chest and leaned back against the headboard. "I've been working on the assumption that Jennifer had been killed elsewhere and her body moved to the trunk because Dorothy told me that's what happened. But I just this minute realized that I only have Dorothy's word that it happened that way."

Next to me, Paul fluffed up his pillow, folded it in half

and stuffed it between his back and the headboard. "I thought Dorothy had an alibi. Didn't you tell me she was getting a manicure?"

"According to Dorothy." I slapped myself on the forehead. "Damn! Why didn't I ask Murray to check that one out, too?"

Paul rolled over on his side to face me. "Don't be so hard on yourself, Hannah." He stroked my arm. "Okay. Let's assume for a minute that you're right and that Dorothy is the killer. What's her motive?"

"Try this. Somehow Dorothy found out that Jennifer Goodall was blackmailing her former boss, Hart, over that contract business. Either Hart himself told Dorothy or Dorothy figured it out. Maybe she ran across her husband's checkbook or something. So, Dorothy killed Jennifer to shut her up, in order to salvage her husband's career."

"Works for me."

"Or, Dorothy really believed her husband was having an affair with Jennifer Goodall and killed her in a fit of jealous rage."

"That works for me, too."

"Or both of the above," I finished triumphantly.

"What I really don't understand is what happened to Kevin," Paul mused. "Here he's all set to go on for the ailing star, it's his big break, and he blows it all by taking some sort of tranquilizer. That just doesn't wash, does it?"

"Okay, let's think about that." I gnawed thoughtfully on my thumbnail. "If Kevin didn't take the tranquilizers on purpose, where did he get them from?"

"It couldn't have been from the dining hall," Paul said, gently pulling my hand away from my mouth. "That food comes directly from the kitchen in family-style serving dishes, and gets passed around the table. Everyone at Kevin's table would have been whoozy."

"Kevin said he picked up a Dr Pepper when he got to Mahan."

"Then Kevin's lying, Hannah. There aren't any soft drink machines in Mahan."

"He didn't have to go to a soft drink machine. The cast and crew have a refrigerator in a little room backstage. We keep a supply of soft drinks in there. You drop a couple of quarters in a coffee can. . . ." My voice trailed off.

I could see myself—was it only three weeks ago?—sitting in the tech room listening to Gadget as he helpfully explained the rules of the fridge. "And I think I know how Kevin ingested the tranquilizer! I just have to prove it! I'll need to have another look at Mahan Hall."

"Hannah?"

"Huh?"

"Can't it wait until morning?"

I burrowed under the covers and wiggled closer to my husband, resting my head in the crook of his arm. "Professor Ives, are you trying to distract me?"

"I certainly am," he whispered, his breath warm against my hair.

CHAPTER 26

Monday morning, early, I dressed in my re- cently acquired jogging gear, jammed a wool cap over a hopeless hairdo, and jogged stylishly off to the Academy, leaving Paul to finish his coffee and newspaper in peace.

At Gate 3, I fished the chain holding my ID out of my cleavage and showed it to the Marine guard, who studied the ID briefly before waving me through. "Have a good day, Mrs. Ives."

"Oh, I intend to, Marine."

Classes were already in session when I let myself in through the door of Sampson Hall and wound my way quickly up the stairs and down the corridor that connects Sampson with Mahan. Once inside Mahan, I made a beeline for the tech room and opened the refrigerator.

Because the show had ended its run, most of the soft drinks had been consumed, but a handful of Cokes, Diet Cokes, and Gatorades remained, some still with labels: BILL G, KAREN—YOU TOUCH-A, YOU DIE. I found none of Adam Monroe's favorite Dr Peppers.

I closed the fridge and looked around.

In the corner by a television set and a stack of videotapes sat a black plastic garbage bag. I'm not terribly fastidious, but the thought of rooting through several days of adolescent garbage with my bare hands made me gag. I swallowed hard, undid the plastic ties, spread the bag open, held my breath and peered into its depths.

Starting with the pizza boxes, I removed the contents of the bag one item at a time, gingerly, sorting them into neat piles around me. By the time I got to the bottom of the bag, I had collected five pizza boxes, approximately twenty miscellaneous twelve-ounce soda cans, ten sixteen-ounce plastic soda bottles, exactly seven wine cooler bottles in assorted flavors (a dismissal offense, but I'll never tell), and a single, plastic Dr Pepper bottle with ADAM MONROE, HIS DRINK scrawled in black magic marker across the label.

I also found a surprise: an empty blister pack that had once contained ten tablets of Zofran, Dorothy's antinausea medication. I sniffed the empty package. It smelled like strawberries. Adam Monroe would never have detected the medicine in his already spicy, fruity Dr Pepper.

As far as I was concerned, it was an open-and-shut case. Dorothy had set a trap for the midshipman playing the Beadle, not knowing the young man had been stricken with mono and that Kevin had already been tapped to sing in his place. But unfortunately, Kevin had drunk the Dr Pepper intended for Adam, with near tragic consequences.

Holding the Dr Pepper bottle by the mouth with my thumb and forefinger, I set it carefully on a shelf along with the empty blister pack, then started shoving the garbage back into the bag. I was making so much noise that I didn't hear someone come in behind me.

"What are *you* doing here, Hannah?"

I tucked the pizza box I was holding into the garbage bag and turned around ten times more calmly than I felt. "Good morning, Dorothy. I was so busy picking up in here that I didn't hear you come in. How's Kevin this morning?"

Dressed in jeans and a blue and gold Naval Academy jacket, Dorothy glared at me from the top of the stairs. Under the baseball cap she was wearing, her face grew dangerously red, and I realized, too late, that mentioning her son's name had been a terrible mistake.

"He's at Bethesda," she snapped. "His eye is infected. But you wouldn't care about *that*!"

"Infected? But I thought the doctor said his eye would be fine."

"Hah!" Dorothy snorted. "What do they know? I told you Kevin needed a specialist! This morning the whole side of his face was hot and swollen, and his eye was glued shut. Kevin reported to sick bay, and the duty driver rushed him to Bethesda, and they've diagnosed—" Dorothy stopped to catch her breath. "He's got peri something, peri . . . peri . . . periorbital cellulitis! That's what it is."

She took two steps down, then paused on the third. "They did a CT scan and found orbital involvement. Kevin could go blind, Hannah, and it's all your fault! If you hadn't insisted on taking me to that goddamn hospital, Kevin would never have been hurt!"

As irrational as Dorothy seemed, I couldn't fault her logic on that one. "I guess you're right about that," I confessed. "But you were very ill, Dorothy. You wouldn't be able to stand where you are today, bitching at me like this, if I hadn't taken you to a doctor for help."

"If anybody had bothered to tell me that Kevin was going on for Beadle Bamford," she continued coolly, "I could have retrieved the soda. Kevin would never have drunk it."

"You put your Zofran into the Dr Pepper, didn't you, Dorothy? That's why you didn't take your medicine. You didn't have any left. You'd put it all into Adam Monroe's Dr Pepper."

Dorothy ignored me. She drifted down the remaining stairs and crossed the room to the wall where members of the cast of *Sweeney Todd* had painted their names, joining the names of countless other midshipmen who had, over the years, acted in Academy musical productions. "See that," she said, pointing to a spot about ten feet up the wall where Kevin had printed KEVIN HART, "JONAS," 2004 in crimson paint.

"Kevin was wonderful in the role," I gushed. "Better than the guy who did it on Broadway, if you ask me."

Dorothy turned furious eyes on me. "Don't you *dare* patronize me, Hannah Ives."

I raised both hands in an attitude of surrender, but in the time it took me to say, "Sorry," Dorothy's hand dove into her bag and came out holding an object that flashed silver in the light streaming down from the ceiling fixtures. "You couldn't leave well enough alone, could you, Hannah? I had everything under control, then you came along to screw things up."

I backed away. "What's that in your hand?" I asked stupidly. It looked like one of Sweeney's prop straight-edge razors, it was so large and shiny.

Without warning, Dorothy lunged.

I staggered back. Something pricked my arm, and when I looked down, I saw that Dorothy had sliced open the sleeve of my brand new jogging outfit. I rubbed my arm where it stung, and when I pulled my hand away, I noticed a dark stain creeping along the edges of the cut.

Dorothy's arm swung up again, and as it began to descend, it suddenly registered that the razor was all too real. Dorothy had attacked me with a box cutter.

I didn't stay to argue with her. I turned and ran.

Behind me, I heard Dorothy's bag hit the floor with a *plomp* as she lightened her load, preparing to take off after me.

I raced up and out of the tech room, crossed the stage and stumbled down the stairs on the opposite side, heading for the door that opened into the hallway near the water fountain. I skidded to a halt in the stairwell. Some damn fool had piled the folding chairs used by the orchestra against the door, blocking the exit.

I turned back to the stage door, but Dorothy was blocking it, box cutter in hand, her face incandescent with rage.

The only way out was up.

I flew up the marble staircase, taking the steps two at a time, with Dorothy hot on my tail. When I reached the first landing, I considered running around the balcony, but I knew I'd have to scramble over theater seats and negotiate the narrow aisles in order to reach the opposite side. It'd slow me down.

Could I hang from the balcony and drop? Not if I ever wanted to use my legs for walking again.

I took a deep breath and continued up, flight after flight.

As I ran, the stairway narrowed. The marble became linoleum. Dorothy was still behind me, but her footsteps seemed to be slowing. Even though I was outpacing her, she and her deadly box cutter still stood between me and the outside world.

At the next landing, I paused and leaned over the banister, gasping for air. Sunlight poured from the skylights over my head, illuminating the stairwell below and Dorothy's bright green hat, two flights down, moving relentlessly upward.

To my left a tall wooden door, decorated with garlands of grapes in an ornate, nineteenth-century style, stood ajar. I pushed the door open and peeked inside. To my right, a pair of double doors led to a neglected classroom. Ahead, just to the left of a trophy case, was a door identical to the one through which I had just entered. I crossed over to it and jiggled the knob, but the damn door was securely locked.

One way in, no way out. If I didn't get out of there soon, I'd be trapped.

I hurried back the way I had come and took the last short flight of stairs, scaling them quickly. At the top was a nondescript door. I grabbed the doorknob, twisted it clockwise and pushed. The door didn't budge.

I jiggled the knob, lunged, and applied my shoulder to the door. Again. And again. It suddenly gave, hurling me headlong into the room beyond. I fell hard, sliding along the floor on my knees. My Naval Academy ID, which had been hanging around my neck on a chain, went flying, skittering along the floor and into the shadows.

With my palms smarting from the attempt to break my fall, I picked myself up and had the presence of mind to slam the door just as Dorothy began plodding up the staircase after me.

I found myself in a vast room, roughly the size of the auditorium I figured must be directly below. As my eyes grew accustomed to the dim light filtering in through several round windows placed at regular intervals even with the floor, I wondered if I had landed in a construction zone. Metal girders connected by bolts and studded with rivets crisscrossed the room, designed, I was sure, to support the weight of the enormous dome that dominated the room like an inverted salad bowl, its surface flocked with insulation resembling clumps of snow. Crude metal ladders led up into the rafters, and fat air-conditioning ducts snaked everywhere, wrapped with bright aluminum-covered insulation.

Behind me, the doorknob rattled. Then the pounding began, so loudly that I was certain Dorothy was using both fists. "You. Let. Me. In."

No way! On my hands and knees, I crab-walked across the floor and crouched under one of the ducts, just as Dorothy burst through the door. She slammed it shut behind her and yelled, "Hannah! I know you're in here!"

I sucked in my lower lip, concentrating on silencing my breathing. In spite of my efforts, it came in ragged gasps. The ice-cold air seared my throat, like a shot of whiskey taken neat.

I listened to Dorothy muttering as she explored her surroundings. I knew that if I stayed where I was, sooner or later she would find me. I prayed she would move away from the door so I could make a dash for it, but she must have figured that out because as she paced, she kept herself positioned between me and the exit.

I needed a distraction. As quietly as possible, I patted the floor, searching for something solid I could throw—like a nail or a screw—but the floor around me was surprisingly clean. I patted my clothing. Nothing. The pockets of my Juicy Couture velour hoodie and matching pants were still too new to have the usual paper clip, stick of gum, or the odd house key tucked into them.

Almost reluctantly, I fingered the jacket's signature J zipper pull, slid it quietly down, then twisted it off the bottom of the zipper, thinking, *There goes $88 plus tax.* First a gash in the sleeve, now a ruined zipper. Some people were never meant to own designer clothing.

With a flick of my wrist, I tossed the zipper pull across the room, where it pinged anemically on the plywood floor.

Thankfully, Dorothy heard it and set off in that direction. "Come out, come out, wherever you are," she singsonged.

Cautiously, I unfolded from my cramped position. Keeping the duct work between me and Dorothy, I crept toward the door, sprinting the last three yards. I tugged on the knob, but once again the door was jammed.

Dorothy spun around and came after me, moving slowly but confidently.

I backed away, easing my way warily along a rough brick wall. A few feet to my right, a short flight of stairs disappeared into an opening in the brickwork. I had no idea where they led, but at least it was out, so I scrambled up the steps, banging my head painfully on the jamb as I charged through the low opening.

I emerged into a passageway that appeared to run between the roof of Mahan and the base of the clock tower. Built crudely of firebrick, the rough mortar tore at what was left of my clothing as I careened down the short corridor and pushed through another door. I closed it behind me, noticed that it had a latch of sorts, and with fumbling fingers dropped the hook into the eye. The primitive latch might keep Dorothy at bay for the time it took me to figure out what to do next.

To my utter amazement, I found myself in the clock tower, surrounded on four sides by giant clock faces, their hands all pointing to IIX and IX. Was it 1:05 already? Then it dawned on my frazzled brain that I was seeing the faces from behind. It was only 11:55.

Directly before me was a room within a room, constructed of white clapboard, like a summer cabin, and decorated with the usual midshipmen graffiti: KATHY AND BEN,'02 and the perennial GO NAVY, BEAT ARMY. From the clicking and whirring emanating from inside the structure, I suspected it housed the clock mechanism.

It took only seconds to explore the room. There was no way out, except for the way I had come and whatever lay at the top of a spiral wrought-iron staircase. Another staircase. I groaned. How many staircases had I climbed that day? I'd run out of staircases soon, and then what would I do? Fly?

Dorothy began cursing and kicking at the door, so I had no choice. I scampered up the spiral staircase, round and round, until my head popped out in the bell tower itself. A single bell, larger than a washing machine but smaller than a Volkswagen, hung from a pyramid of stout wooden beams. I touched the bell, ran my hand over the cold metal.

Floor-to-ceiling windows were set into each wall, covered with chicken wire to keep the pigeons out. A door had been cut into one, presumably to provide access to the balcony. I opened the makeshift door and stepped through.

I was standing outside, on a balcony barely four feet wide that encircled the tower, approximately 120 feet above sea level.

Under ordinary circumstances, a person might have paused to enjoy the view—a spectacular panorama of Annapolis all the way from the Bay Bridge to the Maryland State House dome. But these were not ordinary circumstances. And I wasn't crazy about heights.

On legs of rubber, I grasped the railing and looked down. Patchworks of grass, brick sidewalks, the copper roofs of nearby buildings swam into view. All I could think about was how badly I'd splat should I fall.

In the chamber below, the clock hummed and clanked. I circumnavigated the balcony, searching for a ladder or fire escape, but the only way out was the spiral staircase.

And Dorothy was now standing at the chicken wire door, smack dab in the way.

I reversed direction and ran around the balcony, my feet slipping on patches of ice. While turning a corner, I stumbled on a protruding drain and nearly fell. I managed to recover, but Dorothy gained a few feet on me.

"Hannah, I just want to talk," she yelled.

"I don't believe you," I yelled back, but the wind ripped my words away.

Around and around we ran, slipping, stumbling, staggering as cold and exhaustion took their toll in a senseless chase that could only end badly. There was nothing I could do but confront her.

I whirled around, raised both arms and shouted, "Stop!"

Startled, Dorothy did as she was told. Hundreds of feet below, the winter wind whistled across the Severn River and climbed the sides of the clock tower, lifting the brim of her cap—my cap, I realized with a pang, one of the half dozen or so I had given her. Dorothy's eyes narrowed and she tilted her head, as if wondering who the heck I was. The arm holding the box cutter hung limply at her side.

"Please, drop the knife, Dorothy."

Her eyelids fluttered. She raised her hand. Puzzlement

turned to surprise, as if she were noticing the weapon for the first time.

But my move backfired. Seeing the box cutter only seemed to remind her of exactly who I was and what she intended to do. "Kevin can't be a pilot now," she snarled. With the box cutter held high, she advanced.

"We don't know that, Dorothy," I soothed. "Kevin's in the best of hands. The doctors at Bethesda really know their stuff."

She shook her head. "No. No. It's too late."

The clock beneath our feet whirred and clanked. I realized it was about to strike noon: eight bells. I'd read Dorothy L. Sayers's novel, *The Nine Tailors,* and as I steeled myself for the first deafening *bong*, I prayed she'd made up the part about the bells turning your eardrums to mush.

"Too late for what?" I pressed.

"Ted says you were hanging around the Pentagon. Is that true?"

"Oh, did Ted see me there?" I asked in what I prayed was a conversational tone, although my voice was quaking as violently as my knees. "Why didn't he say hello?"

"We think you went there to stir up trouble," she said, narrowing her eyes.

"I can't imagine why you think that, Dorothy. I was there to visit the memorial chapel," I told her, shading the truth just a tad. "It's profoundly moving."

Below us the clock shifted gears.

"I don't believe you."

"Paul and I had friends who perished in the attack." I'd played the sympathy card, but it was wasted on Dorothy, whose tortured brain knew no pain but her own.

"Ted's going to jail!" she wailed. "Now I have nobody! Nobody!" The wind, as bitter as her words, swept across the balcony and tore the hat from her head, sending it spinning into the trees. She didn't seem to notice.

Her sudden baldness, her vulnerability, tore at my

heart. In that instant I saw the true source of her pain. Ted might go to jail. In a year's time, Kevin would graduate, and who knew where the Navy would send him? Dorothy had no other children and, other than me, no friends. She would be utterly alone.

Dorothy closed her eyes for a moment, then joggled her head as if trying to clear it. "I thought you were my friend, Hannah, but now you've turned on me, too, just like all the others."

Others? What the heck was Dorothy talking about? The vague hints of paranoia I'd detected earlier seemed to have grown to epidemic proportions.

"Everyone ends up betraying me." She swayed, reaching out with her free hand to steady herself on the stone balustrade. "Even you. It really, really hurt when you turned against me."

Coming from a woman who had lied to the police about seeing me at the scene of a crime, I found the statement extraordinary, to say the least. What the hell was going on? Had the chemo made her crazy? But Dorothy was the one holding the box cutter, not me, so I decided it would be unwise to contradict her. She seemed to be crying out for love and support, so I decided to give it to her.

"I *am* your friend, Dorothy. You have to believe that."

"You told on Ted."

"No. I didn't. Jennifer Goodall told on Ted."

Dong.

The clock had been cranking up for several minutes, but still the clang of the bell so close to my head surprised me. It surprised Dorothy, too, because she startled, seemed to recall where she was, and lunged.

Dong.

Her arm came down, and I managed to parry the blow, forgetting until her arm made contact with mine that that was the one she'd slashed.

"*Eeeeeeeah!*" I screamed as pain blazed up my arm, exploding in colored lights inside my head.

Dong.

With my right hand, I grabbed Dorothy's wrist and pushed back. With my left, I found her thumb where it grasped the weapon. I worked my fingers around her thumb and bent it backward as far as it would go.

Dorothy screamed and dropped the box cutter. It hit the balustrade, bounced, and tumbled over the edge. I heard glass breaking as it struck one of the skylights below.

Dong.

Dorothy kept coming. Both arms shot forward like pistons, hitting my chest like a battering ram, knocking the air out of me. I staggered and tried to regain my footing, but slipped on a patch of ice and went sprawling.

Dong.

Dorothy was on me in an instant, both hands around my throat. As I struggled to breathe, I forced my fists between us, brought them together and thrust my arms straight up and over my head, breaking her grip. I brought my fists down again, hard, on the top of her head. She screamed and rolled away, palms pressed flat against her temples.

Dong!

By the time I had struggled to my feet, Dorothy had, too. She slumped against the balustrade, panting. While her attention was diverted, I launched myself at her like a linebacker, sweeping her feet out from under her. She landed on the snow-covered terrazzo, her skull making a sickening crack as it hit the stone.

On my hands and knees, I crawled toward her, appalled at what I had done. Dorothy's eyes were closed. She wasn't moving.

"Dorothy!" I cried as I straddled her legs. "Oh, Dorothy, I'm so sorry!" I felt for a pulse in her neck and was relieved when I found it, beating strong and steady.

By some miracle, Dorothy's cell phone was still clipped to her belt. I slipped it out of its case and with the bell still bonging away behind me, pressed 911, reported our location, and characterized the situation as a stabbing and a head injury. I'd knocked her out, that was for sure, but other than that, I really didn't know what was wrong with Dorothy. I figured we could sort that out when the paramedics got there.

Then I telephoned Paul.

It rang once, twice. Paul didn't pick up. I'd left him at home reading the paper. Where the hell had he gone?

Three rings, four, and the answering machine kicked in. "Damn it to hell!" I said, and mashed my finger down on the star button to skip the message and get straight to the beep. "Paul! Don't ask any questions. Just get your butt over to Mahan. I'm up in the clock tower with Dorothy. Please hurry!"

Beneath my legs, Dorothy stirred. Her eyelids fluttered, then flew open. She began to pitch and turn, struggling to get up.

I set the phone aside, leaned forward and pinned Dorothy's shoulders gently to the terrazzo. "Tell me about Jennifer Goodall," I urged her softly.

Dorothy dissolved into tears. "It was Jennifer this and Jennifer that and Jennifer said and Jennifer thinks," she sobbed. "Ted didn't see it coming, but I did, oh yes, I saw it coming from a mile away. Oooooh," she wailed. "How can a man be so blind?"

"Surely you're—" I began, but Dorothy cut me off.

"Imagining things? That's what Ted used to say, but then I caught him red-handed."

"Do you want to tell me about it?"

A sly look crept over her face. "I read his e-mail. He thought his AOL was password protected, but I figured it out." She laughed. "Men! It's always all about them, isn't it? Think they're so clever." She raised her head a couple of inches from the terrazzo, grimaced, moaned, then lay back. "The password was his license plate number! Is that stupid, or what?"

"What was in his e-mail?" I asked, trying to steer Dorothy back on track.

"She wrote him love notes. They were graphic, totally disgusting. I confronted Ted about it. I begged and I pleaded. His career, his brilliant career, was going down in flames, and all because he couldn't keep his fly zipped!

"He tried to break it off several times, you know," she continued, "but Jennifer kept threatening him. She knew all about what was going on in his office. He was paying her money to keep quiet about it."

Dorothy's eyes were fixed on mine. "It was going to go on and on and on. Somebody had to put a stop to it, and Ted didn't have the balls."

"So who stopped her, Dorothy? You?"

Dorothy squeezed her eyes shut, turned her head to one side. "I sent her an e-mail, asking her to meet me here to talk about it." She turned her face to me again and grinned mischievously. "I used Ted's e-mail account, of course. She thought it was him. And when she got to Mahan, I was waiting by the barber's chair.

"I didn't mean to kill her," Dorothy whimpered, "but she made me so mad! She didn't even bother to deny the relationship with my husband, she even boasted about it!"

"I know about that," I said quietly. "She tried that little trick with me."

"Yes! That's why I knew she was evil, and that she'd never go away and leave us alone.

"I don't know what happened, really," Dorothy continued dreamily. "One minute I'm standing there holding the hammer, listening to her go on and on about how sexy my husband is, and the next minute I'm standing over her. I'm still holding the hammer. She was dead," she said matter-of-factly. "So I put her in the trunk.

"At least I still have Kevin." She wiped her nose with the back of her hand. "Kevin won't let me down, not like his father did."

Dorothy shivered, and covered her bare head with both hands. I took my cap off and slipped it over her head, making sure the tips of her ears were well-protected.

"So, you hit Jennifer with the hammer and put her in the trunk. Then what?" I prodded.

"I guess I panicked. The cast and crew would be showing up pretty soon, so I ran off the stage and wrapped the hammer in the first thing that came to hand and threw it in the Dumpster."

"That was my sweatshirt."

"I know," she sniffed. "I'm sorry."

"How can you tell me you're sorry when you deliberately told the police that you saw *me* throw the hammer in the Dumpster? I thought we were friends, Dorothy."

"I don't know why I told them that!" she wailed, fresh tears cascading sideways down her cheeks. "I get so confused!" She covered her eyes with her hands, her freshly manicured and painted nails a stark contrast to her ravaged face.

I was trying to work out how it was that my fingerprints, and not hers, were found on the hammer, and then I remembered the gloves she always wore to protect her nails.

"Were you wearing your gloves when you hit her?"

She nodded miserably.

"Pick up, pick up, pick up, pick up!" Somebody was chanting in a tinny, faraway voice.

After a confusing second or two, I realized Dorothy's cell phone was talking to me. I must have set it down on the terrazzo after leaving the message for Paul.

I raised the phone to my ear. "Paul?"

"What the hell is going on? I was out sprinkling salt on the sidewalk, and when I came in I heard voices coming in over the answering machine. Hannah, are you okay?"

"I'm fine, Paul, so to speak. Did you hear everything?"

"Yes, I did. And the answering machine did, too."

CHAPTER 27

With Admiral Hart shipped off to Norfolk, Virginia, where the Navy could keep a close eye on him, and Dorothy in police custody, I figured Kevin could use a friend. It had been three days since his mother's arrest, and he was still at Bethesda, but we heard from Emma that he'd turned his room into a command post and was directing his mother's defense from there.

"I'm glad Dorothy's in a hospital," I said as Paul eased his Volvo into the heavy stream of traffic moving counterclockwise around the Washington Beltway. "I couldn't bear to think of her locked up in a cell."

"Dorothy's sick, Hannah. Cheevers won't let her go to jail."

Kevin's father had recommended a lawyer for his wife, but Kevin turned him down flat. When Kevin asked for my advice, I'd sent him to Murray Simon. Nobody, after all, could be more familiar with the Goodall case than Murray. But citing conflict of interest, Murray handed Kevin off to James Cheevers, his colleague at Cheevers, Tanner and Greenberg, a firm that specialized in criminal law. We'd met Jim once, at Concert of Tastes, a fund-raiser for the Annapolis Symphony. Aside from a fetish for novelty ties—on symphony night he'd been wearing one decorated with cellos—Cheevers was the best, and Dorothy Hart, poor thing, was going to need him.

Paul took the Wisconsin Avenue exit and drove the short distance south to the National Naval Medical Center, the multistory hospital with the distinctive central tower, familiar to millions of television viewers as Bethesda, the hospital that had saved the lives of several U.S. presidents and a goodly number of congressmen, too. Paul flashed his Naval Academy faculty ID for the sentry, who waved us through into the parklike grounds.

Five minutes later we left our car on the second level of the parking garage and made our way across a footbridge into the hospital proper.

Paul took my hand and squeezed it three times. I—love—you.

"Me, too," I said aloud. "And aren't you glad you're not married to a criminal?"

"You know what's criminal?" he said, punching the Up button on the elevator.

"What?"

Paul stepped into the elevator and dragged me in after him. After the door slid shut, he pulled me into his arms. "What's criminal," he said before planting his lips firmly on mine, "is how gorgeous you look even with your arm in a sling."

We found Kevin on 5C, in a sterile white-on-white room, sitting up in bed with an IV feeding into his arm. Emma was perched at the foot of the bed, while Jim Cheevers, wearing a wool scarf and a tweed overcoat, occupied the single chair in the room that was reserved for visitors. A Navy lieutenant dressed in khaki, her blond hair twisted into a braid and secured with a silver clip, bent over a computer terminal, typing away. I could tell from her collar device that she was a nurse.

"Hi, Kevin," I said.

The lieutenant turned a dazzling smile on at her patient. "Midshipman Hart, this is your official notification that you are now exceeding the regulation visitor allotment by two individuals."

"Thank you, Lieutenant Aaronson," Kevin replied with no hint of concern in his voice. "I'd like you to meet Professor and Mrs. Ives, from Annapolis."

Lieutenant Aaronson grinned, shook our hands, and relented. "But since you've come all this way . . ."

Kevin winked at Emma. "See. She is putty in my hands."

"Behave yourself, Kevin!" Emma slapped his leg where it rested underneath the blanket.

"Excellent advice, Midshipman," Lieutenant Aaronson shot back over her shoulder as she busied herself again at the terminal.

Kevin's face grew serious. He turned to Cheevers, who, we soon learned, had arrived only minutes before us. "What's going to happen to my mother?"

Jim Cheevers unwound his scarf, shrugged out of his overcoat, then leaned forward, resting his forearms on the briefcase that lay across his knees. "She's been arraigned, but the court has ordered a complete mental and physical evaluation. She's up at the University of Maryland Medical Center right now."

I nodded. "That's *good,* Kevin. My mother was a patient there. They couldn't have been more wonderful."

"Have the doctors found anything yet?" Kevin asked.

Cheevers's flyaway salt and pepper eyebrows hovered over his eyes, round and dark as chocolate drops. He nodded.

I was almost afraid to ask. "Is it the cancer?"

"No, something else entirely. Because of the migraines, the confusion, the problems she was having from time to time with her coordination, the doctors suspected that something was putting pressure on her brain."

Kevin's good eyebrow shot up. "A tumor?"

"Because of her medical history, they suspected a tumor, of course," Cheevers said, "but the MRI showed no evidence of that. They did find something else, though. Your mother may be suffering from normal pressure hydrocephalus, which in spite of the name, isn't normal at all. In layman's terms, it's an abnormal buildup of cerebrospinal fluid in the ventricles of the brain. The fluid is often under pressure and can compress the brain, causing all kinds of difficulties."

"Are you talking about water on the brain?" I wondered. "I thought that happened with babies."

Jim Cheevers nodded. "Exactly. But the disease can occur in adults, too."

Lieutenant Aaronson stepped away from the monitor. "Excuse me for interrupting, Mrs. Ives, but I think I can respond to that. We don't know why, but this condition is becoming increasingly common with older adults. And if you'll allow me to climb up on my soap box for a moment, it's very often misdiagnosed as senile dementia or even Alzheimer's disease because of the symptoms. We get it with the veterans all the time."

"What kind of symptoms?" Paul wanted to know.

Lieutenant Aaronson ticked them off on her fingers. "Headaches, nausea, vomiting, blurred vision, fatigue, irritability, incontinence, personality changes, and problems with coordination. In advanced stages, it can even cause paranoia."

I couldn't believe it. Dorothy Hart was a textbook case, a poster child for the disease. We'd mistaken her symptoms for the side effects of chemo. "Can it be treated?" I asked the nurse.

"It's amazingly simple. Doctors install a shunt in the brain that lets the excess fluid drain away, thereby relieving the pressure."

"So Mom will be cured? Once a shunt is installed she'll be completely normal?"

Lieutenant Aaronson nodded. "More than likely, she'll be completely normal."

Normal. Everyone in the room kept silent while the significance of that word sank in. How could anything be normal when you were being accused of murder?

After Lieutenant Aaronson left the room, Cheevers got to his feet and approached Kevin's bed. "She'll plead not guilty by reason of insanity."

Kevin nodded.

"We'll waive a jury trial," Cheevers continued. "We'll let the judge decide, but, yes, I believe she'll be acquitted."

"Do you think Mom will have to spend any time in jail?"

"A hospital, maybe, but just until the court determines that she's no longer a danger to herself or to society."

Kevin relaxed against his pillow. "Good. That's good."

"Not so fast, young man." Jim Cheevers raised a cautionary hand. "There's still the matter of the attack on Hannah."

I flashed back to the time I had spent in the jail cell, the hours that dragged on like eternity, and I didn't wish it on anyone, especially someone who had been legally insane at the time. "I'm not going to press charges."

"You may have no choice, Hannah," Cheevers interrupted.

"It was an accident," I insisted. "Dorothy and I were dismantling the sets, she dropped the box cutter and it fell on my arm." I glanced from my husband to Dorothy's lawyer, searching their somber faces for any sign of support. "That's my story, and I'm sticking to it."

Paul's mouth gave a twitch of a smile. "Right."

Cheevers adjusted his tie, a masterpiece in bright blue, decorated with battleships, circa World War II. "An accident."

That "accident" had required fifteen stitches. With my bandaged arm, I saluted Kevin's bandaged cheek. "We're a pair, aren't we?"

Kevin grinned.

"How's the eye, Kevin?" Paul asked.

"Absolutely A-okay, Professor. The antibiotics are doing their thing. The IV comes out today, then I'll have to take pills for a while." He tapped his temple with an index finger. "The doctor says the eye will be good as new."

"I was thinking," Emma said from her perch at the foot of Kevin's hospital bed. "It's just like Sweeney Todd."

Cheevers, who hadn't seen the musical, asked, "In what way?"

"Well, you know at the end, where Sweeney kills the poor, mad beggar woman he didn't recognize as his wife? Kevin's mother spiked Adam's Dr Pepper, thinking that he'd be drinking it, but she ended up drugging Kevin instead."

Emma was right, I thought. Sweeney was blinded by revenge, and in the end destroyed the one person in the world that his poisoned heart still loved. And Dorothy? In her obsession over her son's career, she nearly took it from him.

I stepped forward and joined the huddle of people gathered around Kevin's bed. "Kevin, I've been puzzling over something. On the day of the matinee, you went to Mahan, drank the Dr Pepper, went down to the makeup room and *then* went out and got in your car. What the heck did you do that for?"

Kevin smiled. "It sounds a bit weird, doesn't it? It's like this. I was eating Sunday dinner at my sponsors' when I got the call that I'd be going on in Adam's place, so I hightailed it over to Mahan and got into the Beadle's costume."

"It's my fault, I'm afraid," another voice interrupted. Professor Medwin Black, swathed against the February cold in wool from head to foot, bustled into the room, instantly bringing Kevin's visitor count to three over quota. "You may recall that Adam Monroe played the Beadle bald. We had such a good bit of stage business going with it that I insisted Kevin wear a pate."

"Pate?" Paul's handsome brow wrinkled attractively.

"A bald wig," Kevin explained. "We couldn't get it to fit right," he said, continuing the story. "I looked like a kid wearing a Halloween costume from Kmart, so I said the hell with it, I'll just go back to the Hall and shave my head. That's where I was going when the wall ran into me."

Emma rested her hands on her hips. "So, how come you drank Adam's soda, Kev?"

"I figured if I had his part, I could have his stupid soda, too."

"I'm glad you didn't shave your head, Kevin," Emma said, giving him a sisterly peck on the cheek.

"I don't know about that." Kevin grinned. "Simone might find it very attractive."

"Who's Simone?" I asked.

"My nurse. She's hot."

I remembered the attractive blonde who had just left the room after recording Kevin's vitals, and although I suspected my advice might fall on deaf ears, I said, "Kevin! You can't date a lieutenant. She outranks you."

"My God, Kev, they'll fry you for frat!"

"What she said," I agreed, pointing a finger at Emma.

Kevin threw me an exaggerated wink. "If you don't ask, Mrs. Ives, I will never, ever tell."